# While

# We

# Were

# Burning

# While We Were Burning

## SARA KOFFI

G. P. PUTNAM'S SONS
New York

**PUTNAM**
— EST. 1838 —
G. P. Putnam's Sons
*Publishers Since 1838*
An imprint of Penguin Random House LLC
penguinrandomhouse.com

Title page art: Burnt paper edges © james benjamin / shutterstock.com

Library of Congress Cataloging-in-Publication Data

Names: Koffi, Sara, author.
Title: While we were burning / Sara Koffi.
Description: New York : G. P. Putnam's Sons, 2024.
Identifiers: LCCN 2023056501 (print) | LCCN 2023056502 (ebook) |
    ISBN 9780593714959 (hardcover) | ISBN 9780593714966 (ebook)
Subjects: LCGFT: Thrillers (Fiction) | Novels.
Classification: LCC PS3611.O36494 W48 2024 (print) |
    LCC PS3611.O36494 (ebook) | DDC 813/.6—dc23/eng/20231215
LC record available at https://lccn.loc.gov/2023056501
LC ebook record available at https://lccn.loc.gov/2023056502

Printed in the United States of America
1st Printing

Book design by Laura K. Corless

To Eric, one of my favorites

*They're lucky Black people are looking*
*for equality and not revenge.*
—Kimberly Jones

# While

# We

# Were

# Burning

# The Beginning of the End

*When did I lose you?*

I can tell I've lost you by the way you glance up at me from that fucking phone in your hands. You look over at me like I'm another one of your boring clients, someone who's talking too much and taking up too much of your precious time. I smile back at you, not saying a word, because I'm not another one of your boring clients, David.

Because I know how you feel about ramblers and ranters and ravers.

Because we used to feel the same way.

It wasn't my intention to become another hated talker and you know that. You know, or at least you used to know, how much I can't stand the sound of my own voice. Each time I open my goddamn mouth, I want to take a chain saw to each ear and just give myself some peace and quiet, to finally shut myself up once and for all. But there's money to be made from people hearing me talk, right? Isn't that what you told me?

*Getting out of the house might be good for you, Lizzie.*

*Getting a part-time job might be good for you.*

*Getting some fresh air might be good for you.*

I know what you really meant, David.

*That me getting away from you would be good for you.*

I don't even know what you do with yourself with all that time away from me. I used to think you were fucking one of your assistants, but courtesy of Dr. Hannah Whitaker, I know that's just me projecting. She tells me that I want to believe that you're cheating on me because I'm cheating on you, because believing that we're both just as awful as each other makes me feel better about hurting you.

Hurting you?

I don't think I *can* hurt you, David. I don't think there's a single thing I can do to you that would make you pay attention to me for more than five seconds at a time. Do you remember how I used to be able to make your head spin just by wearing one of your ratty band T-shirts and nothing else? How you would get down on your knees and worship my body until the old woman who used to live in the apartment right next to ours would knock against the wall as hard as she could?

You'd always joke about stopping for her sake, for the sake of her brittle bones, for the sake of her bloodied knuckles rapping, rapping, rapping.

But you were never really joking.

You wanted to stop because you care about other people, David. Even when you think they're boring, you force a smile on your face, and you're polite and considerate and thoughtful and seemingly present in all the ways that matter. You would give the shirt off your back to someone who you thought needed it more than you, and I've seen

2

you give the last few dollars you had in your wallet to a begging woman in the street without a moment of hesitation.

And it kills me to know that, David. It kills me to know that the man who cares about everyone he meets, even if he can hardly stand them, doesn't care about me.

Doesn't see me. Looks right past me. Looks right through me.

*When did I lose you? When did I lose you? When did I lose you?*

I almost form the question in my mouth before I brush it away with my tongue.

Asking you would just turn me even more into something you hate, a too-much talker, a time-waster.

Especially because I already know how you would answer.

*You haven't lost me, baby. I'm right here.*

*I'm always going to be here for you, Lizzie.*

And then you would disappear back into your fucking phone.

And I would turn back into the ghost you've made of me, the whisper of the woman you used to love.

# 1

# Elizabeth

Beale Street after five? I'd rather kill myself."

Patricia was leaning against the main lobby's printer, her nurse costume clinging tight to her skin. It was inappropriate for an office setting, in every sense of the word, the blouse cut too low and the skirt too short. Her only real saving grace was that she waited until I'd finished with my shift at the Learning Center to change into it, making sure no one saw her but me.

That seemed to be the rhythm of our entire relationship. Patricia always coming just as I was going. Patricia wanting to tag along on errands that I desperately wanted to get done by myself. Ever since I'd opened the door to her welcoming me to the neighborhood with homemade brownies and a megawatt smile, she'd been around, a little offbeat, a fly in the ointment that was my attempt to *not* have a fly in my ointment.

"Yeah, well, that's what David told me they were up to," I replied, my fingers gliding along the printer's control screen. "Getting a drink at the Absinthe Room."

"So, they're pregaming before the Halloween party tonight." Patricia rolled her eyes, punctuating the end of her sentence. "What is it with men and trying to relive their college glory days?"

I bit my tongue, hard, as a fresh copy landed in the printer tray. I knew for a fact that Patricia had wanted to be a nurse when she was in college and that she'd flunked out of the program. It was one of those stories she'd always come back to, when there were any lulls in our conversations, whenever it seemed like there might be a single moment of silence between us.

I never asked her why. Why she was so hell-bent on reliving something from her past that'd clearly hurt. Why she always felt the need to bring it up again like she was stuck in some modern-day version of *The Rime of the Ancient Mariner*.

Maybe it was the failure.

Maybe Patricia wasn't used to it. Maybe that was the first time it'd ever happened, the first time she'd ever been scarred by anything like it. Like a little kid who can't stop telling people about the first time they ever got a sunburn at the beach.

Failing was a novelty.

"What are you supposed to be, Liz?" Patricia nodded over at my outfit. "You look . . . interesting, at least."

"Stevie Nicks," I answered with a slight shrug. "But maybe without the innate talent and grace, I'm coming off more like a burnt-out hippie?"

Patricia smirked, but she didn't laugh. Like she was amused but didn't want to fully admit it. "Did David buy you that?"

"Nope. I thrifted most of it."

"Thrifted? Why?" Her eyes widened with abject horror. "You and David aren't having money problems, are you?"

"No, that's not—"

"Because you could tell me, if you were," she interrupted. "Jack and I would be happy to help—"

"We're not having money problems." It was my turn to do the interrupting. "David and I are fine. I just think thrifting is better for the environment. That's all."

"Better for the environment?"

"You know, fast fashion and all that." I shrugged again as I pulled a stack of freshly printed copies close to my chest. "I read an article about it online. Recycling clothes is all the rage."

"Okay . . ." Patricia murmured, like she didn't believe a word of what I was saying.

And it took everything in me not to drop the stack of copies back onto the landing tray, pull up the article I'd seen on my phone, and make Patricia digest every word. There was just something about suburbanites and lying. They lied so much that they assumed everyone else was always lying, too. Lying about how much they're pulling in a year. Lying about how wonderful it is to be a mother, a father. Lying about how much they love the holidays, their spouses, their car, their job, their life.

Always lying, lying, lying.

But not me. I long suspected it was one of the reasons I never felt like I really fit in to the rest of Harbor Town, no matter how much they wanted me to. I wasn't interested in crafting some version of myself that I could never live up to. And I wasn't interested in spending my precious time on this planet surrounding myself with people who wanted their lives to resemble SUV commercials: saccharine, sweet, fake.

On a road headed to fucking nowhere.

"Speaking of thrifting . . ." Patricia paused for a moment as she shot me a pleading look. "Have you talked to David about the Neighborhood Watch program?"

*Are you really so removed from reality that thrifting and stealing are the same thing to you, Patricia?* I asked her, solely in my head. *Have you gone so far down the upper-middle-class rabbit hole that you can only conceptualize something as having been bought if there's a designer's name stitched across its label?*

"Uh, no, I haven't."

"Not yet? Or not ever?"

". . . Not ever," I admitted with an apologetic glance in her direction. "Sorry, Patricia. But it doesn't really gel with what we believe in. Besides, the last big Harbor Town mystery was solved in less than twenty-four hours."

"The last big mystery?"

"When that kid down the street thought someone stole his bike," I reminded her. "Remember? It was just in his friend's garage? His dad had brought it over to have the tires fixed."

"That doesn't even count for anything!" Patricia laughed through her argument. "And for all we know, that could've been the first score of a very ambitious thief."

"But it wasn't." I laughed now, too, as I started locking up for the night. It was something Patricia would usually help me with if she was scheduled to stay until end-of-day. She'd been a volunteer at the Learning Center long before I'd ever had a job here, although her knack for volunteering only seemed to kick into high gear whenever her in-laws were in town or there was some #GivingBack social media challenge.

But I knew she wouldn't be helping me lock up tonight, even if she wanted to. Not with how high her heels were, anyway.

"Please? Just float it by David and tell me what he thinks about it?" she begged. "That's all I'm asking you to do, Liz."

"Why does it matter if David and I are involved with something like that?" I asked. "We're still pretty new to the neighborhood. Do people really care what we do?"

"Are you serious right now?" Patricia folded her arms across her chest. "Everyone's obsessed with you two. You're basically the coolest people in the neighborhood, like Barbie and Ken if they weren't trying so hard."

"I don't know what that means, Patricia."

"It means that *yes,* people care what you two do. They care a lot. Why else do you think everyone's tripping over themselves to be at your party tonight?" Patricia scoffed. "Seriously. I've thrown Halloween parties where maybe half the neighborhood came, but your RSVP list was insane."

"It was David's idea. He said it'd be a good way to *establish* ourselves." I chuckled at the thought. "As if we were royalty or something. As if people really needed to know who we were."

"You're right about that. Everyone already knows who David is," Patricia replied. "Which is why having him involved with Neighborhood Watch would be perfect. If the other guys see him doing something, they'll join in, no matter what it is. Everyone wants to be in his . . . orbit."

*Right.*

Of course. Everything comes back to David. Always.

Because David was David.

And I was just David's wife.

It wasn't like that when we first got married. I distinctly remember being my own person and having my own name. It was *David and Elizabeth* everywhere we went.

Until it wasn't. Until David started to work on million-dollar projects. Until David's success was an eclipsing force, the sort of thing that hid other accomplishments in the shadows, no matter how bright they seemed in my hands. And then I was nothing. Still here, still in place by his side, but only seen as an extension, as a ring around his planet, as the woman whose finger he'd deigned to place a ring around.

"So? You'll talk to him about it, right?" Patricia pleaded as she followed me outside the building and toward the parking lot. "Pretty, pretty please?"

". . . I'll think about it." It was the last thing I said before offering her a temporary wave goodbye, knowing that I'd be seeing her again in less than thirty minutes at my house for the party.

And knowing that I was never going to speak a word of this conversation to David.

Ever.

\*　　\*　　\*

"How many more of these do you have left in you?" Jack, Patricia's husband, was slurring his words as he suddenly appeared at my side.

The Halloween party was in full swing now, the foyer of our home transformed into a sea of bodies writhing in time to music, champagne flutes clutched with perfectly manicured nails and candy wrappers littering the marble floor.

And there I was, bored out of my mind, in the middle of it all.

It felt like I was back in college. Back before I knew any of these people existed. Back when I barely knew I existed, either.

I let myself sink into a glass-clear memory, one where I was stuck at some college party a friend had dragged me to without my consent. The only saving grace about the whole thing would be at the end of the night, where I finally met someone worth talking to and we snuck off together to the other side of the house, far away from the boozy crowd. I'd learn by the morning that my savior's name was

David, with bright blue eyes and a smile that'd so often made me lose my train of thought.

*My David.*

It didn't matter that it'd been years since I'd seen him that way, that age. I was never going to forget the way he looked when I fell in love with him. I wondered if that was how he'd always remember me, too, wearing a hand-me-down T-shirt and dark jeans, trying to make myself invisible in whatever room I stumbled into.

I could never understand why he fell in love with me back then, when all I knew how to do was hate myself.

When I didn't even know what love was supposed to feel like.

"What are you talking about?" I looked up at Jack, overbearingly tall as ever, noticing the beer he held in his right hand. The dark brown wrapped around its label complemented the notes of sandy blond in his hair, almost like he'd planned it. "I don't think I understand the question."

"You understand the question!" He cackled. "Come on. I know how you girls are . . . You tell each other everything. Don't act like you don't know what I mean."

"Jack, I have no idea where you're going with this—"

"When's it going to be baby time?" Jack cackled yet again.

I winced twice.

"David and I don't want kids. I don't know what Patricia told you, but—"

"Patricia didn't tell me anything," Jack cut me off as a drunken grin spread across his features. "Let's just say that David may have let something slip, back at the bar."

*Oh.*

I managed to suppress my shock, quietly biting back a *hmm* or a *huh.*

David Smith didn't want kids. When I used to be the kind of

woman who saw herself working on the top floor of some important office building, it was one of the things we'd bonded over. He never wanted a bored housewife, and I never wanted to be bored. Children always seemed like a shortcut to everything we never wanted.

"David and I don't want kids," I repeated, like saying it twice was going to undo Jack's revelation. "Maybe he just had too much to drink."

"Yeah. Maybe." Jack studied my features for a second too long. "Maybe you're right."

Jack took another sip of the beer in his hand before his eyes went wild and wide. "Speak of the devil."

"I thought you said you'd done all your drinking at the bar," David replied as he stepped from around Jack, slipping Jack's beer into his own grip, the bottle glistening underneath the bright kitchen bulbs. David's tone was neutral, completely devoid of judgment, even as he cut his friend off for the night.

It was another reason I loved him so much, his ability to be so impossibly . . .

Kind.

He was always, always so kind.

In a way that most people weren't. In a way that Patricia was always, always trying to be.

"Hi." I offered David a small smile. "Nice costume."

It wasn't a nice costume. It was something he'd clearly bought at the very last second, the kind of thing that just happened to be left on the shelves. He was dressed up as the most generic pirate that I'd ever seen in my life, with cheap fabric covering one of his eyes and an even cheaper faux parrot seated on his shoulder.

But he did happen to look nice in it. Because David looked nice in anything.

"Thanks." He returned my smile, just as Jack ambled off toward another side of our home, his steps shuffling and heavy. "You having a good night so far?"

"It could be better," I said while taking a few steps closer to him, my hands already reaching toward either side of his waist. "I could be hooking up with a pirate."

"Sorry, baby. It was a really long day at work. Plus, going out with Jack afterwards . . ."

"Huh."

"Huh what, baby?"

"Nothing." I smirked. "It's just that Jack said that you wanted—"

*Jack said that you wanted to have a child with me. Because Jack is drunk.*

*Or maybe you're drunk, David, and you don't remember saying it.*

*Or maybe I'm drunk for even entertaining anything that comes out of Jack's mouth.*

"Jack said what?" David smiled down at me, interrupting my thoughts.

"Jack just made it seem like you were really looking forward to *going to bed* tonight," I lied, rearranging Jack's words into a whole new meaning.

"It's not that I don't want to, Lizzie—"

"You've barely wanted to for three months, David."

"I'm just tired, baby. That's all." He sighed. "You know how hard I've been working on closing this deal for the Hanson building."

". . . I know."

"But when all of this bullshit is over," he started with that blinding smile, the one that always shot me right in the heart, "I'm going to rock your fucking world, Elizabeth Smith."

David kissed me on the forehead, chastely, distant-relative-ly, fucking-you-is-not-going-to-happen-tonight-ly.

And with that, he was gone, disappearing into the crowd, the warmth that I'd felt when he was nearby souring into something so frigid and empty.

*   *   *

"Fuck, baby. I bet you look so fucking hot tonight." Nathan groaned on the other end of the line, in the way he always did when he was jerking himself off. The sound was enough to set off sparks all along my skin, the kind that traveled right down to the middle of my thighs.

"Don't. Don't call me that," I breathed as one of my hands followed the sparks down, not stopping until my fingers were inside of my panties.

"Don't call you 'baby'?"

"No. You know that I hate it," I reminded him for the millionth time. "We've talked about this before, Nathan. You can call me anything else but that."

"There's not much else I want to call you," he said, his words dripping and sweet. "Especially when my cock is buried so deep inside of you."

"Nathan . . ." There was a hitch in my breath as I leaned against the broom closet wall, the Halloween party happening right on the other side of me. I knew better than to take such a huge risk like this. I knew better than to be playing with myself when there was a chance one of my neighbors could stumble into the closet by mistake, forgetting the layout of my home, assuming it was the route to the nearest toilet.

But after the way David had brushed me off tonight, I needed it. I needed *him*.

I'd met Nathan after he'd come to give a talk at the Learning Center. He'd strolled into my office, confused, wondering if I knew where the secretary was, profusely apologizing for stepping through the open door. I'd apologized right back, taking accountability for his confusion even though I wasn't the source of it, before explaining that I was one of the instructors at the Center myself and could answer any questions he had in the meantime. He'd seemed taken aback by that, almost like he'd assumed I was a guest there, too, despite him standing in the middle of my office. He then apologized yet again before I brushed it away with a friendly wave, thanking him for spending his time with the students that day, going over how wonderful it was that he was giving back to his community, how important the work we do with students at the Center really is, how much it matters.

By the time I was done with my spiel, he'd been nabbed by another guest speaker and pulled into the right room.

Still, I'd been able to mostly overhear the talk he'd given the kids, espousing the value of a good education, promising that if they stayed in our after-school tutoring programs and committed themselves to good grades, then they'd be able to sign up for an all-expenses-paid summer camp he spearheaded out of Yellowstone. And while the teens' reaction to Nathan seemed to range from exceedingly uninterested to so excited for the chance to see a bear in real life their heads almost exploded, I honestly hadn't had any reaction to him at all.

Not until he'd invited me out for drinks when I got off work.

That was six months ago, and I hadn't seen Nathan in person since. Of course that was by choice. The man only lived a thirty-minute drive away from me in the "wilds" of Cordova.

When I told him I was married, he didn't shy away from my predicament, instead offering up an alternative solution, one where we could indulge in each other, guilt-free and hands-free. At least until I was ready to leave David for good. That was how we started, with long text messages and even longer phone calls. And somewhere between the fourteenth and fifteenth late-night message, Nathan mentioned just how badly he wanted to hear my voice as he jerked himself off before bed.

And I obliged. And obliged. And obliged.

Every single time.

"Come for me, Lizzie," he murmured. "I want to hear you come for me. I want to hear you say my name again, just like that."

"Nathan . . . Nathan . . . Nathan . . ." I said his name with staggered breaths as I came hard against my own hand. My thighs squeezed shut while my stomach clenched tight, my eyes shut tight, too.

*David. David. David.*

All I could picture was him barging into the broom closet, smashing my phone to the floor, and slamming himself inside of me, punishing me for having another man's name on my lips. He was finally fucking noticing me, noticing that I was just as alive as he was, noticing that I have needs and wants and desires and he's always been the only one who could ever tick off every box.

"Lizzie . . ." Nathan's finishing groan ripped me out of my fantasy, putting me right back in the broom closet, where a mop handle was pressing too hard against my shoulder. "You're mine, Lizzie . . . You're all mine . . ."

\* \* \*

"Come walking with me in the morning?" Patricia was standing in the doorway, the party having died down around an hour ago.

"Won't you have your hands full with Jack?" I smiled. "I'm guessing he's going to have a pretty bad hangover to deal with."

"Oh, Jack would be thankful for it," Patricia said, her eyes cutting over toward her parked Porsche Cayenne next to the sidewalk,

Jack's sleeping figure visible in the backseat. "He likes it better when it's quiet in the house after he's had too much to drink."

"Are you sure you want *me* to go with you?" My tone was just as filled with uncertainty as the question itself. "What about the crew you usually walk with—"

"They're going to a yoga expo tomorrow," she interrupted, her expression beaming. "There's a group of traveling instructors and the girls have been dying to try it out."

"And you weren't interested?"

"It's not that I wasn't interested," she continued, the beam on her face shifting into a look of earnest concern. "Liz, I . . . I just want to be a good friend to you."

"You are a good friend to me, Patricia." Even though we'd never be genuinely close, I couldn't deny that she fulfilled the role of *friend*, over and above.

*Shit.*

What did that say about me? That a woman that I'd found various ways to tolerate was the closest thing I had to a fucking friend?

What the fuck was wrong with me?

"I just think that we need to talk," she went on, her voice sounding like it was on the verge of breaking. "There's something going on with you and David, Liz, even if you don't want to talk to me about it tonight. It might not be money, but—"

"There's nothing going on between David and me, Patricia—"

"Is he cheating on you?"

". . . What?" I laughed, half in disbelief, half in fucking terror. "What the hell are you talking about, Patricia? Where's that even coming from?"

"I saw you go into your broom closet," she explained, still sounding so close to a meltdown. "And when you came out . . . your face was flushed, Liz. It looked like you'd been crying."

*Ha.*

*Ha. Ha. Ha.*

*Hahahahahaha—*

"Liz?" Patricia whimpered. "Please. Just go for a walk with me in the morning? You shouldn't be carrying all of this by yourself, no matter how strong you think you are—"

"I'll be there." I nodded as I spoke, as I forced down the laugh of a century. "Just text me whenever you wake up and I'll throw on some jogging clothes."

Patricia sniffled before she pulled me into her arms, holding on to me so tight that I thought she was going to pop me right open. "We're going to get through this together, okay?"

"Okay."

"I love you, Liz." Patricia sniffled again, burying her face against my shoulder. "I love you and I'm always going to be here for you. No matter what."

". . . I love you, too, Pat," I said, lying right through my fucking teeth.

# 2

# Elizabeth

I'd set an alarm for four thirty a.m.

Patricia didn't go for her walks until sunrise, which would've been at around six in the morning, but I wasn't in the mood to take any chances. I'd rather get only a few hours of sleep and pretend like I didn't feel like vomiting my guts out with every step than sleep in and turn into a rumor that would've been whispered on every bored housewife's lips by tomorrow afternoon.

*Oh my fucking God. Did you see Liz?*

*I know she had a party last night, but has she completely given up?*

*Do you think Pat was right? Do you think David's cheating on her?*

*Well, if that's how she's going to look, maybe it's about time.*

"Fuck off," I muttered to the imagined conversation in my head and to the bottle of face wash that'd just exploded against my palm. It was still as full as the day David had brought it home to me as a gift from Seoul, a new product from a new line of expensive skincare that no one was going to have access to for at least the next six months. I didn't know why I was being so careful with it, preserving it like it belonged in a museum, only using it when I really needed to glow.

When I really needed to seem like I was okay.

Irritated, I quickly washed my cheeks and forehead and chin with the too-much face wash that threatened to drip between my fingers. When I was finished, I reached for a razor, the bright pink tones on its body always in such contrast to the foreboding metal teeth. I clicked the device to life, just as I leaned against the bathroom wall while resting my foot on the bathtub's edge. And as a familiar hum began to softly fill the room, I lowered the razor down to the left side of my right leg—

*Shaving cream.*

I clicked the razor off, as the hum it made seemed to reverberate in my brain. This was the trouble with waking up so goddamn early in the morning. It was like there wasn't enough space in my head yet for remembering the small things. Everything about me was still half in a dream, the dream I was supposed to be having right now as I lay in bed.

I reached for the cabinet below the sink, swinging it open toward the bathroom door.

And I heard the smallest of thuds.

It was almost imperceptible, the sort of thing I would've ignored as the ice tumbling down from the ice maker in the fridge, the soft sound of a trash can liner sinking toward the bottom of the container with one too many beer bottles. And while I deeply wanted to dismiss the sound and get back to primping and preening for a repulsive morning walk, the noise came to me again, another small thud, another something that refused to be ignored.

And it seemed like it was coming from right outside my bathroom window.

"Fuck," I whispered to myself again as I moved away from the cabinet and stepped down the hall. I passed the kitchen on my way to the front door, but had to double back for a flashlight, my groggy mind recalling that it wasn't sunrise yet and the sky was empty and dark. Armed with the flashlight in my palm, I walked out onto our front porch, the bitter night blowing cold wind across my bare legs.

I'd anticipated finding a small squirrel or chubby raccoon on the steps of our home, something eager to play around in our trash bins, something that wouldn't have set off the sensors on our security system because it wouldn't have been trying to crack open a window or smash through a keypad. Finding nothing, I turned my attention toward the side of our home, bright light beaming from my hand, my mind aching for more sleep.

But there wasn't anything there, either.

I turned away from the space beside our house, the flashlight trailing ahead of me. And as my sandals sank against the cool grass, I let my mind wander toward pillows and satin sheets, some dreamt-up possibility where I'd be allowed to be in two places at once, on a walk with Patricia and rolled up in cotton and comfort—

Shoes.

*No.*

Heels.

Bright red strappy stiletto heels.

There were two of them, resting on their side, right in the middle of the street. My flashlight had caught onto their soles, and I'd stopped in my tracks.

Had I gone back to sleep?

I bit my bottom lip just to be sure. It was something I'd been doing ever since I was a kid, participating in small acts of violence against myself to make sure I was still in the waking world, to make sure I was still *here*. And as I tasted the most intimate drops of blood on my tongue, I trudged toward the street, awake and here and verifiably alive.

Why would someone leave a pair of stilettos in the middle of the goddamn street?

I crouched down beside them, turning one of the heels over in my hand, flashlight focused on the leather exterior. I didn't know what I was expecting. It wasn't like adults often marked their belongings with their initials, and it wasn't like I'd memorized the shoe size of every woman on the block. Even if I had, it would've been a hopeless endeavor to assign this shoe to anyone in my current state, eyes sticky and brain muddled—

Shadow.

As I turned the shoe over in my hand, I spotted a shadow up ahead, something dimly lit from above a few feet away. Acting on instinct, I turned my head up toward the night sky, curious about what was causing the effect, idly wondering if there was going to be a string of shoes hanging down, lining some unseen cable, the kind of thing that I'd only ever seen in the movies.

But the only thing hanging in the night sky was Patricia.

\* \* \*

Was I screaming?

How long had I been screaming?

My hands were filled with pebbles, marbles, hard things that I couldn't name, things that were digging into my palms, but I didn't care, I couldn't care, I couldn't—

*Helpmehelpmehelpmehelpushelpushelpus.*

There was light creeping across the sky, light creeping up Patricia's body, light reflecting off the fake, plastic stethoscope that hung from her bruised and broken neck as she hung from the lamppost. Her blond hair was framing her face like a halo, like she was glowing with the sunrise, like she was an angel coming down from the heavens and not a dead woman with bare feet.

A Harbor Town angel.

That was what she was, wasn't she? Or at least who she tried to be.

Angels weren't supposed to end up this way, with their tongues lolling out the side of their mouths, their fingers turning cold and blue. Angels were supposed to stay in the clouds, far, far away from us, far, far away from red stiletto heels and cheap stethoscopes and Halloween parties where their husband got so drunk that he probably hadn't even noticed that Patricia wasn't sleeping sound beside him.

"Lizzie? Lizzie!"

David's voice broke through the fog, through the images of angels and demons flickering like a fading film screen behind my eyes.

". . . David." It was all I said as I looked up at him, my body feeling so far, far away from his, so far, far away from everything.

"Lizzie. God. Oh my God." David crouched down in front of me, his hands resting on my shoulders. "Lizzie, baby, I'm so sorry."

"Sorry about what?" My gaze was unfocused, my breathing calmed by his touch.

David's face scrunched up in confusion, his fingers gripping my shoulders even tighter. ". . . You found her, didn't you?"

"Found who?"

"Patricia, Lizzie," he answered. "You found her body."

*Found?*

Past tense.

I formed my fingers into fists, realizing that the pebbles and marbles underneath me had somehow turned to velvety soft fabric. I blinked, and Patricia's hanging body was gone, replaced by a too-bright hallway, its overhead lighting daring to burn a hole through my retinas.

"Jack said he found you in the street," David continued. "He said you were screaming so bad that he knew something had to be wrong. Jesus. I don't even know how he managed to drive you to the hospital in his condition."

I winced at the word *condition,* unable to process the meaning behind the meaning, wanting anything else in the world but to imagine Jack's screams, too. It wasn't hard, though, to imagine the screams. Not Jack's. Not the rest of the neighborhood's, either.

Maybe they'd all been screaming with me.

"The police, they . . ." David's words trailed off for a moment, his words coming out with a shaky breath. "They're saying that she killed herself. That it isn't anyone's fault. That it's not *your* fault, Lizzie."

"She didn't kill herself." My response was so serene that I would've sworn it wasn't even coming from my own mouth, that someone had climbed inside of me and decided to speak on my behalf.

"Lizzie," David started again, his hand moving down to mine, interlacing our fingers. "I'm sorry. I know you and Patricia were close, but—"

"She didn't kill herself, David," I repeated as I turned to look over at him. "We were supposed to go walking this morning."

"I'm so sorry, baby, but I don't think that's really—"

"We were supposed to go walking, David," I interrupted. "She invited me. Just me. If she was going to kill herself, she wouldn't have invited me. She didn't need to. Her friends were all at yoga this morning, anyway."

"Lizzie—"

"She wouldn't have wanted to die in that outfit, David," I rambled, my fingers starting to shake. "She wouldn't have . . . She flunked out of nursing school. It was the worst thing to ever happen to her. If she was going to die, she would've—"

"You can't know what's going on in someone's head when they're at that point, baby." David tried to soothe me, his hand gently squeezing mine. "Even if you think you know a person . . . well, that's the thing about depression, isn't it? You can never know for sure."

I laughed, the sound of it being closer to a bark than anything human. "Patricia wasn't *depressed*, David."

"Trust me. People like that . . . they're really good at hiding it. They have to be or else the people they care about might start to look at them differently."

"Not her. Not Patricia." I steadfastly shook my head. "She was fucking see-through. Everything about her was Saran-wrapped."

". . . I'll be here for you, Lizzie." David's voice was low. "Whatever you need, baby. I'm going to be right here for you."

"Okay." It was the only word I could force out of my mouth in response, the easiest thing I knew how to say.

Because I didn't know how to make David believe that I knew Patricia better than anyone else, even if our friendship had always had air quotes around it. Because I didn't know how to make David believe that Patricia was a lot of things, but she wasn't a flake, and she never would've made plans to go for a walk with me if she hadn't intended on keeping them.

Because I didn't know how to make David believe that Patricia didn't hang herself.

Because I didn't know how to make David believe that Patricia Fitzgerald was murdered.

3

# Brianna

*One Year Earlier*

Brianna Thompson had never understood the point of grave-yards.

It'd been a point of contention for her ever since she was a little girl, unable to understand why she couldn't just be buried next to her pet turtle in the backyard when it was her time to die. The thought of being separated from the small creature she'd cared about, of being forced to spend the rest of eternity next to complete and utter strangers, felt like a punishment she hadn't done anything to deserve.

What made matters worse was the ceremony that came before the burial, though. She'd only been to two funerals before, one for her grandmother and one for her mother. Even so, two felt like enough to make her an expert in how supernaturally awful they always were, how that awfulness lingered through and through. She remembered sitting in the church pew each time, feeling like her chest was going to explode, like she was seconds away from bits of her flying everywhere.

This funeral was different, though.

Because Brianna's chest didn't feel like it was going to blow up.

Because Brianna didn't feel anything.

"I'm sorry for your loss." An older gentleman pulled off his black porkpie hat before he took a seat beside her in the pew. "I know what you're going through has to be impossible to—"

"No."

". . . No?"

Brianna spoke without offering the stranger a second look. "No, I'm not interested in doing this with you. I'm not interested in doing this with anyone, actually."

"I'm sorry, Mrs. Thompson. I just wanted to give you my condolences—"

"There's not a damn thing you can give me that's going to make a difference," she explained, her voice just as casual as if they were discussing the weather. "And I'd rather not waste my time pretending to be nice to you right now. So. Please. Just go."

"I get that you're hurting right now, Mrs. Thompson, but you don't have to—"

"It's 'Miss.'"

"It is?" The stranger furrowed his brow. "I'm sorry. I was under the impression that you and Mr. Thompson were still—"

"We were never married," Brianna corrected as she stood up from the pew. "But just the fact that you thought that kind of proves my point, don't you think?"

"Your point?"

"That you really shouldn't be talking to me right now." She offered the stranger a strained smile, almost like she was trying to hide a pocket-size knife between her teeth. "Have a good rest of your day, whoever-the-fuck-you-are."

Brianna waved at the man before she headed down the aisle of the church, passing by the rest of the guests, each one of them certainly having heard her exchange with Mr. Porkpie Hat. Brianna was unfazed by their silent, hardened stares and rushed whispers, having learned a long time ago to not put too much stock into the opinions of anyone who attended First Lutheran Church, not to put too much stock into the opinions of anyone who wasn't interested in helping her pay her rent that month. She'd never been one for church, anyway, only deciding to hold the funeral here out of respect to her deceased mother.

Brianna's mom had loved church. Specifically this church.

And Brianna knew that she would've wanted to see him buried here.

"You don't have to talk to other people like that." Pastor Freeman softly held out his arm, preventing Brianna from completely leaving the building, her walking now paused on the faded purple carpet that ran all the way from the front door to the altar. "I know you're hurting, but that doesn't give you the right to be disrespectful."

". . . I know," Brianna admitted, her eyes casting downward. There was *one* person whose opinion she'd valued at First Lutheran, and it was the man standing right in front of her. Pastor Freeman had been a constant presence in her life. He'd baptized her. He'd helped her through her confirmation classes when that seemed like a hopeless endeavor.

And he was the only one who'd been there for her that same night, the only one who'd been able to hold on to her, even when it felt like she'd turned into a porous mass, unable to be held or grasped or contained.

"I'm sorry."

"I know." Pastor Freeman nodded toward the church's main hall. "And I know you're going to do the right thing and go back in there."

"I can't . . . I'm sorry. I can't. I can't pretend like I want to hear it. Pastor Freeman, if you make me go back in there, I'm not going to make it. I'm not going to—"

Brianna sobbed halfway through her words, her voice suddenly unrecognizable, the sound emitting from her chest so bent and defective.

"I can't do this!" Brianna shouted, her lips quivering as she folded her arms across her chest, trying to hold herself together, trying to keep her skin from sliding down to her feet. "Please don't make me do this."

"I know you don't want to do this, Brianna," Pastor Freeman whispered, his hands moving to Brianna's arms, adding just enough pressure to keep her still and solid. "But today isn't about you. It's about—"

"I know who it's about," Brianna cut him off.

"Well, don't let me tell you something you already know." Pastor Freeman smiled down at her as he so casually quoted one of her mom's favorite sayings. "If you want me to, I can get started with everything, and you can come in after a few minutes. After you've calmed down?"

"Okay." It was the only word Brianna could make come out of her mouth, the easiest thing she knew how to say.

Pastor Freeman pulled her into his arms, just for a moment, just before he walked toward the waiting pews and the waiting crowd.

And Brianna wondered how long it was going to be until she could hold herself together again, how long until she'd return to something approaching cogent and secure. She knew that she couldn't be this fragile forever, because it would be hell if she spent the rest of her life existing like a raw nerve, easily provoked and easily torn.

But how else was she supposed to exist after something like this? She was already in hell.

She was already burning alive.

*   *   *

"Where are you going?" Brianna asked as she watched Charles move about their cramped apartment, his hands grabbing at clothes, pulling them off the closet rack. There was an immediate contrast between his spare, muscular frame and the huge mountain of shirts, jeans, everything he was holding in his grasp. "And where were you?"

"I already told you that I wasn't going to that bullshit funeral, Brianna," Charles answered while still in motion, the suitcase laid across their bed seeming to get heavier by the second.

"You think I wanted to go?" Brianna laughed, the response undercut by her own slight sob. "I didn't want to fucking go, Charles. I almost fucking left but—"

"Let me guess, Pastor Freeman asked you to stay, and you did exactly what he wanted you to do?"

"Yeah. I did." Brianna's gaze turned to cold steel. "Because he was the only person who was there for me that night."

"Don't," Charles warned. "Don't start with this shit again, Brianna. Not today."

"Then tell me where the hell you're going!" Brianna closed the distance between Charles and herself, her eyes cracked and red, now brimming with fresh tears. "I don't understand how you could leave—"

"Yes, you do." Charles's response was frosted over with ice. "You know why I'm leaving. Don't pretend like you don't."

"Fine." Brianna found herself once again trying to keep her skin and bones all together, her arms crossing over her chest. "You're right. I do know why you're leaving. I just don't understand how."

"How?"

"How you could leave when this was the last place that we . . ." Brianna choked on the phrase before she forced her throat to cooperate. "This was the last place we had him, Charles. That breakfast table out there . . . his bedroom . . . this is it. This is all we have left."

"Which is exactly why I'm letting it go. Do you really think I want to sit around here all day and fucking wallow in it? I mean, look at you, Bri. You've never looked this bad before."

Charles reached out to gently brush his knuckles along the underside of Brianna's jaw, the same way he'd done a million times before. But this time, she moved away from him, the mere thought of his skin brushing along hers conjuring up images of her own vomit pooling at her shoes, of the vomit soon mixing with her skin and blood and hair.

Because if Charles touched her right now, Brianna was going to finally fall apart.

"So, what?" Brianna snapped. "You're just going to run away? You're just going to pretend like none of this ever happened?"

"Fuck you. I'm not running away," Charles muttered. "I just . . . can't. I can't be around here anymore. It's like . . . there's never enough air in the fucking room."

". . . And what do you think it's like for me?"

". . . What?"

"What do you think it's like for me?" Brianna repeated, her voice filling the modest bedroom. "I was *there*, Charles. I was right there. You're talking about how you can't be around *here* anymore? Charles, I can't be *anywhere* anymore. There's nowhere for me to fucking go. I can't sleep. I can't even fucking dream without seeing him all over again—"

Charles cut her off then, desperation lining his tone. "You could always come with me, Bri—"

"I don't want to come with you!" Brianna's frustration wrapped around her every syllable. "I just don't want you to leave! How could you leave when I need you—"

Brianna stopped herself, her frame shaking as she stared over at the man who she'd woken up next to for the last fourteen years. She used to think it was funny how Charles always looked like a different man depending on the time of the day, on the way the light filtered in through their windows. He was an ever-changing piece of art, or at least that was the way she'd once described him in the outer edges of her science notebook, when she should've been listening and taking notes.

But today he'd looked the same as he did yesterday and the day before. Charles's ever-changing nature had come to a standstill, the sadness he tried to hide etched into his face as heavy bags under his eyes, as a beard that was a week past when it last should've been shaved.

"Forget it." Brianna shrugged, her arms still tight around herself. "When are you coming back?"

"I don't know."

"You don't know?"

It was Charles's turn to shrug. "You're trying to get me to commit to something. Why? So you can throw it back in my face?"

"No," Brianna insisted. "The last thing I want is to fight with you right now, Charles."

"That's the last thing I want, too," Charles replied before he leaned down toward her, softly brushing his lips against hers. It wasn't exactly a kiss. It wasn't exactly anything.

But Brianna accepted it all the same, taking a moment to bask in the unanticipated affection. She was so used to the new version of

Charles, the one that always looked the same, the one who seemed like he was half here and half gone, that she was eager to hold on to something she still recognized about him.

His mouth. His lips. His touch.

Unchanging and unchanged.

Even if everything else had forever been changed between them.

"I love you, Bri," Charles said when he pulled away from her. "You know that, right? That I love you more than anything—"

"Don't come back."

"What?"

"If you're going to leave, I don't want you to come back."

". . . You don't mean that." Charles stared down at her, searching her expression for the truth.

But Brianna held firm. "Yes, I do. I mean it. If you leave, I never want to see you again."

"Brianna—"

"If you get to be done with this, then I get to be done, too. You don't get to run away from what happened and just come back whenever you've dealt with it, Charles. You don't get to leave me all alone to pick up the pieces."

"I already told you that I'm not running away," Charles said as he reached for her again, his words pleading and sincere. "I'm not running away, Bri, I just need some time to—"

"You can take all the time you need, Charles. Away from here. Away from me."

"Can you please stop talking like that—"

"There won't be anything left for you here, anyway."

"What the hell does that mean—Brianna!" He called out after her as she left the bedroom, her hands balled into fists at her sides.

But Brianna was already gone. And with every step away from him, she marveled at the feeling in the center of her chest, a new-found jumble of cords somehow keeping everything strung tight together.

And by the time she'd stepped outside of the apartment, her back resting against the faded brick, that same jumble of cords seemed like it was swirling around inside of her in a way she never could've expected. The feeling moved up from her chest toward each side of her head, causing a searing headache, causing her to wince and crouch toward the barely tended grass.

And as she collapsed in on herself, Brianna Thompson brought her hands up to her face and screamed against her palms, the cord still radiating while her veins thumped and thumped and thumped.

# 4

# Elizabeth

Patricia's shoes.

That was what I'd heard that morning, echoing outside of my bathroom window on our empty street. I'd heard Patricia Fitzgerald's heels falling from her corpse and landing on the ground below. It was the sort of detail I wouldn't have known anything about if it weren't for the conversations I'd had with the police. It wasn't the sort of detail I'd even asked about, the information being offered to me as some fucked-up source of solace.

Everyone just kept telling me that it wasn't my fault. That it wouldn't have mattered if I'd sprinted out to the street after I heard the first dead thud of her shoe against the pavement. She would've already been gone by the time I got there. She would've already been a misplaced angel dangling like a life-size Christmas tree ornament from a dark lamppost.

Unfortunately for me, whether it was my fault or not, I hadn't been able to shake that small, sad sound. The week after Patricia's funeral, I jumped nearly every time I heard anything that resembled it, my nerves being shot to shit. I didn't want to be the person on our block who always discovered the dead, who was on track to becoming so accustomed to the sound of a dead woman's pair of heels hitting the asphalt that I would've been able to recognize its tone in a crowded room.

Dr. Whitaker had taken care of me, though, over these past few months. She'd prescribed me Paroxetine, a bottle of round white pills that rearranged my brain until the only thing I was able to focus on was how nauseated I felt whenever I forgot to eat breakfast before taking my daily dose. I was grateful for the savior pills, my fingers no longer trembling against the wheel of my car when I passed by Patricia's house on my way to work, my mouth no longer going dry whenever I spotted the bottle of Korean face wash that still haunted my sink.

"Baby?" David's voice called for me, and I answered it, already making my way toward the living room. I'd taken the day off from the Learning Center, under the guise of taking a mental health day. I'd told my coworkers that I had plans for a massage and a mani-pedi, offering the lie as I playfully laughed, making sure to show just enough of my teeth to seem believably joyous about the occasion.

Of course what I'd really done with my time off was the same thing I'd been doing ever since Patricia had turned up dead. I'd been looking for clues, searching for signs, sifting through every single errant thought that Patricia had ever posted to social media. It was so much easier to carry through with a research plan when I was on my anxiety meds, the edges of my mind free and clear of all that fear and trembling.

So far, David was the only person who I'd shared my theory with, the one about Patricia being murdered. I think at first he'd chalked it up to another aspect of my trauma, something I desperately needed to talk about with Dr. Whitaker. But when I wouldn't let it go, he seemed to understand that it was more than just a theory to me.

That to me, it was the absolute truth.

Which meant that it was something that he desperately needed to monitor.

"There you are." David beamed as soon as I turned the corner into the living room. "How was your day, baby?"

*This is a test.*

David's and my relationship had done a 180 after Patricia. I still didn't know if it was because of how broken up Jack had been after she died, the way he shifted his emotional weight onto David whenever he offered up his shoulder, or if it was because David had been scarred by the possibility that he could've been in Jack's place instead.

It didn't really matter either way. The only thing that mattered was how attentive David had been in the last three months. He'd been so involved with me and my day-to-day that I'd dropped all communication with Nathan, unable to engage in an affair when my husband was always moments away from casually peeking over at my phone screen.

"Baby? Did you hear what I asked?"

*Right.*

The test.

My stomach tightened as I thought about whether to tell him the truth. If I told him how I'd really spent my day off, there was a good chance that he would immediately report it to Dr. Whitaker, since it was the kind of behavior that she would categorize as obsessive-compulsive. But if I chose to lie to him about what I'd been up to, and he was able to see right through it, he still would report it to Dr. Whitaker, but he also would give me a look of utter disappointment.

And I didn't know if I had it in me to handle David's look of disappointment right now.

"It was good." I forced a smile. "I just . . . hung out mostly."

"Hung out?" David gently pressed me for more information, and even though he was only standing a few feet away from me, it suddenly felt like there was an impossibly deep gorge separating us.

"I was just hanging out around the house, David. I just . . . needed to take the day. I don't know. I didn't think that it was going to turn into an interrogation if I just took some time for myself—"

"Were you looking up things about Patricia?" David interrupted.

"I don't really see how that's relevant to what we were talking about—"

"Janice told me that you've been struggling with your lesson plans for the tutoring program," David continued. "She said that she's starting to get worried about if you'll have enough material to go over with the kids for the rest of the year."

". . . You've been talking to Janice?" I couldn't help but wince at his admission, the thought of my boss from work having private conversations with my husband like this was the fucking 1950s, giving him updates about my *condition*.

"Don't be that way," David said, his gaze pleading, probably having noticed my fleeting yet pained expression. "I was the one who told Janice to contact me if she thought that anything might be off with you. Besides, Dr. Whitaker said it can sometimes take a whole community to help with—"

"There's nothing off with me, David."

"You never answered my question, Lizzie."

"Because I don't think it matters."

*Because I don't like your tone right now, David.*

*Because I don't like the way you're looking at me like I'm upside down, like I'm inside out.*

*Like I'm the one who's always, always wrong.*

"It matters, Lizzie." David took a step closer to me. "Please. Just tell me the truth."

". . . So what if I was," I started, my tone already on the defense. "You know how I feel about what happened to her, David. And if you're being honest with yourself, you know that there was something very fucking wrong about what happened, too—"

"You can't keep doing this to yourself, baby." David's face filled with concern, his body tensing up like I'd just said something that terrified him. "If you keep trying to . . . you're only going to hurt yourself, Lizzie. Whenever you go over what happened to Patricia . . . Dr. Whitaker says it's like you're opening the same old wound and starting the healing process all over again."

"She's wrong." I confidently shook my head. "I'm not in the same place I was a few months ago, David. It's not like I'm . . . You said it yourself. You said that the pills have been working. And I've been so much better about doing things around the house."

"You have been getting better, baby." David smiled, which I was sure was an attempt at providing some ounce of comfort, but all it did was unnerve me further. "Which is why I want to make sure that you stay on the right path, okay?"

"I *am* on the right path, David," I insisted. "For fuck's sake, I know how to walk and chew gum at the same time. Just because I'm trying to make sense out of Patricia's death—"

"Dr. Whitaker said that you weren't even close." David's smile faded, just as he'd interrupted me.

"Dr. Whitaker said that I'm not even close to being on the right path?" I let out a laugh, each note of it lined with a harsh edge.

"No," David corrected. "She told me that you and Patricia weren't even that close. That sometimes you talk about her like you two were barely friends."

"Why the hell is Dr. Whitaker talking to you about—I thought all the sessions we had together before Pat died were supposed to be off the table—"

I was hardly able to get through a full sentence, my thoughts bubbling all around my brain, each one threatening to spill out of me. I'd agreed to let Dr. Whitaker and David discuss my sessions after I'd been prescribed medication. I was afraid that I wouldn't be able to trust myself, or whatever I was thinking, and I wanted David to be aware of my every word, my every thought behind the thought.

Because I wanted him to keep me safe from myself.

But I hadn't thought about the consequences. I hadn't thought about Dr. Whitaker slipping up and revealing something that I didn't want David to know about, like Nathan, like the way I'd been feeling in the months before David noticed I was alive again.

"She just thought it was important for me to know," David replied. "She just wanted to . . . Lizzie, what is this really about? If you and Patricia weren't even that close—"

"Yeah, well, maybe Dr. Whitaker is wrong about that, too." I cut him off, everything inside of me brimming with sudden indignation. There was nothing as frustrating as having someone try to put thoughts inside my head, even worse when they were actual feelings.

How the hell could Dr. Whitaker think she ever had a clue about what was really running through my mind, anyway? She only knew what I told her. The woman had a passenger-seat window into the back of my head, but it sounded like she'd convinced herself that she had a bird's-eye view of every fucking crevice.

"Lizzie—" David took another step closer. "I just don't want . . . You know, we never even talked about Camilla—"

"Camilla? Why are you bringing up Camilla right now?" A familiar pit opened in my chest at the mention of her name.

*Don't. Don't spiral.*

*That was such a long time ago.*

*It can't hurt me anymore.*

"Lizzie, please. We have to talk about things even when they're hard—"

"I don't want to talk about any of this anymore, David. You're upsetting me."

"Fine. We can talk about something else." David retreated from the conversation, the wheels clearly turning in his head. "Let's go back to what I wanted to talk to you about before. The idea of keeping you on the right path."

"Is that code for upping my anxiety meds?"

"No." David shook his head. "It's code for getting you some help around here."

"Some help around here?" I glanced around the living room, taking in a chair that had several days of my work clothes thrown over its back, a counter with a few too many Starbucks cups lining it, a painting that I'd bought from a street fair but still hadn't managed to frame resting against a nearby wall. "What? Do you mean like a cleaning service?"

"Not exactly." David sighed as he brought his hands up toward his waist, staring over at me like I was a complicated problem, a business proposal that was missing vital information that'd just landed on his desk. "I was thinking more like an assistant."

I chuckled at the suggestion, already prepared to turn it down.

But before I was able to say a word, David went on, "I'm serious, Lizzie. I think you need someone to make sure you don't . . . I'm just saying that things might be easier for you if you weren't alone all the time. You'd be a lot better with keeping up with your lesson plans if it was all you really had to worry about. If you didn't have so much time to—"

"Is this a real option?"

"What do you mean?"

"I mean, is this something I'm actually going to have a choice in?" I explained. "Or have you already picked out the assistant and they'll be starting tomorrow? Whether I like it or not?"

"It's completely up to you, Lizzie."

*"It's completely up to you, Lizzie"?*

Those words were as loaded as a fucking gun.

I knew what was going to happen if I said *no*, if I insisted that I could manage everything all by myself. It wouldn't be long until Dr. Whitaker was somehow writing me a prescription for an assistant, with David soon running it past our insurance for approval, assuring me that it wouldn't interfere with any of my other medication.

Because this wasn't a choice.

This was the difference between David gently slipping a pill into my hands and him violently forcing it down my throat. This was the difference between him sweetly tucking me into bed at night and tightly wrapping leather straps around my wrists so I'd stay in place until the morning.

This was an inevitable conclusion. And I needed to decide if I wanted it to happen my way or theirs.

I chose mine.

". . . Fine."

"Fine?"

"Yes. Fine," I said, even though it felt like there was bile rising in my throat, my anxious state ironically peaking despite the medication that flowed through my veins. "I'll look into it."

"You promise?"

"I promise."

"Good." David tilted his head toward the front door of our home. "Would you be up for some Thai food tonight? I could go run and pick something up from Nine Thai."

"Sounds perfect." I smiled now, too, despite how eager I was to let out a primal scream.

Despite how much I wanted to rebel against the marching orders he'd tried and failed to disguise as me having an *option* in all of this.

# 5

**HARBOR TOWN HIVE—PRIVATE GROUP**

RULES

1. NO RACISM/SEXISM/HOMOPHOBIA/TRANSPHOBIA, ETC.—Just don't be an asshole, alright? No strike system for this bullshit! One strike and you're fucking nuked!

2. LISTEN TO OTHER PEOPLE—What's the point of asking a question if you're just going to argue about the answer? Try not to be a dick. (Also, note for mods, can we find a substitute for "dick"? Might be an issue here with unnecessarily gendered language for an insult.)

3. NO ANTI-MEMPHIS MEMES/NO BAD VIBES—Oh, you think crime only happens here? Oh, you think our city has an exclusive claim on break-ins and cars getting stolen? L O L F U C K O F F

4. NO SCAMMERS—Sorry MLM Queens and Kings!

5. REAL NAMES ONLY—Because if you wouldn't put your name on it, why the hell are you even saying it? 😄

6. NASHVILLE FUCKING SUCKS—Not a rule! Just a way of life. A peaceful mantra. A tattoo @RogerBanks has on his bicep that is glorious and worthy of praise (we love Roger here almost as much as we hate Nashville).

---

## GROUP POSTS AUTOMATICALLY SORTED BY: NEW ACTIVITY

**SILVIA POTTER—4:56 PM**
Post: Ohmygodddddd! Please tell me that everyone here has tried the new BBQ spot on Union Ave? Little Larry's? I swear to God, I had an orgasm after the first bite.

@SilviaPotter from @AndrewGreer: Is it Black-Owned? The wife and I are trying to make sure we only support Black-Owned businesses for the rest of the year.

@AndrewGreer from @SilviaPotter: Of course! 😊 And yay! Happy to hear you and Theresa are taking on the #EatLocalEatBlack challenge! Eddie and I are doing that, too.

@SilviaPotter from @MattHughes: I was just there last night! FUCKING TRANSCENDENT.

@SilviaPotter from @LarryGibbs: Thanks, guys! Come see me on Sunday and we'll be offering a few items that we're trying out to add to the menu (braised lamb, anyone?)

@LarryGibbs from @KimBowers: Larry, please! 😩 Please add some vegan options! I'd love to support but I haven't touched meat since I was 13.

@KimBowers from @LarryGibbs: Working on it, Kim! You got any dish suggestions?

**ROGER BANKS—3:24 PM**

Post: Hey @all! No need to get into the drama of it, but I just kicked a racist asshole from the group (@FrankieClark). Thanks everyone for reporting his posts! And a gentle reminder that if you have a problem with Black people then maybe this city isn't the one for you? Maybe not even the whole planet.

#FuckRacists #FuckNashville #FuckGentrifiers

@RogerBanks from @AndrewGreer: Good riddance!

@RogerBanks from @JodiHolmes: Just wanted to say thank you for being such a good mod, Roger! And as always #FuckNashville 😳

**ELIZABETH SMITH—2:35 PM**

Post: Hey @all! Does anyone have any good leads on an assistant? I just need someone to help me stay organized. I wouldn't ask, but I'm on anxiety meds now and my brain is frieddddd. Pay starts at $25/HR if there's anyone out there who wouldn't mind thinking for me (and maybe remembering to go grocery shopping when I'm too zoned out).

@ElizabethSmith from @SilviaPotter: You don't need to apologize for asking for help, babe! Especially not if you're medicated.

@SilviaPotter from @ElizabethSmith: I knowwwww but still!

@ElizabethSmith from @JodiHolmes: I'd volunteer to be your assistant for free, Liz! Seriously, you should have no problem finding someone.

@ElizabethSmith from @KariParsons: I think I might know someone! Want me to DM you her info?

@KariParsons from @ElizabethSmith: Yes, please! Ahh! Thank you so much, Kari!

@ElizabethSmith from @KariParsons: No prob, Elizabeth! It's the least I can do for another Harbor Towner 😊

# 6

# Brianna

*Nine Months Earlier*

B rianna! Look! Look at this one!" Vera was sitting right next to Brianna during their supposed study session at the mostly empty campus library, holding her phone only a few inches away from Brianna's textbook.

Brianna took a second to glance at the picture on the screen, soon chuckling quietly to herself in response. It was yet another pitch-perfect pharmacy tech meme, probably from one of the several forums dedicated to future pharmacy technicians who were currently enrolled in some kind of course. Brianna and Vera were taking a six-month course themselves, one offered by a local community college. It was meant to serve as a gateway to an entry-level career, or maybe even something a bit higher on the corporate ladder if they were able to pass the national certification exam.

They'd met on the first day of class, when Vera had casually asked Brianna if she had any hand cream in her purse. When Brianna had questioned why Vera had singled her out for the ask, Vera mentioned something about young brown-skinned girls having to stick together, before launching into a few choice quotes from MLK. She'd managed to spin the moment into a continuation of the civil rights movement, talking about the promised land even as Brianna handed her the cream.

And Brianna had laughed so much that day her ribs were hurting afterward.

They'd been inseparable since then, still making each other laugh, Vera still occasionally asking Brianna for something out of her purse.

"Funny." Brianna nodded toward the meme on Vera's phone just as she circled a phrase on the page in front of her. "Have you seen the one about the lunch breaks?"

"Have you seen the one about the patient trying to refill their hydrocodone too early?" Vera laughed before the sound went suddenly quiet in her throat. "You know, I never really thought about how many drug addicts we're going to have to deal with. I don't know why, I just figured that was going to be more of a problem for doctors. Or nurses."

"Or ER rooms," Brianna added, her attention only halfway devoted to the conversation as she attempted to memorize nearly every word on the pages that she held open.

"Yeah. Or ER rooms." Vera nodded as she spoke. "I was reading about this one guy who was on meth or something and tackled one of the nurses at the hospital where he was admitted. She hit her head on a cart and almost bled out."

"And what happened to him?"

"What?"

"What happened to the guy?" Brianna pressed. "The man who was on meth?"

"Does it matter?"

"Just to me. I've heard enough one-sided stories in my life to know when to ask questions about whoever else was involved."

"One-sided stories?" Vera smirked. "Brianna Thompson, have you secretly been a conspiracy theorist this whole time?"

"I'm not a conspiracy theorist," she answered with a smirk of her own. "I just like to know all the facts about a situation before I decide what I'm going to think about it."

"I get that." Vera hummed before she went on, her eyes drifting down to her own textbook in front of her. "Okay, so, which classification states that a product with a strange color or taste will be recalled by the FDA—"

"Class 3."

"Which technique used in compounding accurately describes the mixing of two ingredients of unequal quantities—"

"Geometric dilution."

"Which of the following is *not* a potential cause of medication error—"

"Wrong doctor. The only eligible causes are wrong technique, wrong time, or wrong patient."

"Jesus Christ, Brianna." Vera laughed again. "If you know everything already, why do you still need to study?"

"Because I don't know everything." Brianna smiled. "And because if I don't hang out with you after class, you're going to do something really stupid, like try to flirt your way to the top of the class with Professor Pierce."

"Flirt my way to the top?" Vera grinned. "Oh, I plan on doing a lot more than flirting—"

"Which is exactly why you need someone here to keep a watchful eye." Brianna laughed now, too. "You don't want to end up failing your certification exam *and* being in the middle of a very messy divorce."

"Hey, if a married man isn't wearing his wedding ring, that pretty much means that he's on the market."

"Another one-sided story, huh? I wonder if his wife still wears the ring he got her."

"Ugh! Don't make me think about it like that," Vera whined as she sat back in her chair. "You're taking all the fun out of it."

"I'm sorry for taking all the fun out of potentially ruining a marriage," Brianna said, her every syllable drenched in sarcasm.

"I hate you sometimes, Brianna. You know that?"

"I hate you, too, Vera." Brianna beamed over at her before she went back to staring down at her textbook, her mind already working through the next few sample quiz questions.

*   *   *

Brianna was bone-tired. After her study session with Vera and their usual ritual of grabbing a few drinks before going their separate ways for the evening, she was feeling like the only thing she had enough energy left for was a good night of sleep. But almost as soon as she walked up to the front of her apartment, she knew that she was going to need more energy than she could possibly muster.

Because Pastor Freeman was waiting for her on the building's front step.

"You haven't been coming to church lately," he started with a smile. "I figured I'd come and collect your tithes for the year in person, just to make it easier for you."

"Of course. Makes perfect sense to me." Brianna smiled right back, even as her eyelids felt heavy and drowsy. "What brings you here so late, Pastor Freeman?"

"I just wanted to check in on you. The church was having a late-night rehearsal with the choir, since Toni won't be here to direct next

54

weekend. She's got this Black Women's Leadership conference to get to in Nevada, but everyone still wanted to get another session in."

"Competition season must be coming up."

"Oh, you know how it is." Pastor Freeman smirked. "Church folk can turn into jackals when it comes to singing gospel, especially when there's a points system involved."

"I always thought that Lutherans weren't much for singing, gospel or otherwise." Brianna took a seat next to him on the steps.

"We aren't," he replied. "But ever since the Baptist church closed down a few years back, we've picked up a few transfers. And my God, do Baptists love their gospel music."

"Amen." Brianna chuckled even as she placed a worried hand across her mouth. She couldn't tell if her laugh sounded *off* or not, and she didn't want Pastor Freeman to pick up on the fact that she'd had a few frozen margaritas with her dinner tonight. It didn't matter that she'd been the legal drinking age for over a decade by now. Getting caught half drunk by Pastor Freeman would still make her feel like the teen girl she was when he'd caught her with a bottle of Hennessy behind her high school.

". . . How have you been holding up, Brianna?" His voice was soft. "Really."

". . . I don't know." She shrugged, looking away from him.

"You don't know how you've been feeling?"

"I don't know how to answer that question, Pastor Freeman," she admitted. "If I tell you that I've been doing good, there's no way you're going to believe me, and you shouldn't. But if I tell you that I've been doing just as bad as always, you're going to try to get me to go to therapy or check me into Lakeside's mental health clinic yourself—"

"I'm not asking you that question so I can judge you," he corrected. "I'm only trying to see how you're feeling. That's it. There's no hidden agenda here."

"You promise?"

"I promise."

". . . Okay, then. Well, to be honest with you, Pastor, sometimes I feel like . . . I feel like . . . like I'm trying to run on two broken legs. But I know that I have to keep running or else I'm never going to move again. If I don't keep moving, I'm going to drown in it."

"Drown in what, Brianna?"

"The darkness. The sadness. The way it feels when I wake up in the morning and want to call out for him, even though I know he's not there anymore. That he'll never be there again."

Brianna's face warmed as tears threatened to spill from behind her eyes. "How am I supposed to get used to him never being there again, Pastor Freeman? How is anyone supposed to get used to that?"

"You don't really get used to it." Pastor Freeman wiped a few errant tears away from Brianna's cheeks. In that moment, he felt like her father, trying to comfort her like a child, trying to make her pain disappear in the dark.

"But you have to keep running," he added as he pulled her closer to his side, Brianna beginning to shake with sobs.

"Why?" she cried out, like she was speaking to no one in particular, like she was waiting for an answer from an omnipresent God. "Why?"

"Because you have too much good left to give this world. Because you have such a light inside of you, Brianna Thompson, and nothing should ever get to put that out."

"What if I'm tired of giving?" Brianna's question was quiet. "What if I'm tired of having all that light?"

"Tell you what. Whenever you get tired of giving, whenever you get tired of running, just call me, and I'll help you get back up on your feet."

Pastor Freeman meant every word of it, Brianna could tell. She could also tell that she wasn't ready to accept his grace or kindness or mercy or pity.

Because the goodness inside of her that he'd mentioned . . .

She'd felt further and further from it every day.

". . . Did you hear about what happened in Florida?" Brianna desperately wanted to change the topic of conversation, her heart aching inside of her chest.

"The execution of Brandon Hodges?"

"The murder of Brandon Hodges," Brianna corrected. "The state put a man on death row and then killed him, with no evidence that he was even at the scene of the crime."

"Which is why Tallahassee's on fire right now," Pastor Freeman added.

"Do you think that's the right thing to do?" Brianna looked up at Pastor Freeman's face, wanting to catch even the slightest change in his expression.

"What? Having riots in the street?" He hummed before he gave her his thoughts. "'A riot is the language of the unheard.' Isn't that what MLK said?"

"Yeah, but what do you have to say about it?" It felt like Brianna was walking a tightrope, like she was just a few seconds away from falling into a dark and painful end, a hole that was going to swallow up every last part of her.

"I don't think what I have to say about it would ever trump what MLK had to say about it." He offered her a warm smile. "But . . . if you're after my personal opinion . . ." Pastor Freeman took in a deep breath before he spoke again. "You know how the Sermon on the Mount goes . . . 'You have heard that it was said, "An eye for an eye and a tooth for a tooth." But I say to you, do not resist the one who is evil. But if anyone slaps you on the right cheek, turn to him the other also.'"

"So, that's what you really think about it, then?" She looked away from him, disenchantment staining every word she spoke, even though she couldn't figure out why.

"I wasn't finished." Pastor Freeman held up a single finger. "Do you remember what it says in Isaiah? When he was calling on his people to do better? To return to God?"

"I don't remember." A strange guilt washed over Brianna, her brain too muddled with margaritas and grief to recall a passage she'd learned years and years ago.

"'Learn to do good. Seek justice. Correct oppression. Bring justice to the fatherless and plead the widow's cause,'" he confidently recited the quote. "That's how I feel about it, Brianna. If there's something that we can do to change things for the better, to change things for the future . . . well, I still believe that we should always try nonviolence first, just like MLK, and see if people will listen to reason."

"But?"

"But there's a reason God had to send down those plagues in Egypt, just to get them to listen, just to get Pharaoh to do the right thing. And there's a reason that Sister Harriet carried a pistol, too."

# 7

# Elizabeth

And you said your name was Antoinette Carroll?" I smiled over at the young woman who was seated on my living room couch. She looked hip in a way I couldn't quite put into words, with the kind of sharp aesthetic and winged eyeliner that I would've killed for when I was younger.

She was my third interviewee for the day, another in a short list of Facebook recommendations to fill the new position of assistant in my life. I felt like an idiot, clinging to a clipboard, my hair up in a professional bun like any of this actually meant anything, instead of it just being a way to placate my husband's concerns about my mental health.

And as soon as I was done holding "interviews," I had plans to get back to my research, following a comment thread Patricia had been in two years ago. The comment thread had gotten quite heated, and from the looks of the profile of the man she'd been arguing with, he had a few White Power tattoos and a hatred for women that ran so deep it'd led to him being involved with the Men Going Their Own Way movement, known as MGTOW.

"That's right." Antoinette nodded without smiling back.

"What a lovely name. Lewis Carroll was one of my favorite authors when I was growing up." I smiled even harder, trying to force her to return the expression. I wasn't unnerved by a woman not smiling. In fact, I was elated at the idea of a woman who never smiled unless it was absolutely necessary.

But in this particular instance, during a job interview, Antoinette not smiling was making me concerned about her adherence to societal norms. Wasn't being unable or unwilling to follow societal norms a sign of being a sociopath?

I wasn't going to hire a sociopath to be my assistant, even if their job was going to be mostly sitting by their phone and waiting for me to call, something I intended to do only on rare occasions.

"Lewis Carroll was a pedophile," Antoinette said, her face still not moving a muscle, her inflection stinging without any hint of anodyne.

"Right." The smile in my expression quickly faded. "I forget."

Antoinette shrugged, and suddenly I felt like I was back in high school, a more popular girl effortlessly destroying my self-esteem with a single comment. Thrown off by, well, everything about Antoinette, I fumbled for my clipboard, looking down at her list of qualifications.

"So, I see here that you used to work in your college's social work department?"

"Just for a few months."

"Oh?" I pressed. "Did something happen that made you want to leave or—"

"My boss was a misogynist pig."

"He was hitting on you?" I guessed, annoyance already burning a hole in my chest as memories of my own misogynist pig bosses came flooding back to mind, each interaction like a paper cut against my younger skin.

"She," Antoinette corrected. "And she wasn't hitting on anyone, but she was obviously jealous of all the other women in the department. It's why she was always on my ass about getting to work on time, even though she knows it's hard for me to get up that early. Which makes her an ableist, too."

"That sounds like it might've been a toxic work environment for you. I'm sorry you had to go through something like that."

I flipped to another page on my clipboard before I continued, "Now that you mention the 'ableist' thing . . . do you think you'd be able to perform the duties of this position, with or without reasonable accommodation? I don't think you'll be doing that much around here, honestly, but someone on a hiring forum said I might as well ask—"

"You can't ask me that."

"Oh, I know." I playfully waved a hand between us, like I was waving away the question, too. "I know that I can't ask anything specific about your disability, not that I ever would be that kind of prying asshole. Trust me, this section is just a formality. I can already tell that you wouldn't have any problems with—"

"Are you seriously suggesting that you're able to tell if I'm disabled or not? Just by looking at me?"

"No, that's not—I just meant that I can't really foresee this being a probl—" I stopped myself mid-sentence, my jaw tightening in retreat. "You know what? Let's forget I even went there. You're right, Antoinette. It was inappropriate. I'll be sure to never visit that particular forum again—"

"Yeah, sorry." Antoinette stood from the couch. "I don't think I can get involved with another boss with an 'ableist' bent. You get it."

Antoinette paused, her ever-present frown deepening even further. "Actually, looking at this house, you probably *don't*."

*Looking at this house?*

I squirmed in my seat, now fully aware that I was sitting in a custom-made chair, something that David had picked up for me on one of his trips out of town. I hadn't even bothered to ask how much it cost, just delighted to have something unique, something all mine.

The rest of our home was like that, too. Filled with things I hadn't asked a lot of questions about, things I wanted and assumed David and I would be able to afford. Even the house itself was one I'd picked out while we drove around different neighborhoods, excited to start a future together in a new city. And while I'd always considered our home modest, not exactly a mansion and not exactly a shotgun shack, I couldn't deny that the price tag was probably heftier than most people could've afforded without help from the bank.

But that was just the price of living downtown, wasn't it? It was the same everywhere, I imagined. If someone wanted to live in a nice neighborhood with white picket fences, fresh baby blue paint on the walls, and elegant white columns holding up each house's frame, there had to be a higher number on the mortgage statement. I didn't make the rules, even though I despised how unfair they were, and it wasn't my fault for craving manicured lawns and an open-concept kitchen.

I knew that I wasn't the *enemy* here, no matter how much Antoinette wanted to make me feel like I was.

No matter how much she wanted to believe it.

"I don't think that's really fair, Antoinette," I started, keeping my tone calm even though I was now fully in defense mode. "I don't think where I live has anything to do with my ability to empathize with—"

"Whatever." Antoinette raised her shoulders before she offered me a smile for the very first time. "Bye, *comrade*."

It was the last thing Antoinette said to me before she flashed what could only be described as a *sarcastic peace sign* and headed out the front door.

\*　\*　\*

"Am I a monster?" I asked David on the phone as I paced back and forth in our living room, my fingers flexing against a green apple. "Are *we* monsters?"

"Baby, what are you talking about?" David was on his lunch break, evidenced by the sound of his rapid chewing. There was also the distinct sound of an office in the background, printers whirring, phones ringing, the faint crashing of fingers on keys.

"I was just interviewing this young woman, you know, the one who was supposed to come in this morning. And . . . I'm a little worried that she had a point about us."

"And what, exactly, was her point?"

"Well, for starters, she said I was an 'ableist.' And unfortunately, I'm thinking she may have been right." I winced, remembering the valid accusation.

Why the hell had I even asked that question about reasonable accommodation?

"Well, if you are an *ableist*, at least that sounds like something you can work on."

"She also made a comment about the house—"

"Hey, now that's where I draw the line," David interrupted, his tone playful. "We can all work through our inherent biases all day long, but I paid way too much for that house to have anyone say something about it."

*Inherent biases.*

I'd smiled at the phrase, a familiar warmth moving through my system. That kind of talk was part of what had attracted me to David in the first place, his willingness to admit that there was something wrong with the way of the world, his commitment to being open to change.

"We," I finally added to the conversation as I leaned against a nearby counter.

"We what, baby?"

"*We* paid way too much for this house to have anyone say something about it," I gently corrected.

"Right. We."

"How's your day been going?" I idly wondered if there was a way to permanently live inside of this moment. It was nice feeling like David and I were on the same side again, that it wasn't me vs. David and Dr. Whitaker.

Or me vs. David and Janice from work.

Or me vs. David and the rest of the whole world.

"It's been going all right," he said before completely sidestepping the question. "Have you heard about the new barbecue place on Union?"

"Little Larry's?"

"I was thinking we could go there for dinner. Everyone's raving about it in the Harbor Town group."

"Ooh, that could be fun." I beamed. "Do you think they have outdoor seating? I love it when you can smell the barbecue on the grill before they even bring it to the table—"

*Brnggggggg.*

*Brnggggggg.*

*Brnggggggg.*

The front doorbell ringing pulled me out of the conversation, my shoulders slightly jumping with surprise at the sudden noise.

"Oh, gotta go." I rushed through my reply. "I think my next interviewee is here."

"Sounds good, baby. I'll see you at dinner. And make sure to kick this one out as soon as she says anything bad about the house."

I laughed at David's joke, the emotion filling my chest to the brim as I hung up the phone. I was deliriously happy with how the midday conversation had gone with my husband, that level of fulfillment seeming like a long-lost relic, a snapshot of the kinds of people we used to be with so little effort.

I was still smiling when I answered the door, pulling it open to reveal a Black woman standing on my front step. She seemed to be around the same age as me, but somehow she was immediately more interesting, like she had a billion stories to tell. Her skin was gorgeous, too, as it shone underneath the sun, my mind instantly going to images of a Black starlet walking down a Hollywood red carpet, a Lupita Nyong'o type beaming for all the cameras.

And as I continued to stare at her, something twisted in my stomach, like a knife pushing deep into my abdomen.

*She was beautiful.*

Too beautiful.

Insecurities started eating away at me, my wispy brunette strands and steel-gray eyes seeming to pale in comparison. If I was the most popular girl in school, then this woman was prom queen.

If I was Miss USA, then she was Miss Universe.

If Patricia were still alive, she would've told me to slam the door right in her face, to not even bother giving her an interview. Only an idiot would give someone like her a chance to be in their home, around their husband, around their children. It was only a matter of

SARA KOFFI

time before she'd become the *preferred* woman of the house, and I'd end up spending the next six months going through a rough divorce, looking even rougher for the wear—

*No.*

I gripped the side of the doorway, making sure the motion couldn't be seen by the woman outside. And as my fingers dug into the wall until some of the paint chipped against my nails, I reminded myself that Patricia and I had never seen eye to eye on these kinds of things, that I didn't need to take her advice from beyond the grave.

I also didn't want to prove young Antoinette *right*, that it'd been a good call to not work with me because I would've been just another misogynistic pig, jealous of the women I hired, unable to see them as anything except competition.

". . . Are you okay?" the woman asked, her concern sounding genuine. "I could always come back another time if there's something going on—"

"No." I shook my head, pulling my hand away from the doorway and folding it behind my back. "Sorry. I was just . . . Are you Brianna Thompson?"

"I am." She smiled, and the knife in my stomach buried itself even deeper.

"Come on in." I returned her expression as flames danced across my brain and behind my eyes, warning bells sounding so loudly in my head.

\* \* \*

I was watching Brianna like a hawk, my gaze only cutting away to ensure that I wasn't overpouring the coffee. I'd offered her a cup of it after she'd taken a seat on the couch, before she crossed her perfect legs and let out a perfect, happy sigh like she had the innate ability to be comfortable wherever she ended up.

"Do you usually like sugar in your coffee?" I forced out the question, my palms moving toward one of our cabinets. "Or do you take it bl— plain?"

"I'll take some sugar with it, please." Brianna's voice was as soft and sweet and perfect as the rest of her. "Honey is fine with me, too."

"Got it." I nodded, reaching for the small container of sugar we kept on hand.

"Your home is lovely," Brianna said as she glanced around the room. "I've always loved the way the homes look in Harbor Town."

"Really?" I made conversation, half listening and half fuming about the situation that I'd gotten myself into, having to interview a supermodel for a position in my home.

"Really. I just love the design, especially when you compare it with the homes out in Cordova. Those places always seem so much less . . . personal. Like they were all built by committee. But in Harbor Town . . . every house looks like someone cared about it, like someone was bringing their daydreams to life."

"What a beautiful way to put it," I replied, something softening inside of me. "That's one of the reasons David and I decided to buy a home out here, too."

"Good choice." Brianna smiled again.

"What side of the city do you live on, Brianna?" I asked, almost finished with making her cup of coffee.

"Oh, I live over in Whitehaven."

"Whitehaven?" I brightened at her response, the sharp knife in my stomach turning into nothing more cutting than Styrofoam. "Oh my God."

"Wait. Are you from there, too?"

"No, I'm not from there, but I might as well be." I hastily set down Brianna's drink so I could take a seat in front of her. "That's where the Learning Center, where I work, used to be before they moved a little closer to Midtown. The people who run the place just thought it'd be easier if the Center was more centrally located—"

I scoffed as I cut myself off, irritated with my brain for focusing on details Brianna probably couldn't care less about. "Sorry. I don't know why I'm going into all that right now. I just wanted to say that yes, I'm familiar with that part of the city, and I absolutely love it."

"Are you a big Elvis fan, then?" Brianna's expression was warm.

And I quickly held up a defensive finger. "Fuck no. Fuck Elvis. Why would I waste my time visiting his old mansion when I could be hanging out where the *real* musicians lived and breathed? I mean, Sun Studio? With B.B. King and Howlin' Wolf? Come on."

"I think Elvis recorded a few songs at Sun Studio, too."

"Oh, he did, but that was years later." I rolled my eyes. "Isn't that how things always end up going? Young white guys trying to chase trends? Don't even get me started on what happened with the Beach Boys and Chuck Berry."

"My mom loved Chuck Berry." Brianna chuckled. "She used to have a whole compilation of his greatest hits playing on repeat whenever she'd clean the house."

"Good choice." I repeated Brianna's line right back at her, even copying the same smile.

". . . Can I ask you kind of a weird question, Ms. Smith—"

"Please. Call me Elizabeth."

"Elizabeth," Brianna started again. "Can I ask you kind of a weird question?"

"Go for it."

"You don't . . ." Brianna stopped for a moment, a thought seeming to flash across her features. "Um, usually when I'm going out for these assistant jobs, I can tell right away why the person is hiring help. But with you . . . I think you might be the most put-together person I've ever met."

I let out a laugh, soon pressing my hand across my chest like I was trying to contain the sound of it. "Sorry, it's just— No. I'm not put-together at all, Brianna, but I do a pretty good job of playing a put-together person on TV."

When the amusement had passed through me, I leaned back in my seat, bringing my own cup of coffee toward my lips. "So, what made you want to get in touch with me about the position? Kari recommended you so highly, I was a little worried that someone else would've already snatched you off the market before we even got a chance to speak."

"Kari recommended you highly, too," Brianna answered. "And I've always trusted her when it comes to being able to read people. She has this whole thing about intentions and energy—"

"Oh, wow. Kari's a tarot card kind of girl?" I smirked at the thought.

"You two haven't met before?"

"We've only talked in the Harbor Town group. You haven't joined it yet?"

"I don't think I can."

"Why not?"

"Because I don't live in Harbor Town," Brianna reminded me with a small smile.

"Right." I returned the expression, a little embarrassed at my moment of forgetfulness. "Still. I'm glad Kari was able to convince you to take a chance on working with me."

"You make it sound like I already got the job."

"Honestly, Brianna?" I leaned toward her, my hands covering my knees. "You're the only person I've talked to so far who hasn't made me want to tear my hair out."

"I'm sorry the applicant pool has been so . . . lacking." Brianna's tone was sympathetic.

"So, you want to try this thing out?" I asked expectantly. "See if we can stand each other for the next week or so? And, to sweeten the pot, if you end up hating me, you can quit within the next seven days and I'll still pay you for the full week."

"I'm in. Just let me know when you want me to start." Brianna's tone was casual and cool.

". . . How about right now?" I grinned. "I've got a dinner date with my husband tonight, and I'd love to get your opinion on potential outfits?" My expression fell for a few seconds, worried that I'd somehow overstepped. "Unless that's completely out of your wheelhouse? Sorry for asking, really. You just look pretty fashionable, and I don't think I've kept up with fashion cycles since 2018—"

"I can help you pick out an outfit, Elizabeth." Brianna's answer was confident as she stood up from the couch, her hands resting on her hips. "Just show me the way to your closet and I can handle the rest."

# 8

# Brianna

*Six Months Earlier*

I can't believe you passed up that job at CVS." Vera pouted as she swirled her frozen strawberry margarita around in its glass. "I would've killed to even be interviewed for that position, and you passed on it like it wasn't anything."

"That's because pharmacy techs only make like thirteen an hour," Brianna explained, her fingers tapping against the bar as she perused the drink menu. "I can make that just doing odd jobs here and there. Besides, I'm going to need to start saving up money if I want to put myself through nursing school."

"You're going to be an amazing nurse." Vera's pout furrowed even deeper into her expression. "And I'm never going to see you ever again."

"That's not true, Vera—"

"You think I don't know how hard nurses have to study? My cousin and I used to go out all the time before she went to nursing school. Now it's all about her shifts at the hospital. And when she's not doing that, she's dealing with her twins or there's something up with her girlfriend. I swear to God, I haven't seen her in two years."

"It sounds like your cousin has a lot of stuff going on in her life besides the nursing school thing."

"Whatever." Vera shrugged. "I'm happy for you either way, Brianna. And hey, maybe now that you passed on that CVS gig, they'll start calling other people in for interviews?"

"Relax, Vera," Brianna offered with a smile. "You're going to find the perfect job for you and you're going to be perfect at it. Seriously. You practically lived and breathed that pharmacy textbook—"

"Holy shit."

"What?" Brianna set down the menu at the bar, her attention immediately going toward Vera. "What is it?"

"Just another reminder that you and me need to get the fuck out of Tennessee." Vera groaned before she slid her phone over to Brianna. "Look at this bullshit."

Brianna gazed down at her friend's phone screen, her eyes quickly scanning it for information.

### LOCAL TEEN LOCKED UP FOR CHILD PORN, LAWYER SAYS CASE IS "THE EPITOME OF WHAT'S WRONG IN AMERICA'S JUSTICE SYSTEM"

**Story Last Updated—3:15 PM—Editor: Wendy Page**

In a story that's gripped the Midsouth, a local teen has been arrested on charges of child pornography. Marcus Anderson, 15, has been accused of spreading pornographic images of a child after he sent lewd photos of himself to a fellow female high school student at Midtown High School.

Anderson's friends and classmates, as well as the female student, have all spoken about the case on social media, heavily suggesting that the exchange of pornographic images was a consensual act on the part of Anderson and the female student. Anderson's teachers, both former and present, have also commented on behalf of Anderson, stating that he's always been a stellar student as well as a star athlete.

Currently, Anderson is being held on bond. His lawyer spoke to the press earlier this afternoon, in a fiery, impassioned speech, stating that this case is "the epitome of what's wrong in America's justice system" and proposing that Anderson's treatment is due to the "color of his skin" and not about the facts of the case.

Meanwhile, a representative for the Tennessee Administrative Office of the Courts states that any exchange of child pornography will be tried to the "fullest extent of the law," and Anderson is in no way being made an example of or part of a larger pattern of cases.

"We're taking care of this case just like we would any other," Eileen Lamb states. "If Mr. Anderson's case warrants a jail sentence, it'll be because we examined all the facts of the case and have determined that the punishment fits the crime the man committed."

"'The crime the man committed'?" Something tightened in Brianna's chest. "How could they even call him a man when he's fifteen years old?"

"How can they call it 'child porn' when he was sending nudes to his fucking girlfriend?" Vera scoffed. "Fuck this fucking state. Maybe I should start applying for jobs down in Atlanta."

"Atlanta would really suit you." Brianna let out a light chuckle as she forced the emotion that was threatening to bubble to the surface back down her throat. She hadn't told Vera a lot about her past, not about what'd happened that awful night, and not about what'd happened between her and Charles, either. "I can see you wearing one of those super short bodycon dresses, maybe pair it with some Louboutins?"

"Oh my God." Vera laughed now, too, even as she finished the rest of her drink. "You know what? Never mind. I don't think I'd be able to keep up with those Atlanta girls. I'd die if I had to stop eating carbs just to look cute enough to compete."

"Hot girl summer is every summer in Atlanta," Brianna joked.

"Are you kidding me? Hot girl summer is every *day* in Atlanta," Vera joked right back.

Brianna motioned toward the bartender just then, grabbing his attention long enough to order another round of drinks. The bartender gave her a quick nod, followed by a sly wink, the man so often hitting on her whenever she showed up at the bar. It never went any further than him asking for her number and Brianna mumbling something about either being too drunk to remember her own phone number or having to rush home to the man who'd been so patiently waiting for her to walk through the door.

Even though she hadn't seen Charles since she'd told him to never come back.

"You should try out a temp agency," Vera suggested, seemingly out of nowhere.

"What?"

"To find odd jobs and stuff," she went on. "I'm sure you already have a system or whatever, but it never hurts to go through the traditional route. Or the less traditional, if you join one of those online services that pull local jobs for you in the area."

"I'll keep that in mind. Thanks for the tip."

"You're welcome." Vera beamed before a mischievous look came over her face. "And speaking of tips . . . I'm pretty sure it's your turn to cover us this round, so you might as well put your card on the table now."

\*　\*　\*

There was always a rush that came with shoplifting.

Brianna would know, since she'd been practicing it for the last month and a half. It'd become something like an addiction to her, a habit she'd found comfort in and hadn't been able to shake, no matter how wrong she knew it was. All she knew was that when she made her way down the aisles of Target or Kroger, when a familiar hole began to form in her heart when she looked over at the strawberry stand, nothing could soothe her besides that extra set of pens in her pocket, that pair of socks she'd slipped into her purse.

And with the rush of theft, the comforting sigh that released from behind her chest when she'd gotten away with it again and again and again, all was right with the world. Today was going to be no different as Brianna pushed her cart past the automatic doors of the grocery store, offering a friendly wave to the older woman who worked security. Brianna wasn't an idiot about her habit, knowing better than to frequent the same store back-to-back, even if their security system hadn't managed to catch up with her.

There was no point in testing fate. Not when this was something she needed.

She turned down the nearest aisle once she was inside of the store, a muffled version of some '70s song playing over the speakers. There was a time before the funeral that Brianna would've been able to enjoy the song that was playing, when she would've noticed the music and been grateful for its groove, its bass encouraging her to tap her fingers along with the beat.

But now she pushed her cart like there wasn't any music playing overhead at all, its tune meaning nothing, its lyrics having the same effect on her as a conversation in a language she didn't understand.

When she reached the baking aisle, grabbing on to a bag of generic flour, her eyes cut over to the pricey baking equipment that hung only a few inches away from her fingers.

Brianna had tasked herself with baking a cake from scratch to celebrate Vera getting a job at Walgreens as a pharmacy tech manager. Vera was technically still on probation for the position, her probationary status so often causing her to downplay the opportunity.

But Brianna knew better. She knew that it was hard to find a pharmacy tech as good as Vera, which meant that unless her friend somehow royally fucked up during her probationary period, she'd locked down the kind of position she'd been hoping for all along.

Which was why Brianna was finding it hard to deny Vera the pleasure of having a homemade cake baked with the best of the best utensils. There were visions dancing around in Brianna's head of those expensive silver measuring cups and spoons, her cake turning out all the better for having them. And since Vera deserved the best cake that Brianna could make, Brianna's palm was already reaching out for the priciest set, not bothering to mentally calculate what kind of dent it was going to put in her shopping budget.

Because the price of the kitchen utensils didn't matter to Brianna, not when she'd be walking out of here with the set for free, anyway.

"What do you think you're doing?"

Suddenly, there was a gruff voice beside Brianna. She turned to find a young security officer, a man who couldn't have been a day over twenty-five, staring back at her. His eyes were narrowed as they followed down Brianna's arm, her motion frozen in time as her fingers curled around the very tip of the utensil set.

"Oh." Brianna smiled, flustered but not shaken. She'd gotten so much better at lying after going through all the fake conversations in her head, the ones that were supposed to go just like this, with someone almost catching her in the act. "I was just trying to find the price of—"

"The price is listed right above it," the officer interrupted, his finger pointing toward the black-and-yellow sign. "Do you want to know what it looked like to me?"

"What?" Brianna's voice was as sweet as honey. "What did it look like to you?"

"It looked like you were trying to steal those utensils," he answered.

Brianna stilled, just for a moment.

And then something began to burn inside of her veins, the fire quickly spreading through the rest of her system, every hair on her skin soon alert and alive.

*She'd barely moved the utensils from their hanging display.*

Which meant that if she was being accused of stealing, this officer was either able to somehow see the near future, or there was another reason he felt so damn confident accusing her of the crime she hadn't yet committed.

"Why did it look like I was stealing?" she shot back. "I was just holding it in my hand—"

"Right, you were holding on to it a little too long." He looked Brianna up and down, his gaze traveling over her coat, her jeans and shirt, a dependable outfit that she'd had in her closet for years. "Do you live around here?"

"I'm sorry?" Brianna raised her voice. "Is there a new law in place saying that people aren't allowed to shop wherever the hell they want to?"

"There's no need to get loud, ma'am—"

"Oh, there's no need to get loud about how some asshole is racially profiling me?" Brianna shouted. "There's no need to get loud about you pretty much telling me to go back to my side of the fucking city? What year do you think this is?"

"Ma'am—"

"Do you think you can just treat Black people like this because of that stupid little badge on your stupid little uniform?" she pressed. "Who the hell do you think you are?"

"Ma'am, please—"

"I want to speak to your manager."

". . . What?" The young security officer's voice slightly trembled. "There's no need for that, I think. I was just going to let you off with a warning—"

"I said," Brianna started as she stepped closer to the man, her eyes boring down into his, "go. Get. Your. Fucking. Manager."

". . . Why?"

"Because I want to talk to him or her about the piece-of-shit racist that they have working for them," she said, her words coming out as calm as the ocean.

"But he might fire me, ma'am," the man murmured, shaking his head. "My manager is . . . he's like you . . . And like I said, I'm sorry. I didn't mean anything by it. I was just trying to—"

"There it is."

"There what is?"

"You're sorry." Brianna smiled as she searched his expression. "That's all you had to say. That wasn't so hard, was it?"

"No, ma'am. It wasn't." The officer began to back away from the conversation. "Have a nice rest of your day, ma'am. And I hope you enjoy shopping with us."

"I will." Brianna's smile remained on her face, a new kind of rush taking over her. As the rush continued to pulse, she slipped the utensils into her coat pocket, making sure she was slightly angled away from the merchandise so that the store's cameras wouldn't be able to easily pick up on her motion.

*Life owed her this much.*

This utensil set. The rush. The absolute luck of the young officer's manager just happening to be a Black man. The look of fear in his eyes when he thought for just a moment that maybe the tables were going to be turned on him, that his commitment to being a piece of shit could've lost him his job.

Her fingers flitted across the hidden utensil set in her coat before grabbing on to it tighter and tighter, until her skin began to crack and bleed, until there were small drops of blood trailing down her fingertips. There was a realization burgeoning inside of her, one that set off a craving she'd never felt before, a desperate hunger she knew could never be satiated with anything she could possibly eat, anything she could possibly drink.

Because life *didn't* owe Brianna Thompson this much.

Life owed her so much more.

9

# Elizabeth

L izzie? You still here?" David called out from the front entryway, my head turning in his direction. I was standing in the living room beside our couch, with different outfits all lined up against it, from flowing dresses to a daring black-and-blue jumpsuit that I'd only worn once, on vacation. Brianna was going in and out of the living room, mixing and matching pieces, trying to decipher my indecisiveness. I currently had on what we'd decided was most likely going to be the winner for the night, a pair of faded blue jeans with a white designer tank. Brianna had pulled it from the very back of my closet earlier, insisting that what was old was new once again, that fashion trends were always in permanent rotation.

After I'd put it on, she'd grabbed for a near-transparent white shawl, which she'd quickly draped around my arms, too. And even though I sort of felt like I was trying a little too hard by attempting to make it seem like I wasn't *trying* at all, Brianna's confidence in the outfit had rubbed off on me.

"I'm here!" I called out in response, now turning the rest of my body to face him, too. "I thought you said that we were going to meet each other at the restaurant?"

"We are. I mean, we were," David corrected, his gaze slowly sliding up and down my frame, his features shifting into a warm, knowing smile. "You look good, baby."

"You look good, too." I smiled back at him, meaning every word of the phrase.

Because David always looked good.

"I just wanted to pop in and drop off my laptop." He held up its case before setting it down on the floor beside him. "Usually, I'd just leave it at the office, but it's one of those nights where they're doing overnight cleaning, and the company wanted us to be on the safe side."

"Right. We wouldn't want one of the cleaning guys accessing all of that supersensitive information," I playfully joked. "Who knows what they'd do with that kind of intel? Move in on a piece of property before your firm has a chance to make the first deal?"

"Hey, I'm on your side." David chuckled. "But you know how it is. It's easier to go along with the silliest of company rules if it means making the big bosses happy—"

David's sentence was cut off by his jaw quickly snapping shut. Worried, I turned to where his gaze must've gone, fear thrumming through my every heartbeat.

But all I saw behind us was Brianna, who'd quietly stepped back into the room. She offered David a nervous wave before quickly folding her arms across her chest.

I looked back over at my husband, studying the tightening of his jaw, the way his eyes moved across her the same way they'd just moved across me, too. He was studying her too closely, his gaze lingering on her features for just a second too long. He shifted his attention back to me when he was finished taking her in, probably assuming that I hadn't noticed his transgression, that I couldn't tell that he'd been pleased with what he'd seen.

"Sorry, baby, I didn't realize we had company." David smiled at me again.

"Hi," Brianna said, her tone business-neutral, as if she were passing a work colleague in the hallway. "I'm Brianna Thompson. And as of this afternoon, I'm your wife's new personal assistant."

I couldn't help but smirk at Brianna's approach to David, the way she was treating him like he was the least interesting man on the planet, despite the way he'd clearly shown that *some part of him* had been interested in her.

"I'm David. David Smith. Nice to meet you, Brianna."

"I'm going to get going, Elizabeth." Brianna gently patted my shoulder before she made her way toward the front door. "I'll see you tomorrow, okay? And remember to call me if you need anything in the meantime."

"I'll see you tomorrow, Brianna." I waved her goodbye, my heart warming at the fact that she hadn't even turned around to give David a final look.

*God.*

I couldn't have been more wrong about Brianna Thompson.

And I'd never been so happy to have been so wrong, as irrational thoughts of Brianna shamelessly flirting with my husband dimmed into nothing, like they were just a light being turned out in the dark.

"I think we should get going, too," David suggested as he held out his hand for mine.

I took his hand without saying a word, interlacing our fingers, the shawl around my shoulders brushing alongside his suit and jacket with our every step.

* * *

There were fireflies dancing around our heads as David and I worked through an order of ribs and pulled pork on the outside porch of Little Larry's. The fireflies were typical for Memphis this time of year, spring coming upon us faster than I'd realized. Soon enough, it'd be time for every other seafood restaurant to start offering crawfish on the menu, the critters ever more popular the closer we crept to summer, although it was hard for me to imagine a bucket of crawfish when I was in the middle of tearing through my third cup of extra barbecue sauce.

*Goddamn.*

This place was *good.*

It was always so deliriously wonderful when the hype about a restaurant matched the experience to a T. From the reviews on the Harbor Town group, Little Larry's was the next coming of Christ, if Christ's only intention had been to open the best barbecue restaurant in the city. And judging from the way the conversation had lagged between David and me after the food had come to our table, we were going to be repeat visitors at Little Larry's altar, the truest of believers to ever follow the Good Word of Smoked Meats.

On the walk back to the car, David had wrapped his arm around my waist, pulling me close to his side. Even on the drive home, his palm was still locked in mine, his free hand expertly maneuvering the steering wheel through Midtown traffic. I relaxed into the passenger seat of the car, listening to the sounds coming through the stereo. There was a song playing on the radio, and I knew it was something from the '70s, even though I couldn't quite place the band. It was energetic and upbeat, the kind of thing I could picture being blasted through nightclubs, women with big hair clapping along to the beat in between checking their makeup in their pocket mirrors.

It was the kind of thing I could picture Patricia forcing me to listen to, once upon a time, whenever we'd run errands in her van.

My skin went cold at the connection between the thoughts, the lingering space between me still being alive and Patricia being very much dead. My most promising lead had turned to dust in a matter of seconds, after I'd managed to follow up on the thread between Patricia and that Nazi fuck that she'd gotten into an argument with. The results of my research had come in bits and pieces, with me hurriedly checking my phone whenever Brianna had been out of sight, whenever she delved deeper into my closet.

The Nazi fuck was harmless.

*No.*

That wasn't quite right. His belief system was hot fucking garbage, and I was certain he'd thought about hitting a woman or two, with his utter inability to make anything out of himself turning his Nathan Bedford Forrest–shaded soul into something unrecognizable and cruel.

But he wasn't dangerous, not in practice. From what I'd been able to gather, it was obvious that he was a coward, always excited to cheer on the destruction of progress, reacting with heart emojis to photos from those White Lives Matter rallies and digitally befriending some of their attendees. But he wasn't interested in joining in on any of the action, preferring to be a piece of shit from the comfort of his home.

"Don't," David whispered, his fingers curling around mine tight.

"Don't what?" I was already deleting all information about the Nazi fuck from my mental case folder for Patricia.

"I can tell, sometimes. When you're gone again."

"When I'm gone?"

"When you're not here in the moment with me," he continued. "When you're . . . when you're off somewhere else in your mind. You were with me the rest of the night, but just now . . ."

"Sorry," I apologized as I turned toward him. "You're right. I should try to stay in the moment."

"I know it can be hard, baby. But you've been doing so well. I'm so proud of you, Lizzie. I really am."

David squeezed my hand even tighter, so tight that I heard one of my knuckles crack under the pressure.

And I offered him a small smile before I went back to looking out the window, my thoughts still as heavy and dark as the night that surrounded us.

* * *

"Come here," David instructed as we slid into bed together. His fingers were already creeping up the sides of my Yves Saint Laurent camisole. David had always been good at this, making his advances seem effortless, like the idea of sex had just occurred to him as a possibility mere seconds ago. It was this exact kind of approach that'd caused me to be so taken with him the first time we'd made love. He'd made me feel like I was the one in control, like I held all the power in the room.

Even though David was the only one holding any cards.

"Really? Even after all that barbecue?" I joked before nuzzling into his neck, loving the feel of his stubble against my cheek. "Are you sure?"

"I'm sure, baby," David said, his hands rising up even higher, his fingertips trailing across my bare back. "You looked so beautiful tonight. I could hardly keep my eyes off you."

"All courtesy of Brianna." David's palms now slipped lower and lower, not stopping until he'd slid a hand between my thighs. "Fuck."

"You like that, baby?"

"Yes." My answer came out clipped, in between a moan. "Fuck, David."

I reached for him, my hand trailing down his frame, searching for the upper lining of his boxers. When I found it, I pressed my fingers underneath the fabric, searching again. And once my fingers were where I wanted them to be, David groaned, the length of him growing harder against my grip. He pulled down my panties then, right before returning his hand to that same place between my thighs, my moans sounding deeper yet becoming so much shallower.

"You're so wet for me, baby." David groaned again as he spread me apart with his fingers, soon pushing two of them inside of me. "Fuck."

I suddenly stilled at the motion, every part of me that was touching him turning numb and removed.

David noticed, his gaze flying up toward mine. "Lizzie? What's wrong?"

"I don't like being touched that way, David," I muttered as I pushed against his wrist, moving his fingers away from me. "You know that I don't . . . Why would you do that?"

"Shit. Lizzie." David pulled his hand away even farther, like I was a burning-hot stove that he'd touched by mistake, an accident that was going to leave him with scars. "I'm so sorry, baby. I'm so sorry. I wasn't trying to—"

"Because you're gone." I spat the sentiment of his earlier phrase right back at him. "Because you're not in the moment."

"What are you talking about, baby?"

"I saw the way you looked at her," I clarified. "I saw the way you looked at Brianna."

". . . What?"

"Is that who you thought you were fucking just now?" I pulled my panties back up toward my waist, my skin flushing red with a worsening case of rage. "Is that why you forgot your own wife's limits in bed? Because you're so tired of fucking me that you have to imagine you're with other women just to get through it?"

"Lizzie—"

"Which is fucking hilarious, by the way." I laughed for emphasis, even though the sound was hollow. "That you somehow went from not being interested in fucking me at all, to not being able to keep your hands off me, without any attempt at explanation. Or is that just another part of my treatment plan? Did Dr. Whitaker recommend it?"

"Lizzie, please," David begged. "Please don't turn this into a bigger deal than it is. Yes, I fucked up, but I wasn't thinking. Maybe you were right. Maybe I'm too out of it from all the barbecue."

I stood up away from the bed as David was talking, slipping a pair of slippers onto my feet, smoothing each side of my camisole down with my palms.

"Baby, where are you going?"

"I don't want a pity fuck, David. If you don't want to fuck me, don't pretend like you do."

"Lizzie—"

"Good night, David," I cut him off, already heading out of the bedroom door. "I'll see you in the morning."

\* \* \*

*God.*

I hated crying. There was always this nagging sense at the back of my head that I could've been doing something more worthwhile with my time, like checking my email, like sticking my head in the oven and hoping for the best. Still, I let myself get on with it, trembling and shaking as I wept in the privacy of the hall bathroom.

I wondered what I would've looked like to someone just peeking in on my life, sniffling in my expensive camisole, my tears probably ruining the integrity of the fabric. My hands were against my knees as I stared down at the bathroom tile, striking the signature pose of a *broken woman*. All I needed was a black eye, and I would've been living out one of those local commercials for a domestic violence shelter, a perfect candidate for their brand of assistance.

Maybe I was a broken woman.

Maybe I wasn't just striking a pose.

Not wanting to give the possibility a chance to sink any further into my psyche, I grabbed for my phone, pulling it into my lap. I aimlessly cycled through all the apps, Facebook, Instagram, Twitter. There wasn't anything that made me feel better. Although, even if there were, I wouldn't have been able to process it. It was all reading like a bunch of indecipherable noise, things that might have meant something if my vision weren't blurry with tears.

I swiped out of the apps and into my recent messages, scrolling through those, too, each one just as impenetrable as the apps. There was something from Janice. There was something from David. There was something from the guy who'd worked on our roof last summer.

And then there was something from Brianna. Her message shone through like a light in a dark tunnel, showing me the way out, my brain able to latch on to it and digest every word. It was such a simple message, too, just wanting me to confirm that I'd given her the right number.

So, I decided to confirm.

ELIZABETH S.
MESSAGES SORTED: NEW

**Brianna T:** Hey there! Just wanted to confirm that this is the right number for Elizabeth Smith? Let me know when you can!

Elizabeth S: Hey Brianna! Yes, this is the right number. Thank you for helping me out today. I really appreciated it.

Brianna T: Of course! That's my job! ☺ Let me know if you need anything else.

Elizabeth S: I do . . . kind of need something else right now.

Brianna T: Right now? Sure, just give me a few minutes to get ready and I'll be over there ASAP.

Elizabeth S: Sorry. I should've been clearer. You don't need to actually come over. I just had a question for you, if that's okay?

Brianna T: Of course. Anything.

Elizabeth S: This might be overstepping, but I was wondering if you had someone else in your life?

Brianna T: Someone else? Like a family?

Elizabeth S: Like a boyfriend or a husband.

Elizabeth S: Or a girlfriend or wife. Sorry. Didn't mean to leave out the other options, just in a weird headspace right now.

Brianna T: I don't have anyone in my life right now. Well, I might. That's up to him.

Elizabeth S: Up to him?

Brianna T: I had a boyfriend, but we had a big fight a few weeks ago and we haven't spoken since. No official breakup yet though. ☹

**Elizabeth S:** Oh shit. I'm sorry. That must be really hard for you.

**Brianna T:** You get used to it.

**Elizabeth S:** You shouldn't have to. No woman should have to get used to feeling like that.

**Brianna T:** Are you okay, Elizabeth? Did something happen between you and David?

**Elizabeth S:** No. Nothing happened. Sorry. I was just being nosy, that's all.

**Brianna T:** Not nosy. Smart. You'd be surprised how many people still let complete strangers in their homes nowadays even though there are a billion true crime podcasts about how that's suchhhhh a bad idea. 😁

**Elizabeth S:** hahahaha seriously! And oh my God, of course you listen to podcasts. Because you have good taste.

**Brianna T:** Hell yeah, I have good taste. Except when it comes to men, apparently?

**Brianna T:** But we'll see. Fingers crossed he starts texting me back tonight.

# 10

# Brianna

*Three Months Earlier*

Requesting access to 9-1-1 calls was perfectly legal in the state of Tennessee.

As long as the calls hadn't also been requested by a police station or involved in a legal case, which would've meant that they were sealed and kept out of public record. Brianna worried that she would find herself in that exact situation, with the call she was looking for kept private underneath some stack of paperwork on a sergeant's desk, completely inaccessible for her to ever see or hear.

The worst part was the not knowing. And it seemed like she was going to be in the not-knowing part for some time, especially since she'd relied on letters coming in the mail to update her on the request. In the meantime, she'd learned how much stamps were going for nowadays, something her generation had been accused of being generally ignorant about. She'd also learned where the nearest USPS centers were to her apartment, their locations not being on her radar until mail had become the focal point of her life.

They didn't make any step of the request process easy, the state of Tennessee. Not only did Brianna have to know exactly what she was asking for, down to the time of the call and general location, if she was off by even a single detail, her request was denied for *insufficient information*. She'd once called to ask what *insufficient information* meant to the office of the Secretary of State, and the curt woman on the other end of the line informed her that there were between two thousand and three thousand emergency calls placed in Memphis per day, with another five thousand placed per day but categorized under a nonemergency.

"With up to eight thousand calls per day, ma'am, you can see how it's difficult for us to locate information that isn't specific enough for us to find," she said, her voice a typical Southern drawl. "We're always happy to help with public records requests, but there's only so much that we can do. Our office is only a few people, including myself."

Today had been different, though. Today Brianna had been hopeful for a more positive result, her fingers eagerly tearing through the letter she'd just received, waiting for a transcript of the call to appear before her eyes like a dream come true.

But her skin went cold as soon as she spotted the familiar refrain: *insufficient information.*

The cold turned to fire in a matter of seconds, the fingers once eager to open the letter now ripping it into pieces. Pure anger was a newer expression for her, but she'd been quite taken with it, loving the way rage felt on her, the way it shaped her into a disparate version of herself.

How the hell was she supposed to get a transcript of that phone call?

She held a hand up to her forehead before she collapsed against the wall in her apartment. Her heart was thrumming inside of her chest at an unsustainable pace, head aching with fresh pain to match. Flashes of that awful night came to her then, unwarranted and unwelcome muscle memory kicking in, making her feel so, so helpless and so, so small.

*No.*

She was never going to be that woman again.

She was never going to let anyone or anything make her feel that way ever, *ever* again.

Brianna stood, her legs starting to move toward the apartment's parking lot, the rest of her going along for the ride. She didn't stop moving until she was sitting in the driver's seat of her car, her mind only joining the equation when she was already on the highway with plans to take I-40 all the way to Nashville.

\* \* \*

"Good afternoon, ma'am."

There was a Tennessee State police officer standing right beside her, offering her a gentle wave and a smile. He was stationed outside of the building's front doors, his demeanor fully relaxed, as if he never expected anything troubling to happen while he was on his shift.

Brianna had to force herself not to flinch away from the conversation, not to avert her eyes and pretend like she hadn't heard the greeting at all. She hadn't had the privilege of liking or trusting policemen ever since she was six years old, ever since she saw a pair of them harass her father over an expired tag on the back of his car.

She still remembered the gun they'd stuck in his face, too.

*Not why I'm here*, Brianna thought to herself as she strained to smile back at the man in uniform. *He's nothing but a symptom. He's nothing but a fucking symptom.*

"Good afternoon to you, too." Brianna beamed before she walked through the building's double doors, her hands clenched tight in her pockets. She took in a deep breath, holding it all the way up to one of the help desks, only then letting it escape her chest in small bursts.

"Hi!" A chipper young woman greeted her, her blue eyes just as bright and sparkling behind the desk. "Welcome to the Tennessee Department of Safety and Homeland Security. What can I help you with today?"

"Hi," Brianna started, nervousness coursing through her, even though she hid it like a pro. "I just wanted to check with your office about something?"

"Sure! What were you wanting to check with us about?"

"I've been sending letters to your off— I've been having this correspondence, mainly by mail," Brianna said, trying her best to sound as professional as she could. "I've been requesting some information from your end, specifically the transcript for a 9-1-1 call. But whenever I put the request in, I get a letter back telling me that there's not enough information?"

"Hmm." The young woman hummed. "I'm sorry to hear that, ma'am. That must've been a frustrating experience for you."

"Just a little." Brianna smiled. "But that's why I wanted to come in person, to see what the holdup might be—"

"You said a 9-1-1 call, right?"

"Right."

"Are you sure it hasn't been pulled for a legal case? Or even for a police case. Although they tend to pull those as soon as it becomes their jurisdiction."

"If that's what happened, would the office let me know? Or would they still file my request as having 'insufficient information'?"

". . . They'd let you know." The young woman hummed again as she stood from her chair. "You know what? Ms. . . . ?"

"Brianna. Ms. Brianna Thompson."

"Right. Ms. Brianna Thompson." The young woman smiled now, too. "Would you mind waiting for just a few minutes out in the lobby? I'm going to see if my supervisor has anyone in her office. This sounds like it might be a little above my pay grade."

The young woman playfully winked before letting out a small laugh.

And Brianna laughed along with her, her nervousness turning acidic, feeling like it was eating right through her stomach. "Of course. I don't mind waiting."

"Great." The young woman offered Brianna a final smile before she disappeared behind a column, her footsteps lightly echoing against the marble floor.

*     *     *

"You must be Brianna, right?" An older Black woman was sitting behind a sizable office desk, every corner of it occupied by beige folders, sheets of paper sticking out by their edges. Brianna was reminded of her high school principal's office, her desk set up in much the same way. Her expression had been similar to the look on this woman's face, too, like she was already tired of their conversation, despite the fact that Brianna had yet to say a single word.

"Yes, Brianna Thompson." She took a seat in one of the black plastic chairs in front of the desk.

"Brianna, I'm Nina Carr. You're lucky that my last appointment of the day never showed. We usually don't do walk-ins—"

"Sorry. I didn't know I had to make an appointment—"

"Not your fault." Nina grinned. "A lot of people don't know we take appointments. I swear, sometimes I think this office prefers for things to be as complicated as humanly possible. Which only makes things harder on our end."

Nina sighed before she went on. "Now, Ashleigh was telling me that you were looking into a request for a 9-1-1 call? A transcript?"

"Right. I've been sending letters to your office for weeks, but each time I get a letter back saying they need more information. I just wanted to see what I was doing wrong? If I'm missing something, I'll make sure to include it in my next request—"

"It might not be anything to do with you, Brianna," Nina cut her off as she turned toward her desktop. "Would you mind telling me what the 9-1-1 call was about?" Nina peeked around the corner of her computer display, flashing a smirk in Brianna's direction. "Not to make assumptions, but you look like the kind of woman who's angling for a top spot at *The Commercial Appeal*."

"You could tell I'm from Memphis?"

"Another assumption, I guess." Nina chuckled. "Whenever a Black person walks into my office, there's a pretty good chance they're not from Nashville."

". . . You're right," Brianna laughed. "I am from Memphis. But I'm not working for *The Commercial Appeal*."

"So, you're not requesting the 9-1-1 call for any journalistic purposes?" Nina's attention went back to her screen.

"No."

"Were you personally involved with the 9-1-1 call? Either as the caller or the dispatcher on the line?"

"No."

"Were you the subject of the 9-1-1 call?"

"No, but . . ."

"But?" Nina's fingers were flying across her keyboard, the changing screens reflected in her thick-rimmed glasses.

Brianna suddenly had no more words to speak. It was the sort of question that she should've expected—

That she had expected—

But somehow she still wasn't ready to answer it, to give it shape, to breathe life into the most impossible pain she'd ever felt.

"Ms. Thompson?"

". . . My son was," she finally answered, the words sticking like a knife in her throat. "My son was the subject of the call."

"Hmm." Nina's fingers stopped moving, her attention once again turning to Brianna. "Would you mind telling me what the 9-1-1 call was about, Ms. Thompson? If it was a nonemergency call, like a car parked in the wrong spot, that'll be in a whole different system—"

"I don't know."

". . . You don't know what the 9-1-1 call was about?"

"No," Brianna admitted. "I can guess the time it may have come in . . . sometime after my son was done with school."

Brianna didn't know why, but she began to shiver. Not the kind she could've hidden by pretending to fidget in her seat. Not the kind that could've been mistaken for an almost cough or an almost sneeze, a passing moment of discomfort. She was shivering like someone had just dumped freezing-cold water on her skin, like she was stranded in the Arctic, ice and snow piling up on her shoulders.

"My son . . . my son . . ." Brianna repeated the phrase, the words tasting like ash in her mouth. "Jay was . . . he was . . ."

"Ms. Thompson . . ." Nina reached across the desk for Brianna, holding her palms up toward the sky.

And Brianna placed her hands in the stranger's grasp, still shivering, ash still coating her tongue.

"I need you to tell me what you think was on that 9-1-1 call, Ms. Thompson." Nina's voice was low. "If you tell me what may have been on that call . . . I'll be able to help you."

"I don't know. I don't know." Brianna wept, and Nina's hands grasped on to hers with even more pressure, like she was trying to hold her together, like she was trying to keep her from spilling out onto her nice marble floor. "Jay was supposed to come home. He was supposed to come home. He always took the same way home."

". . . But this time, he didn't make it home." Nina finished Brianna's thoughts for her.

And Brianna nodded, her cries coming out so rough it felt like they were going to leave little cuts behind her chest. "I don't know what happened. I was driving home from work, and I saw all these police cars. And there was . . . I saw Jay's bike on the side of the road. It was new. His dad and I got it for him because he'd been begging us for a new one for so long—"

Brianna's words were cut off by another one of her cries.

She sounded like she was dying.

"And then I saw him. I saw him. He was lying right there, in the street. I wanted to think he was sleeping," Brianna murmured as a lifeless laugh chopped up her response. "Isn't that insane? I was wishing that my child had somehow fallen asleep in the road. I wanted to believe it so bad that I remember . . . I remember holding him. And rocking with him. The same thing I used to do when he was just a little baby, trying to wake him up without scaring him."

"Brianna . . ."

Nina's grip on Brianna grew tighter. It was something Brianna knew but wasn't really able to feel, like knowing the wind was blowing but not knowing if it was making things colder or warmer. It was a nonfactor in her grief, not affecting the gnawing in her chest or the way her vision grew blurrier and blurrier as she glanced across Nina's desk.

*Nina had a daughter.*

Brianna's eyes landed on a family photo, a younger version of Nina standing beside the woman she was sitting across from in the office today. She had wild pink hair and brown skin, her smile bright as she flashed a peace sign at the camera. Nina's grip on her daughter was tight, too, her arm around her shoulders like nothing could ever make her let go.

"Did they . . . What happened to him?" Nina's voice interrupted Brianna's staring at the family photo, a daydream blown to pieces. She'd been wondering what it would've been like to look back on a photo like that with Jay, taken when he was just a kid.

How embarrassed he would've been to have ever been that young.

"Brianna . . . what happened to your son?" Nina repeated the question, her tone so low it was almost like she didn't want Brianna to hear it.

"What always happens," Brianna answered, her voice suddenly calm, her gaze seeming to stare right past Nina, right past the edge of the world. "That's what happened."

There was silence then. Too long. Stretched out.

Until Nina started to speak.

". . . I'm going to help you," Nina said, her voice trembling with fresh tears. "I'm going to help you with whatever you need. We're going to figure this out, okay, Brianna? If there's a 9-1-1 call in the system, we're going to find it. You hear me? We're going to find it."

"Okay," Brianna replied, still somewhere so far away, the ash in her mouth being replaced with something candied and sweet.

\* \* \*

Nina couldn't let Brianna leave with a copy of the 9-1-1 call.

That's what she'd told her, midway through her search. Apparently, the transcript had been flagged by local Memphis police.

Flagged but never pulled.

It was a hint that the department never had any intention of doing anything with it, but they didn't want it to be readily available for a public records request, either, like the kind that Brianna had been attempting to file. Which meant that if Nina pulled it from the system, it would alert the MPD, which would alert her boss, which very well could end with her stuffing her office belongings into a single cardboard box.

Which was something neither of them wanted to happen.

So, instead of pulling the transcript, Nina allowed Brianna to read a copy of the document, one she printed from her screen instead of pulling from the system. There might've been a trail of Nina viewing the document, but there wouldn't be any notification that the information had been requested and provided. And since she wasn't allowing Brianna to leave with a copy, either, there'd be no real-world evidence that Brianna had ever seen the transcript of the call.

"Here it is," Nina said as she removed the freshly printed sheet from the still whirring machine. "Here's the only 9-1-1 call we have on file that matches the description of everything you told me, Brianna."

Nina kept the transcript in her hand, even as she took a seat on the edge of her desk.

". . . You don't want me to read it?" Brianna asked, her voice low.

". . . Are you a Christian, Brianna Thompson?" Nina asked a question in return. "You believe in God, don't you?"

"Why are you asking me that right now?"

"Because I don't want you to . . ." Nina's words trailed off. "If you're a Christian, if you believe in the Bible, then you know that if you were to hurt yourself . . ." Nina paused as her eyes landed on Brianna's. "What you're feeling . . . I felt it, too."

"You did?"

"My first child. He died, too. Not like . . . not like Jay. I lost him when he was still in the womb. But I remember that pain, Brianna. And I remember what I wanted to do to myself just to get away from it."

"I'm not going to kill myself, Nina—"

"You can't. Do you hear me?" Nina gently rested a hand over Brianna's. "You . . . you have to be strong for Jay. If not for yourself, then for him. Because if you hurt yourself . . . you can't be with him in heaven. And that boy . . . he's still going to need his mama. He's still going to need you, Brianna, no matter what you think."

Nina smiled as she handed Brianna the transcript of the call. "Don't forget what the Bible says, Brianna. In heaven, there'll be no mourning. No crying. No pain. Your son's so happy up there he won't even remember he's hurting and missing you until you show up at the gates. You just have to hold on until then."

Brianna weakly returned Nina's smile as she took the transcript into her palms, her fingers struggling to hold on to it as she looked down at the page. For a brief moment, Brianna quietly hoped that knowing exactly what led to her son's death would grant her some semblance of peace, some semblance of serenity.

Maybe she would see all the pieces moving together for the first time, and that would be enough.

Enough to stop her shaking.

Enough to make the nightmares stop.

Enough to melt away the rage that'd replaced her blood.

# 11

**TRANSCRIPT--SEPTEMBER 1ST--MEMPHIS, TN**
**3:45 PM CST--CALL #3082**


DISPATCHER #27: 911, WHAT'S YOUR EMERGENCY?

CALLER: HI! I'M JUST CALLING TO REPORT A SUSPICIOUS
PERSON? OR, UH, IT MIGHT BE A ROBBERY IN PROGRESS?
MY FRIEND WANTED ME TO--WOULD THIS EVEN BE THE RIGHT
LINE FOR THAT?

DISPATCHER: HAS A CRIME BEEN COMMITTED OR IS ONE IN
PROGRESS?

CALLER: YES. I BELIEVE SO.

DISPATCHER: CAN I HAVE YOUR LOCATION?

CALLER: I'M ACTUALLY RUNNING AN ERRAND RIGHT NOW.
BUT I KNOW--MY FRIEND TOLD ME WHERE IT'S HAPPENING.

DISPATCHER: AND WHAT'S THE LOCATION OF THE CRIME?

CALLER: UH . . . MAYWOOD STREET? RIGHT BEFORE YOU
GET TO THE FREEMAN INTERSECTION. SORRY. I'M SO BAD
WITH DIRECTIONS.

DISPATCHER: CAN YOU DESCRIBE THE PERSON FOR ME?

CALLER: BLACK. TALL. HE'S RIDING A SCHWINN BIKE WITH
A RED BODY. I'M PRETTY SURE IT'S STOLEN. WE'VE BEEN
EXPERIENCING A LOT OF BIKE THEFT IN HARBOR TOWN
LATELY.

DISPATCHER: AND CAN I GET YOUR NAME AND PHONE
NUMBER?

DISPATCHER: MA'AM? ARE YOU STILL THERE?

CALLER: SORRY. OF COURSE YOU CAN GET MY NUMBER. IT'S
901-555-0124.

DISPATCHER: AND YOUR NAME?

CALLER: PATRICIA. MY NAME IS PATRICIA FITZGERALD.

# 12

# Elizabeth

I hated to admit it, but David had been right.

There was an obvious upside to having Brianna in my life, my thoughts seeming less muddled, my actions feeling more decisive. It was like she was an amplifier for my Paroxetine, the medication working in combination with Brianna's highly effective habits. Suddenly, I wasn't the *problem* employee at the Learning Center, not since I'd been turning in my lesson plans on time.

And it felt like I wasn't the *problem* person in my marriage anymore, either. David and I had scheduled what amounted to an emergency session with Dr. Whitaker, after what'd happened the last time we'd tried to make love. I'd thoroughly enjoyed being the one to come in with a list of complaints and grievances, to have Dr. Whitaker focus all of her attention on David instead of zeroing in on me. There was a smug comfort in having the upper hand, and I'd basked in every minute of it.

"Did you want me to pick something up for lunch?" Brianna

asked as she turned the corner into the living room. "I just realized what time it is, and I'm pretty sure there's nothing in the fridge except for leftovers from Cupcake Cutie."

". . . Not since this morning." I slightly winced through the admission. "I had the last two cupcakes for breakfast."

"Lucky you." Brianna beamed.

And I beamed right back, relieved that there was no sign of judgment on her features. I'd been worried that she was going to offer up the kind of response that I'd become accustomed to in Harbor Town whenever I'd confessed that I'd given in to a craving or had more than five hundred calories in a single sitting.

Women looked at me with pity.

Men looked at me with thinly veiled disgust.

But Brianna looked at me as if she were absolutely delighted by the development, as if the only thing that genuinely would've made her happier was if she'd been in my place instead.

"So? What should we do for lunch?" she continued, her hands resting against her hips. "Should I just get our usual order from India Palace?"

"Ooh, India Palace sounds perfect—" I stopped myself as my phone began to vibrate on the table in front of me.

"Sorry, just give me one second—" I offered Brianna yet another half of a sentence before I picked up the call, my heart already racing after spotting Janice's name on the screen.

"Hello? Janice?"

"Elizabeth!" Janice's tone was welcoming and kind. "I'm so happy I could get a hold of you. Since you were off today, I wasn't sure if you'd be looking at your phone."

"I'm always looking at my phone, Janice." I chuckled. "Although now that I say it out loud, I'm starting to think I should do something about that."

"Would you be able to come in today?"

"Oh." I instinctively frowned at the request. "You want me to come in for a shift? Am I covering for someone—"

"Sorry! I should've been clearer," she went on. "I just wanted you to come in for a quick sec."

". . . You're making me a little nervous, Janice. You know, 'a quick sec' is all it takes to let someone know you're letting them go—"

"No!" Janice insisted, her voice strained, as if something were frustrating her to no end. "No one's letting you go, Elizabeth! I just wanted you to come in for a quick surprise."

"Oh." I let out a relieved sigh, placing a hand across my chest. "Sure, Janice. I can come in for a quick surprise. Not a problem."

"Okay. Good." Janice sounded relieved, too. "Just make sure you come in by the end of the day, okay?"

"Will do." It was the last thing I said before I ended the conversation, my attention shifting back to Brianna.

"So, that's a yes to India Palace." I smirked. "But how would you feel about me coming with you on that food run? Apparently, there's somewhere we need to stop first."

*   *   *

"Oh, wow," Brianna whispered almost as soon as I parked in front of the Learning Center.

For a moment, I was puzzled by her response, wondering why she seemed so taken with a place that we'd been to a million times before—

But then I remembered that Brianna and I hadn't been to the Learning Center a million times before.

*I'd* been to the building a million times before, and Brianna had only been working as my assistant for a week.

*Huh.*

It was strange how ingrained Brianna already was in my psyche, despite how little we knew each other. Still, I couldn't pretend like I wasn't comfortable around her, more comfortable than I felt around the majority of people in my general orbit. As pathetic as it sounded, Brianna was on track to being one of my closest friends in the whole goddamn city.

*Yep.*

That sounded pretty fucking pathetic.

"This place looks so nice," Brianna commented from the passenger seat. I looked over at the building and tried to see it from her virginal point of view, the sleek glass doors, the dark metallic silver painted across the bricks. It was a clear imitation of Midtown architecture, as if it'd been constructed to deceive onlookers about how long it'd been there.

But I guess it *did* look nice, for all of its grand pretending.

"I'm guessing it's all private school kids inside and one-on-one tutoring sessions?" Brianna continued.

I shook my head. "That's not how we operate. We serve whoever comes through the doors, as long as the kids live in the Midtown area and go to school in that same zip code. That way, we make sure that we're not only seeing one kind of kid."

"So, the Center is open to kids from that private Catholic school down the street? And the public school a little farther down?"

"Exactly."

"Do you get a lot of kids from the private Catholic school?"

"Not really." I shrugged. "I think most of them, if they need any academic help, stick with the Kumon centers."

". . . What made them change their location?"

"What?"

"Didn't you say the Center used to be closer to Whitehaven?

What made them want to move to this side of town? Where fewer kids would use their services?"

I blew out a heavy breath before I looked over at Brianna. "Well, they tried to sell the move to us as being about offering more 'central access' to the Center . . . but I think you and I both know that's total bullshit. Honestly, I think they wanted to move it so fewer kids could use it."

"But isn't the whole point of the Center to help the kids?"

"Sure, as long as those kids aren't all coming in through the scholarship and grant programs we have set up. We might not be getting all of the Catholic school kids, but we're getting enough of them to help pay for the owner's new Lexus."

"Oh." Brianna's expression fell. "So, it's not really about helping anyone, then."

"We're still helping kids who need it, Brianna, whether the owner's an asshole or not," I said with a bright smile, as I spotted one of my tutoring students walking up to the side of my car.

"Hey! Ms. Smith!" Justin Montgomery was beaming, his head lowering down to greet me at the driver's-side window. "I didn't know you were coming in today!"

Justin was one of the star quarterbacks at Midtown High School. He'd started coming to the Center after his mom noticed a dip in his overall GPA. She was worried that a torn ACL or a snapped elbow or a twisted ankle would be enough to knock her son completely off the college path, no school wanting to offer a full ride to an injured athlete. And since she was determined to make sure her son had a way forward, she'd enrolled him in one of our programs, full-time.

Of course the program's fees were taken care of by the head coach on his team, which I'd presumed was the coach's way of keeping Justin from transferring to another high school before Midtown High was finished riding his coattails to victory.

"I'm not actually here today, Justin," I said, still grinning. "Think of me as a ghost. Janice just wanted me to come in for a few minutes to talk."

"Ooh, not Ms. Janice!" Justin brought a hand to his forehead as he let out a huge laugh. "Don't worry, Ms. Smith! We're not gon' let them fire you! We've got your back!"

"She pretty much promised that she wasn't going to fire me today, so I think I'm safe."

"Yeah, you better stay safe!" Justin laughed again before he nodded toward Brianna in the passenger seat. "Hey, girl. Wassup with you? You doin' good?"

"I'm good." Brianna smiled back at him.

"All right. I'll see y'all later," Justin said before walking toward his mom's easily identifiable pickup truck parked a few feet away. The truck was covered in Midtown High School logos and slogans, each one designed with the school's vibrant black and gold colors.

*MIDTOWN HIGH SCHOOL: WHERE GREATNESS IS BORN*

*I'M A MIDTOWN HIGH MOM*

*MIDTOWN HIGH PTA: WE DON'T PLAY!*

*MY SON IS A MIDTOWN HIGH TIGER*

*#OFFICIALTAILGATEBRIGADE*

". . . Do you two know each other?" Confused, I turned back toward Brianna.

"No." Brianna shook her head. "Why?"

"I just thought that—Justin was talking to you like you two knew each other."

Brianna chuckled before she replied, "That's just how we talk to each other sometimes."

Slightly amused, I opened the driver's-side door. "Or maybe he was trying to hit on you."

"Is that something the students here do a lot? Hit on teachers?"

"I wouldn't necessarily say it's a Center-only problem. More like something that's been happening since the very conception of the school system."

I waited for Brianna to meet me on my side of the car before I continued, my mouth shaped into a wide grin. "Besides, you're not a teacher. Which means you're fair game. Plus, you're a total smoke show. Don't be surprised if some of the admin staff take a swing at asking you out, too."

"Flatterer." Brianna playfully rolled her eyes.

"I think you mean, truth-teller—" I started to reply, but my words were cut off by the sound of something breaking, something shifting, something crumbling toward the ground.

"What the fuck?" I turned my attention back toward the building, my feet already heading toward the sound's origin. It seemed like it was coming from behind the building. Soon I was proven right, my eyes locking on to a man in an orange shirt and a yellow vest, his hard hat firmly in place on his head.

But he wasn't alone.

There were five, six, seven of them, with a large van parked behind the Center, speaking into walkie-talkies while they continued to break the building apart.

"What are you doing?" I asked, my breaths coming too quickly, my thoughts threatening to turn into fuzz and static.

*Please. Don't.*

*This is all I have left of her.*

*This is all I have left of Patricia.*

Memories, like always, came in a flood.

*Patricia hastily handing me her camera so she could take a selfie* in front of the building. Patricia forcing me to try one of those awful vegan recipes for barbecue mac and cheese in the break room. Patricia narrowing her eyes at my outfit before she broke out into a smile, telling me she hated me for buying a dress she wanted first—

"Elizabeth!" Janice's voice rang out. "There you are!"

She easily maneuvered around the working men as she made her way over to me. "Oh! And you must be Brianna! Good! You're here, too! How lovely to finally meet you!"

"Nice to meet you, too, Janice." Brianna beamed back. "Elizabeth has told me so much about you."

"Good things, I hope?"

"Great things."

As Janice smiled brightly at the compliment, I took a step toward her. Everything about Janice was always *too eager*, her faux-confident demeanor hiding a fragility that echoed throughout her box-dyed red curls and upcycled jacket. "Janice? What is this? What's going on? Are they tearing down the—"

"No! No one's tearing down a thing," Janice started. "They're renovating a wing of the Learning Center."

"Oh." I nodded, still a little confused by the situation. "Is that why you called me down here?"

"Yes!" Janice clasped her hands together, brimming with excitement. "This is a gift for you, Elizabeth. From Jack Fitzgerald."

". . . A gift? For me?"

A chill went down my spine as I folded my arms together as hard as I could, trying my best to keep my focus on Janice's face as I fought the urge to vomit all over the crumbled bits of building on the ground. Something told me that the workers wouldn't appreciate having regurgitated cupcakes and frosting splattered everywhere.

*Fuck.*

*What the fuck is happening right now?*

Jack hadn't spoken to me in months. Why would he want to give me *anything*?

"It's in honor of Patricia, of course," Janice continued, a smile stuck on her face. "He knew how much this place meant to her, how much you meant to her. He just wanted to do something in her memory. For you."

". . . How nice." I struggled to find the words, my mind turning into nothing but pink, pink mush.

*For me?*

*Why would Jack do this for me?*

*Why would Jack do this to me?*

"Oh, and there's one other thing," Janice said while fishing something out of her jacket pocket. A few moments later, she was offering me a set of keys, the ring resting against her palm.

"I can't believe I almost forgot part of the reason I called you down here." She chuckled.

"What do these go to?"

"Patricia's old office," she answered. "I figured you might want to get in there and go through things before—well—the guys will eventually have to renovate that part of the building, too. If there was anything you wanted to keep . . . I just think you should have the first pick."

". . . Jack didn't clear out her office?" I was stunned, paralyzed by the information. "The door was always closed, so I just assumed—"

"It's a hard thing to do, you know," Janice interrupted. "Such a hard, hard thing."

*Of course.*

*Poor, poor Jack.*

This wasn't a gift at all. It was a trap. It was another man in a long line of men passing down the task of emotional labor, assigning it to the closest woman in the queue.

It was bullshit. It was cowardice.

And now, just like for every other woman, it was my problem to deal with, too.

# 13

# Brianna

P atricia didn't work here.

Brianna thought it almost as soon as she and Elizabeth entered the office. Despite the framed photographs on the desk and the motivational posters on the walls, it was obvious to Brianna that this was the office of someone temporary, someone who only used the space on occasion.

It was the office of someone who wanted to be *seen* working, meticulously placing hints that maybe they were, whiffs of productivity set out as a meal to be tasted.

But everything was just empty, empty calories.

It was all too neat. Too everything-in-its-place.

Too perfect to be anything but pretend.

Of course they were dedicating a wing of the Learning Center to this woman. Of course they were giving her the chance to take up even more space to do nothing. Brianna's mind was racing, a gnarling, gnashing sensation at the back of her head.

Even in death, Patricia was allowed to occupy more room than she deserved.

Maybe more than Brianna ever would. Still, despite Brianna's opinion of the previous office holder, she could tell that being in the space was having an effect on Elizabeth. Her hands were shaking as she picked up a file folder off the woman's desk, even as she set it back down.

"Elizabeth?" Brianna started from across the room. "Elizabeth, are you okay?"

"Yeah ... I ..." Elizabeth said, sounding like she was somewhere on another planet, like she was operating on a wholly different plane of existence. "I just ... I don't know if I can do this right now."

Brianna offered Elizabeth a comforting hand, gently resting it along her back, even as she struggled to come up with something to say, something that didn't sound too canned and too rehearsed.

Something that didn't sound like she'd already run this exact scenario a million times in her head.

". . . Something happened to her, didn't it? The woman whose office this used to be?" Brianna murmured, hoping against hope that it came out sounding natural. "Your ... friend?"

Elizabeth laughed, even though it'd torn through her like a cry. "Yeah. Something happened. Something happened, and now it's like no matter how far I try to get away from it, it's always hanging over my fucking head. All I want is to . . ."

Elizabeth paused for a moment, her trembling fingers brushing away fresh tears.

"All I want is to be able to feel better. All I want is to be able to get through one fucking day without . . . having to remember. Without having to think about it. Don't I deserve that, at least? Just one fucking day to myself?"

"... What happened to her, Elizabeth?" Brianna's words were gentle and low.

"... She died," Elizabeth answered, keeping her gaze on Brianna. "It happened a few months ago. She . . . according to the police, she killed herself. But I . . . I was the one who found her."

Elizabeth's shaking returned, her body trembling, all at once.

Brianna lowered her hand toward Elizabeth's palm, Elizabeth's fingers softly flexing against hers.

Then Elizabeth's trembling stilled, her hand calm against Brianna's.

"I don't . . . I've never thought she killed herself, Brianna. She wouldn't have done something like that. The night before, we . . . she told me that she wanted to go walking with me the next morning. It wasn't like Patricia to say something she didn't mean. If she was going to kill herself . . . she would've just told me good night."

". . . Have you told anyone else? About what really happened to Patricia?"

"I tried. I tried going to the police, but they said there wasn't anything to . . . they said that the right bones were broken, around her neck. They can tell when you kill yourself and when someone else kills you. I didn't know that. Did you know that?"

Elizabeth roughly sniffled before she went on. "I tried telling David about it, too. But he . . . he just thinks that I'm crazy. He thinks being the one to find her body . . . he thinks that set me on some impossible task. Like I'm taking responsibility for something that's not my fault."

Elizabeth lifted her gaze toward Brianna, her stare boring right into her.

"But I know I'm not crazy, Brianna. Something happened to her. Something happened to her, and I just . . . I don't know how to be okay, knowing someone hurt her and it's like . . . no one even cares that they're getting away with it. God . . . who would ever want to hurt her? Why would anyone ever do that to Patricia?"

*Why would anyone ever do that to Patricia?*

For a moment, Brianna's grip on Elizabeth's palm went slack as images flashed behind her eyes.

Jay's blood running down his shirt. Jay's blood everywhere.

A makeshift noose. A body that was almost too heavy. A car that almost wouldn't start. A white woman begging for her life, her irises pleading.

Brianna knowing it didn't matter how much the woman begged.

Because she'd already made up her mind.

Patricia Fitzgerald was going to die that night.

The buzzing of Elizabeth's phone brought Brianna's hand back to life, her gentle grip returning. Elizabeth offered her a warm smile before she drew her palm away from Brianna's, soon using it to pull out her phone.

"Oh God. It's Janice. Again." Elizabeth's tone made her sound exasperated. "I'm not . . . I can't . . . Can you go see what she wants? She might still be outside with the renovating guys."

"You sure you don't want to go out there yourself?"

"No." Elizabeth firmly shook her head. "She can't see me like this, Brianna. Ever. She needs to think that I'm okay. That I'm processing it. If she sees me bawling my eyes out, I'm sure it'll find its way back to David and then back to my therapist and then I'll end up on a new cocktail of meds and I can't go through all of that again—"

"I've got you," Brianna interrupted with a small smile. "I've got you, Elizabeth."

Elizabeth returned the expression, just as she handed Brianna her phone. Brianna asked a question with her eyes, looking down at the device before looking back over at Elizabeth.

"Oh. Right." Elizabeth reached for her phone again, concentrating on the screen. "There's some security thing. On the phone. If you're going back through the door we just came in. I'm sure Janice has the alarm turned off with the students here right now, but just in case she doesn't . . ."

Brianna subtly shifted closer to Elizabeth, close enough to get a glimpse of the screen as she swiped and typed, putting in the security information, putting in her phone's password, too.

Close enough to memorize every last number, letter, and special character.

When she was finished, Brianna moved just as subtly away from her, Elizabeth soon handing her the phone yet again.

Brianna then smiled as she pulled the phone into her grip, right before she headed toward the office door. "I'll be right back, okay?"

* * *

"How's she holding up?" It was the first thing out of Janice's mouth as Brianna approached her behind the building.

Brianna squinted away from the direct sunlight in her eyes, her hand operating as a makeshift visor. "Holding up? What do you mean?"

"You don't have to do that." Janice shook her head. "You don't have to pretend like you don't know about . . ."

She waved a hand toward bits of building that'd crumbled to the ground, as if that were enough to explain what she meant.

Oddly enough, for Brianna, it was.

"Right. Patricia." Brianna nodded. "Elizabeth may have mentioned her once. Or twice."

". . . How did she say that she died?" Janice's voice slightly quivered at the end of her question, like she was hiding something underneath it that she didn't want Brianna to see.

"She said that she killed herself," Brianna answered, calm and collected. "Why? Is there something—"

"No. There's nothing." Janice offered Brianna half of a smile. "That's good. I mean, it's not good, but—" Janice took a deep breath before she went on. "You're new in Elizabeth's life, Brianna. You have no idea how hard things have been for her ever since Patricia died. I'm just . . . happy to see that she's back on the right track—"

Janice paused, her eyes going toward Elizabeth's phone in Brianna's grip. "Oh. You have her phone?"

"Yeah, she just wanted to make sure I'd be able to get in and out of the building without setting off any of the alarms." Brianna chuckled. "I didn't even realize this place had such a fancy security system."

"Not that fancy." Janice chuckled, too. "It's just an app. Like one of those smart homes, you know? Actually, if things keep going well with you and Elizabeth, I could get you set up on the app, too? She's probably going to get tired of always handing off her phone."

"Maybe so." Brianna beamed. "But in the meantime, was there something you wanted to talk to Elizabeth about? She noticed you calling and I was heading back to the car, anyway, to grab a filing crate from the trunk—"

"Right! That's right!" Janice suddenly snapped, as if a thought had come down to her like lightning. "I just wanted to let her know about the big reveal for the renovations."

"Won't that be a few months away?"

"Not the big one." Janice winked. "The big one won't take too long at all. Here. I'll just send Elizabeth an email about it since she's otherwise occupied. But you should write the date down in your calendar, too."

"Will do," Brianna replied as she took a step closer to Janice. "Any hints? On what the big reveal is going to be?"

"The only hint I can give you"—Janice leaned toward Brianna

with a playful conspiracy in her tone—"is that I think Elizabeth is really, really going to like it."

\* \* \*

"I'm sorry for being such a headcase, back at the Learning Center," Elizabeth apologized as she took a big bite out of the burger between her palms, sniffling as she spoke. "That's why David wanted me to have an assistant, you know. Because I'm out of my fucking mind."

"David was the one who wanted you to have an assistant?" Brianna asked in between swirling her french fries around in a small barbecue sauce container. The pair had decided to go through a drive-thru instead of picking up anything to go, Brianna suggesting that indulging in junk food might be just what Elizabeth needed after being forced to rifle through Patricia's office.

Forced to deal with her dead friend's leftovers before she'd even had lunch.

Elizabeth had readily agreed.

"He said it would help me stay on track," she answered. "He just . . . he means well, Brianna. He really does. I just feel like sometimes . . . he has this version of me in his head. And anytime I deviate from it . . ."

"He's not hitting you or something, is he?"

Elizabeth laughed at the suggestion, the sound genuine and sweet. "David? God, no. He would never. If he even thought about something like that, he'd cut off his own hand before doing it. The man is a saint."

"Well, it's nice that he cares about you."

Elizabeth turned toward Brianna with one eyebrow raised. "You'd think so, wouldn't you? You'd think that having a saint on your side would make everything perfect."

"Still, having a saint on your side has to help, right?"

Suddenly, there was a heavy silence between the two women, Elizabeth's expression shifting like she'd been absolutely stumped by the question, like no one had ever asked her anything like it before. Brianna stayed still beside her, holding her breath as she waited for Elizabeth to come to a conclusion, her own emotions seeming to mystify her.

". . . It used to be. David and I used to really be something. I mean, even from the first moment we met . . . it was like we were burning. Like we were on fire for each other. I don't even know how things got off track. It's not like we had a kid. But something . . . something's different. Something changed."

"How long have you two been together?"

"Ever since we were in college." Elizabeth smiled as she spoke.

"Maybe that's it, then," Brianna suggested as she pressed her neck against the car's headrest. "You met when you were kids."

"I said we were in college, Brianna." Elizabeth chuckled. "I'd hardly call that meeting when we were kids—"

"But you were," Brianna insisted. "Even if you felt like you were already grown up, you weren't. You were kids in love, and now . . . well, everything's always so much harder when we grow up, isn't it?"

"You sound like you're talking from experience."

"Maybe I am." Brianna smiled. "I met Charles when I was a kid, too."

"Charles? That's the name of the asshole who won't text you back?"

"Hey, that's Mr. Asshole to you," Brianna joked before waving a hand. "And it's not his fault. Something . . . changed between us, too. I think I'll always love him, but sometimes . . . the hurt's just too big to fix."

"Shit. Did he cheat on you?"

"Nothing like that." Brianna shook her head. "Charles was a lot of things, but unfaithful wasn't one of them. He had a lot of issues about that. Stuff to do with his dad."

"Then what was the hurt?"

"Just . . . growing apart." Brianna forced out the lie, even as a sob threatened to tear right through her. "It's like death by a million cuts when it happens that way. You don't even see it happening until there's nothing you can do to stop the bleeding."

"I'm sorry." Elizabeth finished with her lunch, crumbling the wrapper paper into her fist. "Fuck men. Right?"

"I *wish* I didn't want to." Brianna's response came out deadpan with an expectant smirk between her lips.

Elizabeth's laugh was stuttered. She nearly doubled over in the driver's side of the car, her arms wrapping around her waist.

And Brianna joined in the laughter, too, amused at her own joke, and oh-so-very-proud of herself for holding the mask in place.

For never letting Elizabeth see her for who or what she really was.

# 14

# Brianna

Patricia Fitzgerald had friends.

Too many friends.

So many friends that Brianna hadn't been able to narrow them down, not even after following the woman week after week. So many friends that Brianna had lost count of the myriad brunches, friend dinners, drop-ins, pop-ups, all the little things Patricia had been invited to and shown up for.

She was a nonstop flurry, a breeze blowing all around Memphis, an ever-present sundress and a smile.

Which meant that it could've been any one of them.

Any one of the people Patricia had sat and laughed with, shared a meal with, spun around for in her latest gown, could've been the one who'd told her to call the police on Brianna's son. The one who'd made it a priority for Patricia, something so urgent she'd had to call on the way to work. The one who'd given Patricia just enough details for the police to show up and—

Brianna steered her thoughts away from the ending of that sentence, her mind flinching away from the memories. But those same memories were the reason she was here, why she'd devoted so much of her time to trying to find a back door into the Harbor Town neighborhood. She'd had to find a back door because there was no other option. It wasn't like she'd ever be able to afford to live on this side of town, and it wasn't like she had any of the relevant experience the women of Harbor Town were looking for in a Black woman, mainly revolving around taking care of their children and *not* fucking their husbands.

Or at least not looking better than them if they did.

Which was why when Brianna saw Elizabeth's post in the Harbor Town group, it felt like fate. Brianna had joined the Facebook group under a fake name, Kari Parsons, keeping her posts so vague no one would've been able to pinpoint exactly where she lived in the neighborhood. She'd also made sure to ask for travel recommendations almost every week, sourcing tips for Airbnbs in cities all around the country, Kari being the kind of woman who was on the go.

The kind of woman who it wouldn't have been strange for any of her neighbors to not have met face-to-face, the opportunity so often eluding them.

Until this afternoon, Brianna had everyone who lived in Harbor Town on her suspect list, including her new boss and her saint of a husband.

But there was something about Elizabeth.

She wasn't like the other ones, the ones Brianna had seen come and go on Patricia's social calendar. Besides seeming to be barely on it, Elizabeth was rarely around Patricia's other friends. She was mostly an island unto herself, giving admission to nothing and no one. Her isolated nature, combined with her work at the Learning Center, made Brianna start to suspect that Elizabeth never would've called the cops on a *child*. Because unlike Patricia's other friends, Elizabeth would've known what calling the cops on a *Black child* could do, the consequences that could come from it.

She was too close to it, too surrounded by it.

She just knew better.

Which meant that she was the one person whom Brianna could rule out.

Still, that left David Smith on Brianna's suspect list, the saint himself now walking into the kitchen just as Brianna finished cleaning the last plate in the sink.

"Is this what Elizabeth has you doing now?" David asked with a disappointed sigh. "I'm sorry, Brianna. I signed us up for a cleaning service to come once a week, but I think it may have slipped Elizabeth's mind—"

"She didn't ask me to do it," Brianna interrupted. "Elizabeth had a hard day. She's taking a nap upstairs. I just wanted to help out where I could."

Brianna wanted to use any unsupervised time in Elizabeth's home as wisely as she could, too, scrolling through social media feeds, jotting down the names of the few friends that Elizabeth and Patricia had in common online, all the people who'd been tagged in pictures with them both.

All the people who might have convinced Patricia to interrupt her busy day just long enough to make a phone call.

"Oh." David sighed again, his tone shifting to one of relief. "Well, thank you for that. Did you plan on sticking around for dinner, too?"

"No."

". . . That's it?" David chuckled. "Just no?"

"No, thank you," Brianna said before flashing David a sarcastic smile.

"Wow. Message received." David chuckled again, and Brianna

noticed the way his cheeks dimpled with the act of it, a youthful grin soon resting on his features. In that moment, Brianna understood at least some of Elizabeth's angst over losing him, a man who was objectively handsome by any metric. It was difficult finding men like David in the wild, men who were handsome, high achievers who not only took care of themselves but seemed to be invested in taking care of the people around them, too.

Brianna knew exactly what losing that kind of man was like.

"Can I ask you something?" David continued. "And please, let me know if you think I'm overstepping."

"Sure." Brianna shrugged. "You can ask me anything."

". . . Is it because I'm white?"

". . . What?" Brianna slowly blinked. "I'm sorry? I don't think I understand the question?"

"It just seems like you hate me," David went on with a sly smile. "But you don't know anything about me. I was just wondering if this was because I'm a white guy or—"

"Are you accusing me of . . . being prejudiced against you?" Brianna was hardly able to get the words out, confusion and suspicion prickling up her spine. "Because you realize that your wife is white, too, right? And I don't think she'd really share the same opinion—"

"I don't know, Brianna." David folded his arms across his chest. "I think we might seriously have a problem here. I mean, I know that reverse racism isn't real, but I'm starting to feel like this might be the one time it's actually happened in all of human history."

David winked when he was done speaking, a few seconds later letting out a hearty laugh.

Brianna's anxious state alleviated at the sound of it, a soft breath escaping between her lips.

"Sorry. I'm sorry. Was that too far? I don't want you to think I'm an asshole. I was just trying to break the ice a little bit." David held up his hands, defending his position. "I know you're not prejudiced, Brianna. Trust me."

"Who's the prejudiced one now?" Brianna joked. "Isn't it pretty presumptuous to assume that I'm *not* a total bigot? Just because I'm Black?"

"I don't think you're not prejudiced because you're Black. I think you're not prejudiced because I've developed a sixth sense for it."

". . . Really?" Brianna scrunched up her nose in disbelief.

"I kind of had to," David answered. "Working in real estate in the South, you'd be surprised how many of these assholes—" He stopped himself as a wry smile came over his face. "Actually, you know what? You *wouldn't* be surprised."

"No. I probably wouldn't be."

". . . Where'd you go to school, Brianna?"

"Graceland High, before it was torn down."

"They tore it down?"

"They said not enough kids lived in the neighborhood to justify it still being part of the school system." Brianna rolled her eyes. "The truth is that they just needed space to build a new apartment complex. Not so anyone in the neighborhood could actually live in it, because it's not like we could've ever afforded thirteen hundred dollars a month in rent. It was just so the people who own it could rent it out to tourists."

". . . Because Graceland High must be right next to *the* Graceland."

"You got it."

". . . Shit." David sighed. "What about where you went to college?"

"I didn't go to college," she admitted, suddenly concerned about his line of questioning. "Is that going to be a problem? It's not like I don't have plans to, I just—"

"Oh. No. That doesn't matter." David shook his head. "Sorry. I'd just assumed. I feel like everyone around here is practically wearing their framed degrees around their necks."

"I don't know. People around here seem nice so far."

"How many of them have you met, Brianna?"

". . . No one, really." She grimaced after she spoke. "But your wife is nice? So, I'm guessing her other friends are probably pretty nice, too."

"Has she mentioned anything to you about Patricia?"

Brianna noticed that David's voice had that same underlying worry, that same undeniable concern as Janice's voice had earlier.

Like he was absolutely terrified of Brianna telling him the truth.

"Not really," Brianna lied, her response gentle and soft. "She mentioned that they were friends, and that she . . . recently passed away. But she hasn't said much about her since then."

"Okay." David nodded to himself before he went on, everything about him seeming so unsure. "Will you . . . just be sure to keep me posted, Brianna."

"About what?"

"About if she brings up Patricia again. My wife . . . she means well, she really does. But sometimes she can get a little . . . obsessive about things she has no control over. And I just want to make sure she stays on the right path."

\*   \*   \*

". . . Mom?"

Elizabeth had answered an unexpected knock on the front door, and from her seat on the couch, Brianna heard her voice shaking. It'd been a week since their impromptu Learning Center visit and Elizabeth's subsequent meltdown in Patricia's office. Since then,

Brianna had tried to be extra attentive to her, half empathetic, half not wanting her only connection to Harbor Town to become so sedated she didn't need an assistant at all.

"I don't understand . . ." Elizabeth murmured. Neither did Brianna. Was that really Elizabeth's mother?

Brianna watched Elizabeth stand eerily still in the doorway, like she'd been frozen solid. She didn't know much about Elizabeth's parents, other than that they were somewhere up North, maybe Boston or Seattle. One of those cities where whenever someone said the name of it, Brianna's mind conjured up images of snowflakes and snowstorms. But the woman on the other side of the door didn't look like she'd ever known the meaning of the word *cold*, with her Hawaiian-style sundress and bright pink sandals.

She was Elizabeth from a bizzarro universe. An older version of her daughter with more exposure to sunlight and serotonin. Everything about her seemed like it was plucked and perfect, too, from the expensive-looking watch on her wrist to her immaculately shaped eyebrows. Honestly, it was like the woman had just wandered off a movie set—

*Wait.*

*Is Elizabeth's mom famous?* Brianna wondered as she stared over at the woman, her mind shuffling through internal photographs of movie stars on the red carpet, trying to pick her out of the mental lineup. It wouldn't have surprised Brianna if she'd happened to be in the presence of some starlet from the '70s, especially since it would've explained Elizabeth's nature, too.

A famous mom with cameras following her wherever she'd go . . .

And a kid who wanted to stay out of the spotlight, desperate to keep what she could to herself.

Tale as old as time.

"What don't you understand, darling?" Elizabeth's mom let herself into the home, her eyes bright and sparkling. "Didn't you get my messages?"

"No. I didn't." Elizabeth's tone was flat. "Are you sure you sent any?"

At that, her mother laughed, her watch jingling as she playfully snapped her fingers. "Oh my God. You're right, Mini! I'm so sorry. I was *thinking* about telling Alexandra to send you a text or email you or something, but then I got distracted by something your father said about redoing the pool. That's where his mind has been lately, trying to find these tiles that we bought two decades ago. I've told him that he's wasting his time and so many businesses go in and out—"

"Don't call me that."

"Call you what?"

"Mini," Elizabeth answered. "You know I don't like it."

Elizabeth's mother rolled her eyes in response. "Yes, yes. We all know what a grown-up you are now, *Elizabeth*. But can't you give your mother this just once? It is my birthday, after all."

"And you came here? For your birthday?" Elizabeth's eyes were locked on her mother's. "Why?"

"Why did I come to visit my daughter for my birthday?" Her mother laughed yet again. "Is that what the story is now? Are you casting me as a monster in your head—"

Suddenly, the woman's attention was on Brianna, giving her a once-over with an appraising smile.

"Naomi Campbell, as I live and breathe." She smirked before moving closer to Brianna. "Just kidding, of course. I know you're not Naomi. She and I go way back. But I can tell you this much, she would've been terrified of you back in those Milan days. Stunning. Just stunning."

". . . Thank you." Brianna was hesitant to speak to her, sensing the tension between mother and daughter. At no point did she want

Elizabeth to think she was on anyone else's side but hers, not now, when everything could still fall apart.

"I'm Dawn." She held out her hand for Brianna to take. "And you are?"

"Brianna." She accepted Dawn's handshake but dropped her palm much faster than she normally might. "I'm your daughter's assistant."

"You work for my daughter?" Dawn's jaw was wide open.

"She's helping me keep everything together," Elizabeth cut into the conversation. "After what happened to Patricia—"

"Who?"

". . . Why are you really here, Mom?" Elizabeth sounded so defeated. "What do you want? Did David call you?"

"I told you." Dawn smiled as she spoke. "It's my birthday. And I want to spend it with my mini, with my special girl."

\* \* \*

"Do you think Tom Cruise ate here while he was making *The Firm*?" Dawn perked up as she took a seat beside Brianna at the restaurant's table. "I bet he did. Do you think they had him sign a menu somewhere?"

"I wouldn't know," Brianna replied. "It's my first time here."

Brianna looked around Capriccio Grill, something unspooling in the center of her stomach. She was so nervous her fingers were nearly trembling as she held the menu, like at any moment someone was going to ask her to leave, ask her to prove that she could afford to ever eat here. She had a distinct sense of un-belonging, of being a stranger in a very strange land.

But when she glanced over at Elizabeth, she could tell they weren't experiencing the same thing. Surrounded by chandeliers and bottles of wine that probably cost thousands per bottle, Elizabeth didn't seem nervous at all. She seemed annoyed, her mouth forming a pout even as David draped an arm around the back of her chair. It was easy for Brianna to imagine Elizabeth being seventeen again, a moody teenager wearing black makeup and spiky jewelry, doing everything she possibly could to piss off her parents.

Doing everything she possibly could to keep their attention on her for one single second.

"It's wonderful you stopped by for your birthday, Dawn." David grinned. "I'm surprised James let you get away from him for a day. You two are practically attached at the hip."

"Oh, don't get me started on James." Dawn grinned right back at him. "I was telling Mini, earlier, that he's been obsessed with fixing up the pool lately. He probably hasn't even noticed that I've left town yet. Him and those contractors—"

"It's Alexandra, isn't it?"

"What was that, darling?"

"That's why you're here," Elizabeth continued. "Dad's fucking your assistant, Alexandra. This time, at least. It's why you didn't give us any warning you were coming to visit, because you didn't want her to know you were leaving town . . . because you didn't want her to put it on your shared calendar with Dad. You don't want him to know that you already know."

"Baby, let's not make assumptions—" David interjected.

"It's not about assumptions, David." Elizabeth smiled over at her mother, the expression so taut Brianna wondered if it was hurting her to keep it on her face. "It's about patterns. Once a scorned woman, always a scorned woman. Except she never does anything about it."

"Mini, how about we keep things civil? We wouldn't want Brianna thinking that her employer is severely undermedicated." Dawn

WHILE WE WERE BURNING

smiled right back at her daughter, her expression just as tense and tight. "Or have you moved on from antidepressants to something stronger?"

"What's that supposed to mean?"

"It means that I always knew how you would turn out, Mini." Dawn let out a tired sigh. "I always knew that you'd be pretty. I always knew that you'd fall in love and have a beautiful life. And I always knew that they'd find you dead with a bottle of pills in your hand—"

David jumped in again. "Dawn, let's not—"

"You get those genes from your father, you know," Dawn went on. "The ones that make you so sad, despite us giving you the world. Oh, poor little Elizabeth! She's gotten everything she's ever wanted and she can't stop crying about it—"

"I got everything I ever wanted?" Elizabeth half laughed, half scoffed. "How would you know? You were barely ever there!"

"Don't. Don't make me out to be a bad mother when I was always there for you—"

"I don't have to make you out to be what you are, *Dawn*."

"I think we should quit while we're ahead here," David remarked. "Dawn, if you need a place to stay, I can rent you a room somewhere—"

"At least my friends don't kill themselves." Dawn smirked in Elizabeth's direction. "What number are we on now, Mini? Two, right? Camilla and that neighbor girl of yours. You know, some people might call that a *pattern*. Now, what does it say about you if people keep killing themselves just to get away from you?"

". . . You're evil," Elizabeth murmured as she shot up from the table. "You're fucking evil. That's what you fucking are."

David reached out his arm. "Baby, wait—"

But Elizabeth was already halfway out the door.

With Brianna close behind her.

*   *   *

The Mississippi River.

Brianna smiled just at the sight of it, the warmth that was coming down across the back of her ears and neck. She rested her head against her knees, with her feet tucked underneath her. She was sitting beside Elizabeth on one of the benches placed next to the river, far enough away that a rough wave couldn't bring anyone down, but still close enough to feel the spritz of the water when the wind hit it just right.

This had been one of Brianna's happier places, when she was still able to be that happy. She could still see Charles lifting weights at the outdoor gym near the river, right before he'd jump into a pickup game of basketball. She could still hear him complaining about what was written on one of the statues dedicated to Tom Lee, a Black man who'd saved white people from drowning in the river one night.

## A Very Worthy Negro

"I'm sorry about all of that back there," Elizabeth started, ripping Brianna out of her warm daydream and bringing her right back down to cold reality. "My mom and I . . . we have a complicated relationship."

"I can see that." Brianna nodded. "Sorry things couldn't be . . . less complicated."

"One of the many reasons I never wanted to have any kids." Elizabeth chuckled, but it seemed lifeless. "Nobody else should ever have to deal with that woman."

"Wouldn't that be up to you? Whether or not your kids got to see her?"

"You think anything is up to me when Dawn is around?" Elizabeth chuckled again. "I barely got away from her when I went off to college. And the only reason she didn't ruin me and David is because she didn't really meet him until we were already engaged."

"You think she would've tried to ruin you and David?"

"I think that woman is so full of sadness that she can't help but spread some of it around," Elizabeth answered with a small smile. "She's just doing what she was taught. Get married. Stay married, even if you're miserable. And learn how to take it out on everyone around you."

Elizabeth paused for a moment before she went on. "To be fair to my mom, my dad is kind of the world's biggest asshole. He's been cheating on her ever since they said 'I do,' I think. I'm guessing he's partially responsible for who she is now. Sometimes I . . . sometimes I think about what she was like before. Before she met him. Before she had me."

"Heartbreak has a way of changing people," Brianna offered just as a phantom stabbing pain thudded against her breastbone. "It's hard . . . getting back to whoever you used to be."

There was silence between them then, the only sounds the gentle swishing of the waves and the chatter of people hastily jogging past them behind the bench. It was so quiet that Brianna could hardly take it anymore, the pain in her chest reaching a harsh crescendo, her brain needing to concentrate on something, anything else, before it imploded between her ears.

"Who's Camilla?"

"What?"

"Your mom mentioned her, back at the restaurant," Brianna went on. "She . . . Did she . . . hurt herself?"

"... She did, yeah," Elizabeth murmured. "Freshman year of college. She was my dormmate. She jumped off the roof."

"I'm so sorry to hear that—"

"She was my only friend, too, before David," Elizabeth cut into Brianna's reply. "Which made her feel like my whole world."

Elizabeth then turned toward Brianna, her eyes wet with sudden tears. "Do you have any idea what that's like, Brianna? Losing your whole world?"

The images came to her so fast that she couldn't make them stop.

Birthdays. Sleepovers. Frosting. Stuffed teddy bears.

Cradling her baby in her arms.

Cradling her baby in the street.

"And now, with Patricia . . ." Elizabeth trailed off. "Fuck. It feels like it's happening all over again. Like I'm just . . . spiraling. Like I don't know how to make any of it stop. If I could just . . . I just want to make it right. I just want to fix it. I just want to—"

Brianna interrupted Elizabeth by resting her head on her shoulder.

Elizabeth quieted at that.

Before she rested her head against Brianna's, too.

# 15

# Elizabeth

I
s it problematic if I say that we look like twins?" I asked, my eyes
scanning Brianna's outfit up and down. She was wearing a gray
tank-top-and-sweats combo, her sneakers practiced and worn. "I
don't want to be one of those I-don't-see-color people—"

"Is it problematic if I say that I think you totally stole my look?"
Brianna smirked. "Seriously. What are the odds?"

I smirked right back at her as I closed my front door behind me.
"Thanks for coming out with me today. You really didn't have to."

"No, thank you. I needed a reason to get back into working out.
Or at least doing something halfway healthy."

"Oh my God, Brianna. Don't tell me you're one of those women."

"One of those women?"

"The ones who look like goddesses and don't even have to work
out." I couldn't stop the frown from taking over my face. "It's not
fair. The rest of us are forced to pay in blood whenever we eat a goddamn carb, and what? They just bounce off you like nothing?"

"That's a popular misconception, actually," Brianna started, her tone corrective. "That how you look on the outside is any way reflective of inner health. If you're living off Red Bull and Donettes, no matter how skinny you are, that's going to catch up with you, eventually."

"Oh, I don't care about inner health." I waved a hand in the air between us, hoping that it'd emphasize what I was saying. "If I don't look good, there's literally no point."

"So, you're saying you'd rather be sickly and gorgeous?"

"Literally all I heard you just say is 'gorgeous.'"

Brianna broke out in a laugh, and I heard my own laugh following right behind her. A few moments later, and we were speed-walking, side by side, down the street.

I'd invited Brianna to walk with me around the neighborhood before we both got ready for whatever Janice had planned at the Learning Center. I still had no idea what the big reveal was going to be, but Brianna had told me that Janice mentioned that I was *really going to like it.*

Which probably meant that Janice was going to drag me up on some makeshift stage and force me to be the center of attention.

Which meant that I needed to *glow.*

There was no way in hell that I was going to have a grand reintroduction back into Memphis society with bags under my eyes or unplucked eyebrows. If I was going to be the sad sack of the day, I was at least going to be a *hot* sack of sad. Yes, I'd been crushed by the death of my best friend—

*But didn't I look surprisingly good for a traumatized woman?*

"Oh my God. I can already feel my heart trying to beat out of my chest," Brianna said, her feet pumping right next to mine. "Is this place built on a hill?"

"I told you we shouldn't have had that cake last night."

"Please! They were slices from Muddy's!" Brianna scoffed. "What were we supposed to do? Throw them away? Besides, David wanted us to have them."

"Yeah, because he saw that I was counting calories for Janice's big show. It wasn't him being nice. It was straight-up sabotage."

"Well, I, for one, would welcome that form of sabotage each and every day."

"You would say that, Ms. Carbs Don't Stick."

"Hey! Don't body-shame me!" There was a grin under Brianna's tone.

"Uh, it is literally impossible to body-shame someone whose body is perfect," I started, my words lined with a laugh. "Besides, you body-shame me every time I have to stand next to you! That has to be, like, bullying by proxy. Honestly, I should probably sue you."

Brianna cracked up, loud, and I felt a sense of pride radiating across my skin.

Only friends could make each other laugh like that.

\* \* \*

"What the hell is that?" I pointed up at the building, where what used to be the Learning Center's logo was now covered in a dark blue shroud. "That definitely wasn't here yesterday."

I was standing among a crowd of people, all taking their place in front of the building. As I expected, there was a makeshift stage near the front door, with a nervous Janice pacing back and forth across it. She was dressed to the nines, in what I could only describe as a *power suit*, her jacket as impeccably wrinkle-free as her not-a-strand-out-of-place updo.

"I'm guessing that's the big reveal?" Brianna speculated, her hands going toward her hips. "Maybe they're revamping the sign to match the future renovations?"

"All this over a fucking sign?" I rolled my eyes, unable to keep the annoyance off my face and out of my words. "Come on, Janice. This could've just been an email—"

". . . Elizabeth?" A familiar voice cut me right to the core.

". . . Jack?" I could barely look over at him, my gaze cutting away like a faulty TV screen.

How was I supposed to look at him without thinking about Patricia?

Without remembering the too-soft sound of shoes falling on a darkened street?

"I'm so glad you made it." Jack's tone sounded like it was lined with a warm smile. "How have you been holding up?"

"I don't want to do this."

"Do what—"

"I don't want to have this conversation right now, Jack," I continued, my eyes finally lifting up to meet his. He seemed taken aback by my response, hastily leaning away from me as if he'd gotten me mixed up with someone else entirely.

Like I was a party foul he hadn't meant to make.

"I just don't want to stand around and pretend like everything's fine." I finished saying what was on my mind. "Like we mean anything to each other, really. That's not ever how we were, Jack. We were always on different sides."

". . . I didn't see it that way. I didn't know that we were on different sides." Jack's words were stilted and stalled, like an afterthought he'd accidentally spoken out loud.

"I just mean that we don't have to do this fake kumbaya shit." I shrugged. "You don't have to check up on me. And I don't have to check up on you. We can just . . . be. Can't we just be, Jack?"

"Message received. Loud and clear." Jack nodded before his attention shifted over to Brianna.

For a moment, it looked like he wanted to say something to her.

Maybe introduce himself. Maybe apologize for my outburst.

Maybe tell her to stay the fuck away from the woman with conspiracy theories about how his wife ended up a dead angel slowly swinging in the Harbor Town wind.

His hesitation was soon replaced by indifference, Jack brushing by us almost as quickly as he'd entered our atmosphere.

*Good fucking riddance.*

# 16

## Brianna

Brianna wasn't breathing.

She was still stuck in Jack's earlier gaze, her own eyes desperately trailing his as she'd waited for him to speak. Instead, he'd simply walked away, leaving Brianna in a daze of confusion, the sense of it creating a fog around her every thought.

She didn't understand. She couldn't understand.

Jack was the only one who could've pulled the trigger, but he'd never even reached for the gun.

"Sorry about that." Elizabeth turned to look over at Brianna. "Hopefully that wasn't too unpleasant—"

"I'll be right back," Brianna said, already walking away from her. "I just need to go to the bathroom really quick."

"Okay. Hurry back," Elizabeth pleaded as she offered her a wave goodbye. "If I have to get up on that stage without you, I'm definitely going to scream."

"No screaming necessary." Brianna smirked as she continued to put distance between the two of them, soon disappearing into the crowd.

*   *   *

He didn't remember her.

That had to be it.

Jack just didn't remember her.

Brianna forced down deep breath after deep breath, her hands pressed against the inside of the bathroom stall.

It was almost too good to be true.

Months ago, Brianna was quietly sitting in her car as she watched the front door of an unmarked building. Jack had just parked several spots away from her, but she couldn't see if he was still sitting in his car, too, having lost sight of him after they both pulled in.

Suddenly, Jack appeared beside her car window with a wide, welcoming smile on his face.

"I know what you're doing," Jack started.

It took everything inside of Brianna not to set her foot on the gas, not to peel out of the parking lot and never be seen again.

". . . What are you talking about?" Brianna stared up at him, giving him her best doe eyes.

"You're procrastinating like hell." Jack grinned. "It's okay. I was nervous the first time I came to AA, too." Jack then gave her a friendly shrug. "Do you want me to walk you in? Sometimes it helps to just . . . not be going inside by yourself."

Brianna let out a shaky breath before she stepped out of her car. A few moments later, and she was walking inside the building with Jack, side by side.

As each person took turns confessing their pain, Brianna was worried that she wouldn't be able to fake it. Not the tears. Not the sniffling.

WHILE WE WERE BURNING

And especially not the pain.

Which was why she decided, just for a moment, to let the truth seep out of her. She'd never struggled with drinking, but she did recall feeling as if she had done it too much and too often, especially on some of those nights with Vera at her side. So, that was what Brianna confessed to the group.

That she'd lost her child.

That she was sure there was a connection between the loss of her son and the amount of alcohol she ordered on any given night.

It was almost freeing, getting her son's death off her chest in a room full of people who seemed eager to sympathize. She wondered if this could be enough for her, to just have a room full of sympathy, to just have people willing to listen and willing to understand.

But when it was Jack's turn to speak, every mention of Patricia's name sent chills down Brianna's spine.

There was just something about the way he spoke about his wife in the present tense, a way that Brianna would never be able to speak about Jay ever again.

And that contrast, between who was past and who was present, was enough to make her realize that *no*, it wasn't going to be enough to get her feelings out to a willing crowd.

Something still needed to be done.

Something just as permanent as Jay's life being stolen away from her.

\* \* \*

"Thank God. There you are." Elizabeth smiled over at Brianna. "Were the bathrooms suspiciously clean? Almost like Janice is showing them off?"

"The bathrooms were the regular amount of clean." Brianna smirked. "Did they already make the big announcement or what?"

"I think they're about to—"

"Welcome, everyone! To the Learning Center!" Janice announced into the large mic she was holding in her grip. She now stood perfectly still on the stage, no longer anxiously pacing, her nerves seeming to have settled down. "Thank you so much for joining us today!"

"Here we go," Elizabeth murmured, her arms folding tight across her chest.

Brianna quietly watched Elizabeth, taking in her body language, idly trying to read her mind.

A few minutes passed with Janice speaking about how great the Center was for the community, for the children. How great it was that Jack had made such a sizable donation, too.

She then, of course, pulled Jack onstage beside her.

He graciously took the mic from Janice before launching into his own speech about how much Patricia loved the Center, how the renovations were overdue, how honored she would be today. When he was finished with his speech, Jack motioned for one of the renovation guys to pull down the shroud.

And as the Learning Center's new title came into focus, Brianna's vision blurred and her stomach retched.

THE PATRICIA FITZGERALD LEARNING CENTER

*No.*

*No. No. No.*

*This can't be happening,* Brianna thought, frantic and wild. *This cannot be happening—*

Her panic was interrupted by the feel of Elizabeth's hand suddenly gripping her own impossibly tight.

"Elizabeth?" Brianna forced out the question, despite the sickness pooling inside of her. "Elizabeth, are you okay?"

". . . How am I ever supposed to get past it?" Elizabeth's words were so low that Brianna barely heard them.

Before Brianna had a chance to respond, she spotted Janice motioning for Elizabeth to come join her onstage. There was a warm smile on her face, her hand rapidly beckoning like an excited game show host.

But Elizabeth wasn't moving, her fingers still pressed against Brianna's, her body perfectly frozen in place.

She then looked over at Brianna, tears behind her eyes, a question not far behind it.

"You don't have to," Brianna whispered. "You don't have to get up there if you don't want to."

That seemed to be all Elizabeth needed to hear as she started to walk away from the crowd, from Janice, from the stage . . .

Soon they were moving away from all of it, hand in hand, Elizabeth pulling Brianna along and Brianna willingly taking every step, wanting to put as much distance as she could between herself and the pain of seeing Patricia's name in big, bold letters, like she was a must-see attraction.

Like she was someone who was never going to be forgotten.

*   *   *

"No, she loved it, Janice. She really did," Brianna lied through her teeth on the phone. "Her leaving early had nothing to do with you or the ceremony. It was really wonderful. It's just that she was already feeling sick this morning and I talked her into going out. I thought it would be good for her to see the whole thing, especially if it was for Patricia.

"Are you sure?" Janice's question came out shaky. "Oh God, Brianna. I don't want to be what sets her back—"

"You didn't set her back, I promise," Brianna calmly interrupted, even as she paced back and forth across the living room floor. "Oh, and can you make sure Jack knows about what happened today, too? I wouldn't want him thinking Elizabeth walked out on the event."

". . . Okay." Janice let out a sigh of relief on the other end of the line. "I'll make sure Jack knows. Is she feeling any better, though?"

"Oh, she's good for now. Thank you so much," Brianna replied. "And thanks for checking on us, Janice. Not to mention everything you did today, too. We can't wait to see the renovations when everything's all done."

Brianna ended the call, resting her phone against the living room table. When she looked across the room, she noticed Elizabeth shamelessly staring over at her, her attention never leaving Brianna.

"You look like a ballerina when you pace like that," Elizabeth started. "Super graceful."

"Thanks?"

"Just saying, you could've been a gymnast or something." Elizabeth shrugged. "Not me, though. I'm all arms and all legs."

"Isn't that what they usually say about models? As a good thing?"

"Aww. You always know just what to say." Elizabeth placed a hand over her heart. "I'm really going to miss you, once David locks me up in the nearest asylum. Or who knows? Maybe they'll let me have a pen pal."

"I don't think you'll have to worry about that. I mean, I'm pretty sure I just fixed it." Brianna smiled. "Which means we should be good."

". . . Actually, no. I don't think we're good." Elizabeth shook her head. "At least, I don't think that I'm ever going to be good again."

". . . What's that supposed to mean, Elizabeth?"

". . . I don't know," she answered with a small shrug. "I really don't know, Brianna. I don't think . . . I don't know if this is the sort of thing that I get to ever feel better about. I think the world is going to keep going on without me, marching forward like I don't matter, like what really happened to Patricia doesn't matter."

"Elizabeth—"

"Are you hungry?" For the first time, there was something cold in Elizabeth's tone.

"Are *you* hungry, Elizabeth? You just had a super emotional moment—"

"I'm going to make us something for lunch." It was the last thing Elizabeth said before she pulled herself up to her feet.

And then she was gone.

\* \* \*

Brianna didn't know what to do.

It was a rare feeling, the lack of direction, the helplessness. Still, it coursed through her veins as she watched Elizabeth slice through a bell pepper on a cutting board. Brianna couldn't explain it, but despite her putting out Elizabeth's fires, giving her a believable cover for opting out of the rest of the Learning Center's unveiling ceremony, it felt like a distance had developed between them.

And any distance between them meant that Brianna could be cut out of Elizabeth's life at any second.

But that couldn't happen. She'd worked too hard to get this far.

She'd done too much to ever turn back now.

But what would make her indisposable? Indispensable?

What could permanently sew her to Elizabeth's side?

"I'm going to help you." The words flew out of Brianna's mouth.

". . . What?" Elizabeth stopped mid-chop, her knife held partially in the air.

"I'm going to help you," Brianna repeated, beaming over at Elizabeth from across the kitchen counter.

"Help me with what?"

"With . . ." She glanced around the room before lowering herself even closer to the counter with the demeanor of someone about to say a set of nuclear launch codes out loud. "Patricia. I want to help you with Patricia."

". . . Why?"

"What do you mean, 'why'?"

"I mean, why?" Elizabeth pressed. "I haven't exactly been a picture of mental health today, Brianna. Why would you ever want to spend your time helping me with the one thing everyone else thinks I'm crazy for believing?"

". . . Because I don't think you're crazy, Elizabeth. I believe you."

"You believe me?" Elizabeth seemed unsure, even as she spoke the phrase. Once again, she shamelessly stared over at Brianna, her eyes wide, her lips hanging slightly open like she was in a state of disbelief.

Brianna held her breath as she waited for Elizabeth's next move, her lungs nearly bursting with the effort.

But then Elizabeth repeated herself, the words so much gentler. "You believe me . . ." She flashed a small smile. "Thank you for believing me, Brianna."

Brianna returned the expression, her lungs thanking her, too, as she took in a deep breath. "So, where do we start?"

# 17

# Elizabeth

I've been going through all of her social media," I started as soon as I opened up my laptop on the living room table. "It seemed like it was the easiest place to begin, even though it's going to take me years to get through everything."

"Do you have access to Patricia's passwords?" Brianna took a seat across from me at the table, her own laptop pulled open, too.

"No," I bitterly admitted. "And the only person I could get them from is Jack, but there's no way that he'd ever . . . Let's just say that he's another nonbeliever."

"Everyone's a nonbeliever until you prove them wrong." Brianna shrugged. "And if you don't think you can get them the honest way, it might be worthwhile to guess them."

"Guess them?" I was already shaking my head. "Wouldn't that send alerts or something? Or freeze up her account so we couldn't look at it anymore?"

"That depends. Was Patricia super tech-savvy?"

"I wouldn't say super tech-savvy, no."

"In that case, she probably wasn't using a password randomizer."

". . . A password what?"

Brianna lightly chuckled. "Sorry. My true-crime-podcast side is showing again. There are a few apps out there that can connect to your browser when you're setting up passwords on websites. The passwords are usually super complicated, but since they're stored in the app, you never have to remember them yourself."

"Oh."

"But I don't think we have to worry about that," Brianna went on. "If Patricia wasn't into technology like that, she probably just used a normal combination password, just numbers and letters, maybe a special symbol."

Brianna paused for a moment, a soft hum escaping her. "Do you know when she met Jack? Like, the actual year?"

"2006," I answered, my tone confident. "I remember the year because she always made such a big deal out of being married around the same time as Tom Cruise and Katie Holmes. She was a really big fan of hers."

"She was in *Dawson's Creek*, right?"

"I think so? I never really kept up with that show."

"Do you know her Instagram account handle?" Brianna continued, everything about her so much more serious than usual. It was strangely comforting to see her like this, though, as if Brianna had solved a million murders before and Patricia was just another one on a list she needed to cross off for the year.

"It's @PatriciaFitz85," I replied. "She wanted to go with her whole last name, but it was already taken. She was pretty pissed off about it."

"Okay, so, we have Jack, we have 2006, we have Katie, and we have Joey—"

"Joey?" I interrupted Brianna's list.

"Joey Potter," she clarified. "That's who Katie Holmes played on *Dawson's Creek*."

"Right." I nodded. "Now what? We're just supposed to combine all of that until we're able to—"

"Got it."

". . . Wait. What?" My eyes went wide as I stared over at Brianna. "What do you mean, you 'got it'? Are you telling me that you're already logged in to her Instagram account?"

"Well, from what you told me, Patricia loved her husband, but it sounds like she loved Katie Holmes more," Brianna explained. "And then I figured since her handle had an 85 in it, that meant that she was a kid when *Dawson's Creek* was airing. From there, I just guessed that it wasn't really about Katie Holmes. It was about the connection Patricia felt with Joey Potter."

Brianna turned her laptop around to face me as she finished with her thoughts. "And that's how we get to a password that's not so obvious it's a security hazard, but obvious enough for Patricia to remember for herself. P-O-T-T-E-R-2-0-0-6."

". . . Who are you, Brianna Thompson?" My jaw was nearly on the floor, so impressed with Brianna's tactics. "I mean, seriously. Are you secretly a genius or something? Did you use to work for Apple? If I check your phone, will I see Tim Cook on your speed dial?"

"I'm just a girl who listens to way too many podcasts, hacking into your friend's social media for you."

I smirked at Brianna's *Notting Hill* reference as I typed Patricia's Instagram password onto my own keyboard, my eyes watering as it went through, her dashboard springing to life.

*Holy shit.*

It was like I was finally able to see behind the goddamn veil. It'd been so frustrating trying to keep track of Patricia's conversations online, especially whenever she'd deleted a comment or it seemed like she'd abandoned a heated back-and-forth.

But now?

Now I had access to everything, my fingers anxious to start the search.

"You should start with her DMs," Brianna suggested, seemingly reading my mind. "With things like this, from the way you described what happened to her . . . it sounds like whoever hurt her already knew her, like it might've been a crime of passion."

"How are we going to be able to pinpoint who they were, though?" I frowned as I noticed the unblinking *272* near the top of Patricia's inbox, signaling there were 272 unopened messages waiting for me. "Shit. Was she really this popular?"

"It looks like things were picking up for her as an influencer. I'm seeing a lot of collab offers. That's a good thing, right?"

"Of course things were picking up for her. That's when the worst thing that could happen in your life is supposed to happen, isn't it, when everything else is going—"

I cut myself off mid-sentence, my eyes landing on a particular message in Patricia's inbox. She'd been exchanging messages back and forth with someone whose Instagram handle was @TheBabyGuru.

> @PatriciaFitz85 to @TheBabyGuru: Hi! I saw you were doing at-home consultations this week.

> @TheBabyGuru to @PatriciaFitz85: Hi! ☺ Yes, I am! I love your page, by the way. Your homemade birthday cakes look so gorgeous.

> @PatriciaFitz85 to @TheBabyGuru: Thanks! ♥ Would you be available to come over this Friday? I'm in Harbor

> Town. We'd have to meet up before
> 6pm, though. My husband gets so
> weird about this kind of stuff.

@TheBabyGuru to @PatriciaFitz85: Of
course! And I completely understand
about your husband. A lot of men are
skeptics, but I'm confident that my
results speak for themselves. And if you
don't see the results you want, I offer
full refunds and exchanges! 🔮

> @PatriciaFitz85 to @TheBabyGuru:
> Perfect 😊 How does 3pm sound?

@TheBabyGuru to @PatriciaFitz85: I'll
be there ✧ All I need is an address.

"Who the fuck is the Baby Guru?" I murmured before clicking on
the username. It only took a few seconds before my screen was pop-
ulated with moonstones and amethyst crystals, each posted photo
more aesthetically pleasing than the last. When I clicked on one of
the posts, one that featured who I'd assumed to be the owner of the
account, a young blonde wearing a chic yoga outfit complete with
expensive tennis shoes and a peridot hanging around her neck, my
attention went right toward the comments.

Thank you so much, Baby Guru! You've changed my life forever!!! I
can't wait to welcome our bundle of joy in a few months.

Really? You still have to exercise? Don't you get enough of a
workout dealing with us stressed out clients L O L love ya, girl!
Keep it up! You're looking 🔥 🔥 🔥

OMG IF YOU'RE LURKING IN THE COMMENTS LIKE I WAS TWO
WEEKS AGO YOU NEED TO GET IN CONTACT WITH THIS LADY
RIGHT NOW! SHE'S THE REAL DEAL I SWEAR TO GOD

"... Patricia was trying to get pregnant?" I mumbled as I scrolled through the rest of the comment section below the image, so many women sending overzealous thanks and well-wishes to the gemstone pusher in the shot. "... Patricia was *struggling* to get pregnant?"

Suddenly, everything was coming on too quick.

My breaths.

The light in the room.

The way my fingers felt against the keys.

And then everything was coming on so fast that it wasn't coming on at all.

"Elizabeth? Elizabeth!" Brianna called out for me, just as the room around me started to spin.

Just before all the air went out of my lungs, all at once.

# 18

# Brianna

Brianna was only about halfway through her mental checklist when Elizabeth had her panic attack. And while it was a slight deterrent to her plans for the afternoon, it wasn't enough to slow her down entirely. A part of her was grateful for it, worried that her facade was cracking, that she'd made a mistake by showing how easy it was for her to guess a dead woman's password.

She didn't know how much longer she could extend her true-crime-podcast-lover alibi, especially since she'd never listened to one.

Because she didn't need a true crime podcast to tell her how to handle a body, how to properly cover up a crime, how to get away with murder without really trying. The answer had been the same for most of human history, or at least it seemed that way to Brianna. If someone wanted to get away with something so drastic, all they needed to do was have zero connection to the victim. It didn't matter if the crime scene was littered with evidence if the police had no idea where to look, even worse if the person they were looking for wasn't even in the system.

Still, Brianna didn't want Elizabeth getting any ideas about her, especially not after she'd volunteered to help her solve Patricia's murder. It was a strange cognitive dissonance, helping her new friend try to figure out if her old friend had been murdered, all the while already knowing the answer. It was like a game of cards where Brianna knew them all by heart, guessing at the future when she already knew the outcome.

It was also another way to ingratiate herself with Elizabeth. After that disaster of a lunch with Dawn, Brianna realized that Elizabeth's isolation wasn't solely due to her own choices. She was a woman who'd lost someone young, a woman who'd been turned cynical by it, too. She'd never really had anyone, before or after, and Brianna had a feeling that Elizabeth would be receptive to someone supporting her, believing in her, not calling her crazy when she spouted off about her suspicions.

Especially after Janice's big reveal turned so sour.

Plus, if Brianna could become that person for Elizabeth, if she could become her new right-hand woman, she'd have access to everything she needed, everything that she ever could've dreamed of. All the missing puzzle pieces about Patricia's life were right in front of Brianna, stored somewhere in Elizabeth's brain.

And all Brianna needed was for Elizabeth to trust her enough with the key.

". . . Are you still going through everything?" Elizabeth asked, from her place on the living room couch, her arm folded across her forehead. "Did you finish going through all the DMs?"

"Most of them, I think," Brianna answered with a small smile. "Are you feeling any better, Elizabeth?"

"I don't know." She sighed, her eyes closing with the effort. "I just didn't . . . There was something about seeing all that stuff about the baby. Just the thought that she spent all that time and effort trying to get pregnant, when it wasn't going to matter anymore."

"We should make a list," Brianna suggested, her tone neutral and unaffected.

"A list of what?"

"Suspects."

". . . Like who?" Elizabeth sat up on the couch, her hands folding into her lap. "Did you see something suspicious in her messages?"

"Maybe," Brianna replied. "But it's going to be a lot easier to compile everything if we can see it all at once."

Brianna was telling the truth. It *was* going to be easier to compile everything once she could see it all at once, including everyone who Elizabeth would consider a close friend of Patricia's, everyone who could've aided her in the worst mistake of her life.

"Okay." Elizabeth nodded. "Do you want me to start the Google Sheet and invite you to edit it, too—"

"We can't use anything that goes into the cloud," she cut her off mid-sentence. "Or anything that's going to live on your computer."

"Why not?"

"Because of David," Brianna explained. "I may not know a lot about him, but something tells me that he's watching your devices like a hawk. And if he catches wind of what we're up to—"

"Fuck." Elizabeth groaned as she stood up from the couch. "You're right. I never even thought about that before."

Elizabeth's eyes closed again before she spoke. "I'll go get us something to write on."

It was the last thing she said before heading up to her bedroom. A few minutes later, she'd returned to the living room with a small brown box, stacks upon stacks of blank white letterhead filling it up to the brim. She offered Brianna one of the paper stacks, holding it out to her, clenching tight to its edges like she was holding on to an ancient tome, something that had the power to change the course of human history.

"What is this?" Brianna was amused by the amount of paper Elizabeth was handing her way. "Did you use to run a printing company from home? Or . . . ?"

"It's just a bunch of letterhead from my old job." Elizabeth's voice was lined with just as much amusement. "Well, not really my old job. Just the Learning Center's old location in Whitehaven. Janice had ordered everyone in the office a bunch, but when we switched locations, an order came down from the owners that we weren't allowed to use it anymore." Elizabeth shrugged after the revelation. "Most people probably just threw theirs out, but that seemed like such a waste to me, you know?"

"No point in wasting it when there's so much of it." Brianna smiled. "Did you happen to have a box full of pens, too?"

"Pens. Right." Elizabeth playfully snapped her fingers before she scurried back up the stairs to her bedroom, leaving Brianna behind. Brianna was still smiling to herself as she pulled one of the sheets of paper toward her, casually reading over the letterhead printed against its upper edges.

### THE LEARNING CENTER—WHITEHAVEN
DIRECTOR—JANICE LOESKE
PHONE: 901-555-0124
ADDRESS: 1227 MAYWOOD STREET, MEMPHIS, TN 38116

\* \* \*

*Maywood Street. Right before you get to the Freeman intersection.*
Brianna couldn't breathe.

*Maywood Street. Right before you get to the Freeman inter-section.*

There were things locking into place, an unseen key clicking against a mechanism, gears chugging forward, her every sense set on fire.

*Maywood Street. Right before you get to the Freeman inter-section.*

She was moving before she'd even realized she'd started to move, no longer able to stay seated, no longer able to stay underneath the same roof as Elizabeth, the same roof as anyone.

*Hi! I'm just calling to report a suspicious person?*

*My friend wanted me to.*

*Maywood Street.*

Brianna whimpered as she fell to her knees, right outside Eliza-beth's house, hidden from any curious neighbors, although she wouldn't have cared if anyone had spotted her. Nothing in the mo-ment seeming like it mattered anymore, things shattering around her faster than she was able to keep up.

She didn't want to be right.

She *couldn't* be right.

Because if Brianna was right, then that would mean that she'd let herself cross out the woman who actually—

She'd let herself actually feel bad for, actually feel anything for—

God.

How could she have gotten everything so wrong?

"... Brianna?" Elizabeth's voice was light as she called out for her. A few seconds later, she'd found her, resting beside a wall outside of the home. Elizabeth's frown was deep as soon as she spotted Brianna.

"What happened?" Elizabeth crouched in front of her, her palms going out to rest on Brianna's knees. "Brianna, what's—"

"He was in an accident," Brianna lied, knowing that she needed to come up with something that was going to explain away her crying, that was going to explain away her trembling.

"Who?"

"Charles. They don't know if . . . I don't know if he's going to be okay."

"Oh my God. Brianna, I'm so sorry—"

"Could I stay here tonight?" Brianna's question came out low. "I know it's . . . I know I shouldn't be asking you that. It's just that you're . . . so much closer to the hospital. And I don't know if I'm going to be . . . I don't know if I should really be alone tonight."

"Of course you can stay here tonight, Brianna. You can stay for as long as you need, okay?" Elizabeth said as her palms flexed against Brianna's knees.

". . . Thank you, Elizabeth." Brianna flashed Elizabeth a slight smile, her mind already working its way through all the possibilities.

Working its way through the various potential letter and number combinations that would give Brianna access to Elizabeth's phone.

\*     \*     \*

"Are you sure you don't want to go up and visit him at the hospital?" Elizabeth took a seat beside Brianna on the living room couch. "I could come with you, if you wanted me to—"

"No." Brianna shook her head, interrupting Elizabeth's response. "It's . . . Some of his family members are there with him now."

Brianna turned toward her, her mind racing with what to say next. "We have a . . . complicated relationship. And I don't think hearing me get into a screaming match with his mother is really what Charles needs right now, not in his condition."

It was partly true, which was probably why it'd sounded like it was fully true as it came out of Brianna's mouth. She'd had a complicated relationship with Charles's mom ever since her senior year of high school, when she'd decided that she was going to keep the baby. It didn't matter how many times his mom offered to pay for an abortion. It didn't matter how many times she'd tried to make Brianna see reason, swearing that she was ruining both of their futures by holding on to a *mistake* they'd made in the backseat of Charles's handme-down Toyota Camry.

Brianna was just as stubborn about having her son as she was about moving in with Charles after high school, renting out the only apartment they were able to afford. And when she'd found out that he'd been saving up what little money he could to try to buy her a ring, she'd insisted they put that money toward fixing up the Camry. Two years down the line, Charles brought up the idea of a quick courthouse ceremony, wanting to make things official between them, wanting to make sure that their son grew up in a *real* home.

But Brianna had resisted the definition.

*Real home.*

They already had a *real* home together. They already had a *real* home with Jay.

There was nothing that a piece of paper could do to make things any more real between them, and since neither of them had any major assets, there was never going to be a need to split things evenly down the middle, either. There were never any upsides to being as broke as they were, but Brianna had appreciated how simple it kept things, how easy it was to fill out her taxes when she never had to check too many boxes.

"Maybe when his mom's gone, then." Elizabeth offered her a small smile. "Is there anything you're craving for dinner—"

"He should've called 9-1-1," Brianna interrupted her again, casually planting the seeds of a discussion that she'd already devised.

There were rarely any organic moments between Elizabeth and Brianna, not with how often Brianna had anticipated what Elizabeth was going to say and how she was going to say it.

Not with how often Brianna had tried to predict Elizabeth's every thought.

". . . What do you mean?" Elizabeth's brow furrowed. "He didn't call 9-1-1 after he got into an accident?"

"No, because he knows that when you call 9-1-1, they usually send a police cruiser, too," she continued. "He . . . he's always had this problem with the cops. Even after getting into his accident . . . he didn't want to call 9-1-1, so he went to a neighbor's house. He almost bled out on their doorstep. Thank God they called for an ambulance as soon as they could."

"I get that." Elizabeth gave Brianna a sympathetic nod. "Not wanting to call the cops."

". . . You get that?" Brianna gently pressed.

"Yeah. I do," she replied. "I've heard the same thing from a lot of the students I work with at the Learning Center, that you're not supposed to call the cops unless you absolutely have to. And with the way the police treat Black people in this country—" Elizabeth waved a hand between them. "It's like, *fuck*. You know? What's the point in calling for help if all they're going to do is make things worse?"

"So, you don't call the cops when you're in trouble?" Brianna sounded just as wounded as she felt, a split second of real emotion showing through the phony, plastic-wrapped moment.

"Not unless David or I were literally dying," she answered. "And even then, only if there's nothing else that we can do about it. Although honestly, even if we were dying, the only thing the cops would probably do is help us get to hell just a little bit faster."

Brianna laughed, hoping that the sound hadn't come out as rehearsed as it was, how hollow it was.

Elizabeth laughed, too, before she casually rephrased an earlier question.

"So? Dinner? What were you thinking?"

* * *

Brianna was wearing one of Elizabeth's T-shirts, combined with a set of her shorts. She hadn't planned on wearing anything of Elizabeth's, but the woman had practically emptied out her closet, searching for an outfit for Brianna to sleep in for the night.

She'd settled on a T-shirt that looked like she'd worn it while either fundraising or campaigning for Bernie Sanders, a candidate who Brianna had voted for twice herself. The shorts Elizabeth had picked out for her had reminded Brianna of the kinds of clothes she'd see people wearing on TV whenever they were headed to the beach, bright floral patterns going down along each side.

Although, right now, the beach was the furthest thing from Brianna's mind as she stood over the kitchen counter with Elizabeth's phone in her palm. Elizabeth had been charging her phone during dinner, a generous spread of Chinese takeout, complete with sesame chicken and shrimp fried rice. After dinner, Elizabeth and Brianna had split a bottle of wine while sitting on the living room couch, their conversation a mixture of innocent gossip from around the neighborhood and shared moments of pain, the women commiserating over their fraught history with romance.

Well, Elizabeth was commiserating.

Brianna had simply been mirroring her, making up whatever sounded good in the moment, whatever she felt would make Elizabeth comfortable enough to keep talking. It was a phenomenon she'd read about when she'd been idly looking into different personality types, a suggested reading from the professor who helmed the nursing classes she'd been planning to take someday. In one of his prere-corded lectures, the professor had practically sworn that the thirty-page research paper would be useful when working with the public, teach-ing future nurses how to manage various expectations and confron-tations with their patients, even teaching them how to spot when someone might be withholding vital information, too.

But for Brianna, the part that'd stayed with her was the mirror-ing. It was terrifying, at first, that there were people out there who were experts at making others feel at ease even when they shouldn't be. And while the research paper had only explored mirroring as a potential red flag that a patient was being dishonest, wanting nurses to be aware if someone's details suspiciously aligned with ones they might have mentioned about themselves during the introductory con-versation, wanting nurses to be aware if a patient's accent sharpened or softened to match their own, lulling them into a false sense of kinship, Brianna couldn't stop thinking about all of the other possi-bilities of becoming someone's mirror, too.

What would it be like on the other side of that glass? Knowing that there was no real separation between the reflected images, knowing that at any moment she had the power to reach through and close the gap, shocking whoever stood across from her?

What would it be like to have that much power over someone? The power to destroy them from the inside out. The power to crack their world into pieces while they stared, slack-jawed, their eyes filled with disbelief at the betrayal.

Because mirrors were only supposed to give. Give someone a re-flection of themselves. Give them exactly what they wanted to think about themselves, too, whether it was for better or for worse. Give people hope that the years had been kinder than they'd initially wanted to believe. Give people hope that maybe their hair being out of place hadn't been why their date hadn't called them back, why they hadn't tried to make a move during the last act of that movie they'd seen together last week.

*Give. Give. Give.*

Give until the person standing on the other side was satisfied, satiated, safe.

Mirrors were never supposed to *take*.

". . . What are you still doing up?" David's voice floated over to Brianna, her body going still at the sound of it. She slowly turned to offer him a smile, noticing the briefcase he was clutching in his hand.

"Nothing," Brianna lied, noiselessly setting Elizabeth's phone down behind her. "I thought . . . Elizabeth told me that you were taking an overnight trip?"

"Yeah, I was." David shrugged. "Turns out, I didn't need to. Which is great, because I fucking hate having to fly to Chicago just to sit around a table and listen to someone drone on about building codes."

". . . If you weren't on an overnight trip, why were you at the office so late?" Brianna couldn't help herself, an utter inability to let an unsolved puzzle remain on her radar. Brianna hadn't been able to figure out David Smith since the day she'd met him, everything about him seeming to throw her curveball after curveball.

She knew that he loved his wife, but from the way Elizabeth talked about their relationship, it was almost like he'd been abusive, the woman nearly in tears whenever she'd recounted their most recent years together. She knew that David had to be a hardworking business type, based on his zip code and lifestyle, and yet whenever he was around her, it felt like he wanted to come off as laid-back as possible.

Even now, as he stared over at her with a slightly disheveled tie, Brianna wondered if there was another contradiction waiting for her at the end of his next sentence.

". . . Because I don't always like coming home," David murmured the truth as he walked up to Brianna at the counter. He sighed after he spoke, the sound seeming to unravel inside of him, like a too-tight coil finally coming loose. "Shit. I'm sorry. I shouldn't have—I don't know why I said that."

"Because it's true," Brianna suggested as she subtly raised her shoulders.

"Just because it's true, that doesn't mean I'm not an asshole for thinking it."

"Did something happen with you and Elizabeth? Because if we're both being totally honest . . . she sounded like something happened with you two, when we were talking after dinner."

"Nothing happened . . ." David broke into a pained laugh. "Fuck. I don't know. Everything happened."

"What's that supposed to mean, David?"

"It means that sometimes it doesn't matter how much you love someone. It means that sometimes there's just . . . sometimes there's an expiration date you didn't notice before."

". . . Are you talking about divorce?"

"I don't know what I'm talking about." David shook his head before he folded his arms across his chest. "But whatever I'm talking about, I should probably be saving it for Dr. Whitaker, not burdening you with bullshit emotional labor, because that's not part of your job description."

"It's not emotional labor when I'm the one asking the questions." Brianna smiled. "But . . . I'm sorry for pushing the issue. I think I was just looking for something to take my mind off—"

"Right. Elizabeth told me about what's going on with your . . . husband?" David's voice went up at the end of his sentence, almost like his tone was lined with an inappropriate hope.

"Long-term boyfriend," Brianna clarified.

"Are you two still together? Because from the way Elizabeth described it . . . I mean, she used the term 'complicated,' so I had no idea what I was supposed to do with that, really."

Brianna chuckled at David's response. "'Complicated' is a good word to describe it."

"What complicated it?" David's words came out low. "Was he sleeping around?"

Just then, David's face tightened before he quickly asked a follow-up question. "Was he hurting you?"

"It wasn't anything like that," Brianna's voice was calm. "I think it was just a symptom of . . . growing up and growing apart."

"Are you still going to try to make it work? If he . . . if it turns out that he's okay, after what happened to him."

"I don't know. I don't think so. I think that I'll always care about him, though, no matter what. But . . . I don't think we'll ever be together, ever again. Not like we were. There's just too much history."

"How long were you two together?" David said as he took another step toward Brianna, closing the space between them inch by inch.

"Since we were in high school."

"Since high school? Really? And you never wanted to have any kids?" David wondered out loud.

"I could ask the same about you and Elizabeth, couldn't I?" Brianna smirked, even though David's question had sliced her right to her core, her fingers inconspicuously tightening on the kitchen counter's edge for support.

". . . I wanted kids," David confessed. "I still want kids. I always did. I just . . . Elizabeth always seemed so sure that she didn't, and I was so sure that I loved Elizabeth that I figured that she knew what was best for the both of us."

David's face fell as he went on. "I've been thinking that maybe I was wrong about that, though. Trying to edit out parts of myself so I can . . . so Elizabeth can be happy. It's been that way since we first met, you know, as soon as I realized that, to her, I was just a living cardboard cutout, that I was just a blank slate for her to project all of her bullshit onto so she could always come out on top—"

David's phone vibrated, loud, in his front pocket, interrupting David before he had a chance to finish his sentence.

"I should probably get that," David mumbled. "And then I should probably go to bed."

"Good night, David," Brianna replied with a warm smile.

"Good night, Brianna." David didn't take his gaze away from her as he spoke . . .

And Brianna's gaze lingered on him, too.

# 19

## Elizabeth

I couldn't sleep.

It'd started a few weeks ago, with any semblance of rest eluding me. At first, I didn't mind the extra hours in the days. I was still researching everything I could about Patricia, Brianna and I comparing notes and compiling information, no matter how trivial. After Charles's recovery in the hospital, it'd seemed like Brianna was just as energized as I was to try to solve the case, to find answers that no one else was looking for except for us.

But as the days dragged on, blurring into each other, sunsets bumping into sunrises bumping into sunsets bumping into sunrises, I realized that what I'd accepted as a blessing had become a curse. Suddenly, I was always tired, always half present, always half struggling. I'd attempted to replace my lost sleep with caffeine, but that would only get me so far, still not making up for the sluggishness that was dragging down my veins.

*Fuck.*

In any other situation, this wouldn't have been such a problem. I'd just tell David that I was having trouble sleeping, and he'd show up tomorrow night with the perfect little pill, something that would knock me out nearly as soon as I swallowed it down my throat.

But I couldn't go to David. If I went to David, he'd go to Dr. Whitaker, and Dr. Whitaker would go right back to me, asking me a million invasive questions about my lack of sleep, wondering if there'd been a major change in my life recently. And since there was no way in hell that I was going to admit to either of them that *yes, there has been a major change in my life recently, I've never been so damn close to finding out what happened to Patricia*, I knew that I needed to come up with another solution.

". . . Are you feeling okay, Elizabeth?" Brianna asked, her notepad in her lap as she sat across from me at the dining room table. "You seem a little zoned out today."

"I'm fine," I instinctively lied, my social programming kicking in. I was way too used to people asking how I was doing but never wanting to hear a real answer, so used to it, in fact, that I struggled to give a real answer even now, my mouth tripping over the words.

"I . . . actually . . ." I set my own notebook down on the table. "I'm not feeling okay. I haven't been feeling okay for the last few weeks."

"Oh." Brianna frowned. "Do you think it's because of the stress?"

"The stress?"

"Elizabeth, we're literally trying to solve your friend's murder. You can't pretend like this isn't stressing you out. All the dead ends. All the possible suspects. Your next-door neighbor could be—well, we know whoever did this has to be a psycho, so we can start there."

"And, statistically speaking, probably white," I added. "At least judging from Patricia's friend lists. I never really noticed before, but I don't know if anyone in her immediate friend group had anything other than German-Irish ancestry." I leaned toward Brianna as I lowered my voice. "That's weird, right?"

"I don't think it's that weird for a white person to have mostly white friends." Brianna shrugged.

". . . But in Memphis?" I grimaced as I spoke. "Look, I'm not saying that I'm the president of the Rainbow Coalition, but you have to admit it's a little weird."

Brianna lightly chuckled. "Fine. It's a little weird, but I don't think that makes her a bad person. It's easy to get caught up in the same circles. Why do you think some people still hang out with the friends they made in high school?"

"Jesus Christ. Could you imagine?" I grimaced again as a full shiver went down my spine. "If I seriously had to keep up with the same people I cared about when I was in high school? I wouldn't even know where to start—" I held up a hand, a spark going off in the back of my brain. "Holy shit."

"What is it? What's wrong?"

"What if we're not going back far enough?"

"What do you mean?"

"All of this stuff with Patricia . . ." My words trailed off as I finished working through the thought that was sending energetic jolts through my much-too-weary mind. "We're only looking at what she posted on social media around the time of her death."

"Well, that makes sense, right? Since she posted so often—"

"Right, but I'm saying that we're spending way too much time on what's recent," I clarified. "What if we need to go back a few years? What if we need to . . . get out on the streets and start cracking a few skulls?"

*Cracking a few skulls? What the hell?*

It was a phrase I knew didn't belong in my mouth. Didn't belong in my brain.

And yet I hadn't been able to stop it from getting past my lips.

I was too damn tired to gatekeep my own tongue.

Brianna frowned. "I don't know about that, Elizabeth. I don't know if I'm really built for skull cracking."

"Have you ever read *The Count of Monte Cristo?*"

"No, but I saw the movie when I was in school," she answered. "That's the one with the guy from *The Passion of the Christ,* right?"

"Right." I nodded, a small migraine forming in what felt like the very middle of my brain matter. "I don't know why I never thought of it before. I mean, here we are, thinking that this was some kind of in-the-moment crime of passion . . . but what if this was planned for years? What if this was someone who'd wanted to hurt Patricia for a really, really long time?"

"Oh my God." Brianna's eyes widened, as if my words had finally taken root. "Oh my God, Elizabeth. What if you're right? How awful would that be?"

"We need to add a column to our enemy list," I shot back, the migraine spreading even as I attempted to will it away. "We need to figure out who the hell Patricia has pissed off throughout her whole lifetime— Fuck!"

I groaned, doubling over against the table, no longer able to deny that there was pain shooting right through me.

"Elizabeth?" Brianna's tone was filled with concern as she made her way over to my side of the table. "You know what? I think it might be time to take you to the hospital—"

"No!" I shouted, much louder than I'd intended. "Sorry. I just . . . I can't go to the hospital, Brianna."

"Why not?"

"Because if I go to the hospital, David will know. If not today, then soon enough. I'm on his insurance. They always send a copy of whatever's left on the bill to the house."

"So, what do you want me to do?" Brianna made herself eye level with me, her hand gently rubbing a circle into my back.

". . . You wouldn't happen to have any sleeping pills, would you?" I tried to make my voice sound as sweet as possible. There really was no *sweet* way to ask someone if they had access to prescription-strength medication, especially since I planned on mooching off said prescription.

"Are you sure that's a good idea, Elizabeth?" Brianna's hand continued in circles against my back, just as gentle as before, as if my request hadn't fazed her a bit.

"Please," I begged as I looked over at her. "Please, Brianna. I just need to sleep. Once I can get some sleep, I'll be good to go, okay? It's all I need."

". . . Okay." Brianna offered me a small smile before moving away from me. "If that's all you need, I think I can help you with that."

*　*　*

By the time I woke up, on the couch, it was dark outside the windows. My limbs felt like they'd been twisted ten times over, each one broken before being snapped back into place, heavy and molded. I'd only started taking the sleeping pills a few days ago, but their effect was stunning and stark. Still, I was thankful for the dense sensation of sleep, the familiar tiredness of opening my eyes post-slumber. I was thankful for Brianna, too, the angel of a woman who'd asked one of her friends about me *borrowing* a few of her leftover sleeping pills in the first place.

She'd told me that her friend, Vanessa, had lost her child late last year. There'd been a hit-and-run accident, and Vanessa had barely made it to the scene in time to say goodbye. After the accident, she'd been beside herself, her grief eating through her, paralyzing her, keeping her stuck in place. It'd gotten so bad that Vanessa had stopped sleeping. She'd gone to a therapist's office to talk about it, but since all she could afford was a shitty, mid-tier service provider, courtesy of her shitty, mid-tier health insurance plan, the therapist hadn't done much for her outside of giving her a prescription for sleeping pills.

But Vanessa wasn't like me. She didn't need sleep. She needed comfort. She needed to know that she could keep going on and that tomorrow was going to be different, that maybe it was even going to be better. Vanessa had thrown the pills into one of her drawers at home, the bottle forgotten as she found other avenues for her own version of therapy, which had entailed going to church more and spending quality time with her friends, friends like Brianna.

She'd only remembered the bottle when Brianna had asked her about it today, according to Brianna. She also didn't mind getting rid of them, her grief salved and sated by time. I almost wanted to call the situation *convenient*, that I'd been gifted just what I'd needed by the universe. But I knew that there was a dead child on the other side of my convenience, the irony of it not lost on me as I sat in a former slave state on stolen land.

God.

There was a dead child on the other side of everything.

". . . Baby?" David was sitting on the very end of the couch, his eyes staring back at mine. "Are you awake?"

I nodded before bringing myself onto my elbows, sluggish and slow.

"How are you feeling?"

"Why? Did Brianna say something?"

"No. Brianna didn't say anything. I just . . . saw my wife passed out on the couch and wanted to make sure that you were okay. You usually don't take a nap unless you have a bad headache or—"

"That's what I had," I interrupted, maybe too eager to respond. "A really bad headache."

"But you're feeling better now?"

"I am."

"Good." David smiled for just a moment, the expression soon fading from his features. "Baby, there's something I wanted to talk to you about." David took in a deep breath, seemingly holding it in his chest. "I think we need to have a talk with Dr. Whitaker."

"Why would we need to do that, David?" I pressed, adjusting my position on the couch, feeling an urge to be so much closer to him. "I've been doing so much better, haven't I? You don't think that I'm finally on the right path—"

"I think you're keeping something from me, Lizzie."

"Keeping something from you?"

"You're not . . ." David started and stopped, his words trailing off mid-sentence. "It's like there's a wall up with you."

"We already went through this with Dr. Whitaker, David. She said one partner feeling shut out while the other one is grieving isn't abnormal—"

"The wall was there before Patricia, Lizzie," David quietly corrected. "It's been there. Maybe for years. There's been something off between us for a while now, and I think we both know it."

"David—"

"Sometimes I don't think you see me. I don't know what you see when you look at me, Lizzie. Sometimes I—Lizzie?"

David's hand was on my shoulder, trying his best to still my weeping frame. I hadn't even noticed that I'd started crying, my body shifting into the motion without much effort, tears flowing and clouding my vision. My fingers were buried deep in the blanket that covered me, twisting at its thread, working further into its fabric.

I was here and I was nowhere.

I was halfway gone.

"Lizzie, baby." David's voice was low. "Please. We're just having a conversation—"

"I can't lose you, David," I said, my voice so calm and so disconnected. "I can't lose you."

I wasn't pleading with my husband to stay.

I was letting him know that he couldn't leave, that it was as impossible as building a townhouse on Saturn's rings or swimming across the Atlantic Ocean all in one day.

That there was nowhere for David Smith to go where I wouldn't follow, even if that meant following him off a cliff, diving headfirst into the endless nothingness of death and darkness.

But even in the dark, I'd find him.

Even in the dark, we'd be together again.

Always.

"Who said anything about leaving, Lizzie?" David whispered. "I just said that we need to talk to Dr. Whitaker—"

"Is it someone you met at work?"

"Lizzie, this doesn't have anything to do with—" He stopped, his gaze searching up and down my frame. "Do you really think I'd ever do something like that to you? That I would cheat on you?"

I snorted out an ungraceful laugh before I hid the expression behind the back of my hand.

". . . Did I say something funny?" David asked, clearly confused by my reaction.

"Sorry. It's just . . . you realize that you've spent the last year trying to get me to believe that Patricia killed herself? Something that I told you was never something that she would do?"

"I don't see what that has to do with anything—"

"You're telling me that you would never cheat on me because it's not something that you would do. So, which is it, David? Do people never break character? Or do people just do whatever the hell they want?"

". . . You're upset, Lizzie. And you're trying to take it out on me—"

"Of course I'm fucking upset, David," I shot back. "My husband is trying to leave me, but he's too much of a fucking coward to just pull the fucking plug."

". . . Fuck this." David stood up from the couch before he started to head toward the front door.

"David? Where are you going?" My legs wanted to follow him, but I was still too, too heavy, the sleeping pills in my system weighing my blood down like lead.

"I'm going out. Let me know when you've calmed down, and maybe we can have an actual, productive conversation like two adults."

# 20

## Elizabeth

Elizabeth? What's wrong? I came over as fast as I could—"

"He's done with me, Brianna," I interrupted as I pulled her into my home, my fingers lightly digging into the fabric of her sleeves. I'd sent her an SOS text only moments after David had left our home, my hands feeling like the only part of me with enough energy to function. "He's finally fucking done with me."

". . . What are you talking about?" Brianna offered me a barely-there smile. "You're not talking about David, are you?"

"He hates me," I continued, my hands going up toward my waist, my breaths becoming shallower and shallower. "Brianna, he . . . he pretty much told me that he wants a divorce."

*And then I'd finally go from being halfway gone to fully off-world.* My mind raced with the realization. *Out of sight, out of mind, out of body.*

*Out of David.*

*Out of me.*

*Out of breath, I'm out of breath, I'm out of—*

"Fuck! This is so fucked!" I yelled at no one in particular, my voice cracking with the effort. "How could he even be thinking about this right now? He knows how fragile I am. He knows how much support I need just to fucking—fuck!"

I took a seat at the bottom of the nearest staircase, my words becoming jumbled in my head, further turning into a clusterfuck inside my mouth, too.

". . . Could you go get my Paroxetine from the bedroom?" I begged as I looked over at Brianna. "I feel like I'm having a fucking panic attack."

"Of course. Anything you need." She nodded before she went around me, her footsteps soft, light, comforting. When she returned with the pill bottle in hand, I slipped it away from her palm, hastily popping two pills onto my tongue.

"I'm not supposed to be having fucking panic attacks. See? You see what happens when David pulls this kind of shit? Everything fucking falls apart."

"Did he really say he wants to get a divorce?"

"He said he wants to talk to our therapist," I clarified. "He said . . . he said that I have a wall up, that I've had one up for a while. And that he thinks I don't . . . that I don't *see* him."

"What do you think he meant by that?"

"I don't fucking know, Brianna." Exasperation lined my tone. "The only thing I do fucking know is that if David and I actually go through with a separation . . . I'm so fucking fucked."

"Why?"

"Because when we got married, I was young and I was in love and like a goddamn idiot, I thought that we were going to be together forever." I groaned, irritated with my past self for her misplaced, romantic optimism. "I didn't even think about the word *prenup*. And if David had tried to bring it up, I would've called the whole thing off."

"Why would you need a prenup, Elizabeth?" Brianna slowly sank down beside me on the staircase. "Do you think . . . you think that David would try to make it hard for you? Separating?"

"I don't know," I admitted. "I don't know what he's thinking. But since we don't have any kids together . . . if he really wanted to punish me, Brianna, he could. He could drag me straight to hell."

"He wouldn't."

"Brianna, you don't—"

*You don't know him.*

*Maybe I don't even know him.*

*Maybe I don't know anything.*

"He wouldn't do that to you, Elizabeth," she insisted. "He just wouldn't."

". . . And if he did, I wouldn't have anything, Brianna," I replied, tears springing to my eyes with every syllable. "If David wanted to take everything from me . . . I don't have anything. Do you understand? None of this is in my name. Even my own fucking car isn't—"

I was crying again, my face wet and my voice trembling. "And I can't go back to my parents, Brianna. I mean, Jesus Christ, you've met my mom . . . I wish I could tell you that the rest of my family is any better, but they aren't. Not really. I don't want anything to do with them. All I ever wanted was David . . . and without David, I don't have anyone—"

"You have me, Elizabeth Smith," Brianna said, her arm wrapping around my waist, pulling me closer to her side. "You're always going to have me, no matter what. I'm always going to be here for you."

". . . Even when I can't afford to pay you anymore?" I turned toward her, earnestly searching her expression. "Even when David kicks me out on my ass and I'm just another homeless woman ambling around on Poplar?"

"Please." Brianna playfully rolled her eyes. "You're never going to be homeless, Elizabeth. If worse comes to worst, you can always come stay with me. And if you can't afford to pay me, all that means is that I need to find another job."

Brianna smiled, wide, before she finished with her thoughts. "But that doesn't change the fact that we're friends. And I'd never let my friend end up out on the street ambling around, even if she does unnecessarily pepper words like 'ambling' into normal conversations."

Brianna gave me a gentle nudge in the side, a laugh soon escaping her chest. I found myself laughing right along with her then, my head moving down to rest on her shoulder, my tears seeping through her T-shirt.

". . . I don't want to lose him, Brianna," I murmured. "I really, really don't."

"No one said you had to. Just keep an open mind when you go to talk to your therapist. And don't catastrophize. Things aren't always as bad as we want them to be—"

Brianna's words were interrupted by the doorbell, its sound ringing through the hallway.

"See?" Brianna smiled. "I bet that's David right now, back to apologize or make up or whatever it is you two do after a big fight."

I offered her a smile in return as I moved away from the staircase, absent-mindedly running a hand through my hair. I knew there was no way I could look like I hadn't just been weeping my heart out, but maybe there was a chance I could look a little less run-down, a little more like the woman David had once fallen head over heels in love with.

By the time I reached the front door, my breathing had returned to normal, my anxiety settling down farther in my stomach. It wasn't quite gone, but it was sated, enough for my hands to stop shaking, enough for me to preemptively beam at David as he stood on the other side of the doorway.

Although the expression disappeared from my face as soon as I realized that it wasn't David standing on the other side of the doorway.

It was Nathan Andrews.

". . . Elizabeth." Nathan smiled after he said my name, his features shifting into a grin. "There you are."

". . . What the hell are you doing here, Nathan?" My words came out cold, my skin suddenly icy and frigid. "Are you out of your fucking mind? Why would you ever—"

"What are you talking about, Elizabeth?" He quirked an eyebrow in my direction. "You're the one who wanted me to come over."

"Nathan, what the fuck? I haven't spoken to you in months—" I stopped myself mid-sentence, holding up a hand between us. "Is this some kind of fucking mind game? What? Is this your way of asserting your bullshit dominance as the *man* in the relationship? Which isn't what we had, by the way. You know that, right? We were never anything more than—"

". . . Lizzie?" David's voice was low as he appeared by Nathan's side. He paused for a moment, looking him up and down, each second that ticked by causing my anxiety to resurface throughout my veins. I wondered what David was thinking as he looked at Nathan, as he noticed the similarities in their build, as he considered that Nathan was nothing more than a less handsome version of himself, less charming and less interesting, too.

Molded in David's image, but not quite the same. A copy of a copy. An image in a funhouse mirror that was vaguely recognizable but with each feature wrong enough to know that something *was* wrong.

"I'm sorry." David offered a hand toward Nathan. "I don't think we've met? I'm David Smith."

"I'm Nathan Andrews," Nathan confidently shook David's hand, like there shouldn't be any friction between them.

"Are you . . . a guest of Brianna's?" David guessed before he looked at her over my shoulder.

"Yes," I answered on Nathan's behalf, my mind moving a million miles per minute. "Yes, Nathan is a guest of Brianna's. We—they— met at the Learning Center while I was on one of my shifts."

"Oh." David nodded in understanding, turning back toward Nathan. "So, you work at the Learning Center, too?"

"Only sometimes." Nathan was seemingly going along with my fresh lie. "I work with a youth summer camp that specializes in nature trips. The Learning Center brings me in to offer scholarships to the kids a few times a year, and educate them a little on the program, too."

"Wow." David smiled. "That sounds like such fulfilling work."

David then nodded toward the inside of our home before he continued, "Were you planning on joining us for dinner, Nathan? I'm sure we could find a place for you at the table."

"Actually, I think Nathan and Brianna were just leav—"

"I'd love to stay for dinner, David," Nathan interrupted as he shot me a solemn look. "I can't wait to see what we'll be having."

*　　*　　*

When I was in college, I'd gotten into an argument over a short story by Harlan Ellison. I'd never cared much for his writing, and this short story wasn't any exception. The argument had come about while I was half drunk at a party, with Francesca Oliver repeatedly getting into my face, pointing a pink, unmanicured finger toward me

WHILE WE WERE BURNING

as she accused me of just not being smart enough to pick up on the nuances of his writing, just not being *interesting* enough to relate to it.

At the time, my retaliation tactic included going up to a half-drunk David, my very hot boyfriend who'd just happened to be the best-looking guy at said party, and kissing him until my lips were sore. When I was finished, I went back over to terminally single Francesca, making a quick joke about not needing to understand Harlan Ellison because I wasn't going to die alone like she was.

The joke wasn't funny, but people still laughed.

And Francesca slunk away to another corner of the room with her proverbial tail between her legs. And yet, if it was possible right now, I would go back in time to offer Francesca a much-deserved apology.

Not for making a joke at her expense, though. She'd rightfully earned that moment of derision.

I would've apologized to her because she'd been right about that Harlan Ellison story.

"I Have No Mouth, and I Must Scream."

That's what it was called.

And as I sat at the dining room table next to my husband, right across from the man I'd once had a semi-passionate affair with, a man who'd been staring over at me like I'd murdered his mother in cold blood, I finally understood every word that Ellison had written.

*I have no mouth.*

*And I must scream.*

"So, have you two been on any dates yet?" David made conversation with a smirk, his fork held a little ways away from his mouth. "When Lizzie said that you two 'met' at the Learning Center, I figured that was the first step toward something a little more romantic?"

"We're just friends," Brianna casually clarified the lie. "I was . . .

intrigued by the nature program Nathan works for. It seems like something I might want to get involved with over the summer, if the program would have me."

"Could you do that program and still work for Lizzie? Or would we have to find a temporary replacement for you while you're away?"

"A temporary replacement," Nathan responded this time with a lie of his own. "But you might want to start looking now. From what I've heard about Brianna, it's going to be pretty damn hard to find a replacement for her."

Brianna lightly chuckled before she waved off the compliment.

Nathan then turned his attention over to David as he went on. "What do you do for work, David? Eli— Brianna told me that you're in real estate?"

"Oh, don't get me started on real estate." David chuckled now, too. "It's the most boring dinner topic in the world."

"I don't know. It doesn't seem so boring to me. Selling Memphis to the highest bidder one property at a time. I was just reading an article the other day that said we're the number one place that Gen X-ers are moving to right now. Although I'm sure you already knew that."

"I did, yeah." David smiled. "It's my job to know as many boring facts as you could possibly imagine."

". . . Right." Nathan smiled in return, but I knew there was venom behind it, his eyes slightly narrowing as he stared back at him. "How does that make you feel? Knowing that your whole job is to make Memphis more unaffordable for the average Joes who live here?"

"I wouldn't say that's my job at all, Nathan—"

"Knowing that your main responsibility at work is to help this city gentrify as fast as it can?" Nathan went on, not giving my husband a chance to respond. "To push out everyone at the edge until it feels safe enough for the white flight crowd to send their kids back to buy up all the houses?"

David's friendly expression finally broke into bits and pieces.

". . . I think it might be time for you to leave my home, Nathan." His tone was calm, even though I knew there was fury raging inside of his chest. "I don't mean to be uncivil, but since you seem to be looking to get a reaction out of me . . . let's just say I'm not interested in giving you what you want tonight."

"Yeah, me and Elizabeth both."

"Nathan, don't," I quietly pleaded with him, my words coming out so muted I wasn't sure if they'd even made it over to his ears.

"What the hell was that supposed to mean?" David pressed. "What the hell is he talking about, Lizzie?"

"I'm talking about the fact that you don't fuck your wife," Nathan replied. "I'm talking about the fact that if you were worth a damn in bed, she wouldn't have gone home with me the first night we met."

Something cracked down my spine, all the air in the room being sucked through an invisible vacuum, its hose stealing oxygen right out of my lungs.

Any chance I had of not breaking evaporated in front of me.

Nathan was staring at me. David was staring at me, too.

Brianna was the only one giving me any grace, her head turned toward a different corner of the room, her expression half hidden from view.

*Fuck. Fuck. Fuck.*

I had to say something.

I desperately willed my jaw to move, my teeth to finally click back into place . . .

"Nathan!" I finally found my scream, his name tearing through my throat. "Stop!"

SARA KOFFI

"No, Elizabeth! You're the one who needs to stop!" Nathan shouted in return. "You need to either stop lying to him or stop lying to me! You told me that you were going to leave him, and then you just . . . disappeared. Do you have any idea how that felt? To have the woman I love disappear right out of my life?"

". . . The woman you love?" David repeated the phrase as he looked over at me, his eyes wide with surprise. "Lizzie, do you . . . you two love each other?"

I returned his surprised expression, his question a clean, sharp slice to my chest.

Did I love Nathan?

How could David even ask me that?

How could he not know that he was everything to me?

"David, I don't love him—"

"Don't," Nathan interrupted. "Don't you dare say that you don't love me, too, Elizabeth Smith."

"I don't love you, Nathan," I confessed. "I'm sorry. I love David. I've always loved David—"

"Did you love him when you were fingering yourself to the sound of my voice on the phone? Did you love him when you told me that I owned your pussy? That I owned every piece of you?"

"He's lying! David, he's lying—"

". . . Is he?" David murmured as he looked over at me. "Is he really lying, Lizzie? Or is he just saying something that you don't want to be true?"

David's expression was pleading and compassionate, something behind his eyes so fatally sincere, like he was offering me his last bit of rope at the edge of a cliff. I opened my mouth to speak before snapping it shut again, not wanting to sink even further into the lie but nowhere near ready to admit the truth.

I couldn't do it. I couldn't be the reason David's expression

194

shifted from compassion to hate, from wanting to believe me against all odds to looking at me with nothing but disdain.

I couldn't be the one to finally snuff out what little light was left between us.

"I can't fucking do this." David barked out a pained laugh as he stood up from the dining room table. "I can't fucking do this anymore, Lizzie—"

"David, please," I started as I reached out for his wrist.

"Don't touch me," David said, moving his arm far away from me, already turning toward the front door. "And don't follow me."

"David? David!" I stood up from my seat, too, determined to close the distance between us. I reached for him again, but by then it was too late; he was already on the other side of the door. "David, please! Just wait—"

"Don't," Brianna added as she was suddenly standing right in front of me. "I'll take care of David. You . . . take care of Nathan."

"Brianna, no. I need to go to him—" I stopped speaking mid-sentence, suddenly out of breath, suddenly out of everything.

Of course it made sense that I was struggling to be coherent, given that my heart had just walked away from me, given that the man I loved had just punched a hole straight through my chest and left me bleeding out in his wake.

"I'll make sure he doesn't get too far, okay?" Brianna insisted. "But if you try to talk to him right now, Elizabeth, you might actually lose him for good. Right now, he just needs to calm down. And he needs to remember why he chose you, why he loves you. If you let me take care of him, I can try to keep him focused on that."

Brianna reached for my wrists, her touch tender and light. "Just . . . trust me, Elizabeth. Can you do that? Can you trust me to take care of this? To take care of you?"

". . . I trust you," I said with a shaky breath. "I trust you, Brianna."

"Good." Brianna smiled before she turned to leave the room.

And I turned back toward Nathan, the coldness in his eyes replaced with something warm and inviting.

"I'm so sorry all of that had to happen that way, Elizabeth, but at least now we can finally be together—"

"Get the fuck out of my house, Nathan. And if you ever try to contact me again, I'll chop your dick off and eat it for breakfast."

# 21

# Brianna

avid? David!" Brianna ran after him, following him all the way back to his parked car on the other side of the street. There wasn't any room left for him in the parking spot in front of his home, the space being taken by Nathan's and Elizabeth's vehicles.

"David, stop!" she yelled, even as he stepped inside the driver's side of his car. By the time David turned on the engine, Brianna had slid into the passenger seat, settling against the leather as she tried to catch her breath.

"Get out of the car, Brianna."

"No," she shot right back. "I'm not going anywhere. I'm not letting you leave like this."

"Are you seriously sticking up for Elizabeth right now?" David scoffed. "Jesus Christ. I know that we're paying you well, but I didn't realize we were paying you *that* well—"

"It's not about sticking up for Elizabeth," she argued. "It's about not letting you throw something away just because you're in the wrong frame of mind. I just don't want you to—"

*I just don't want you to get hurt.*

Brianna stopped herself before she could finish letting out the thoughts in her head, shaken by the fact that they'd come to her in the first place. Why did she care if David got hurt?

Why had she even come out here at all?

"I'm not going back inside of that goddamn house, Brianna."

". . . Okay. Fine. We can go somewhere else."

"We?"

"I told you, David. I'm not letting you throw your whole marriage away," Brianna continued. "Wherever you want to go, let's go. But I'm not letting you make a mistake you can't take back just because you're pissed off."

". . . There's a new apartment site I've been meaning to check out." David pulled away from the curb. "One of the investors had a question about interior design."

"Is that part of your department?"

"Everything's part of my department when you're at my level in the company." He sighed. "Every last damn detail."

"Okay." Brianna nodded again. "Then, I guess, lead the way—"

"Did you know?"

"What?"

"Did you know about Elizabeth and Nathan? Have you been . . . have you been covering for her this whole fucking time?"

"No," Brianna murmured. "I had no idea. Not until he showed up at your doorstep. Honestly, I . . ."

"Honestly, you what, Brianna?"

"I don't know. I don't know how to process it," she admitted. "Elizabeth . . . whenever she talks about you, it's obvious how much

she's in love with you. I just don't understand why she would ever . . .
do something like that."

"Because she's a selfish bitch."

"You don't mean that, David," Brianna said, her tone lined with
disappointment.

And David winced. "You're right. I'm sorry."

Brianna watched as David reached for the radio dial without
looking at the radio at all. Soon, whatever happened to be playing on
104.5 FM was blasting throughout the car. It was all noise to Brianna, though, indecipherable from the wind that whipped around his
car as he sped through the Memphis streets, from the slight sound
of her own breath catching as they drove over a particularly deep
pothole.

When they made it to the apartment complex half an hour later,
David pulled out his key card, an affirmative beep sounding as the
gates opened wide. He then got out of his car and walked toward
the building, barely acknowledging Brianna's presence at his side.
She wondered if he'd somehow gone into mental autopilot, his eyes
looking around but not really seeing, his footsteps retracing a path
they'd gone down a thousand times before.

"David." Brianna's voice was gentle as they stepped onto the elevator.

"Yes?"

". . . What's this building going to be called?"

"What?"

"There's no sign on the front of it. And I couldn't read what it
said underneath the 'coming soon' posters that were on the gate."

"The Front Street Fortress."

"Wait. Really?"

"No." David laughed, the sound just as pained as it was during dinner. "But it might as well be called that. That's the point of it, right? To keep people who don't belong out."

"David—"

"You know what the worst thing was? About that asshole tonight?" David stepped out of the elevator, heading toward the unit near the very back of the hall. "That he was fucking right about me, Brianna. Everything he fucking said about me."

"David, he was just trying to get under your skin—"

"Yeah, and it fucking worked." David laughed again before he unlocked the unit's front door, soon walking through its entryway. "This is all I fucking do now, Brianna. Make things more comfortable for assholes who wouldn't be caught fucking dead on the *wrong side* of the city. Make sure they feel safe enough to rent overpriced apartments and invest in overpriced condos."

Once Brianna was through the front door, David slammed it behind them. He then walked up to Brianna and backed her into the wall, towering over her, their bodies so close that Brianna inadvertently shivered with anticipation.

"I'm a fucking sellout, Brianna," David said, his gaze locked on hers, ocean blue staring into earthy brown. "This isn't . . . I never wanted to end up like this. I never wanted to end up as just another piece of shit who makes everything worse. I should fucking know better and I—"

Brianna's lips were on David's then, interrupting his spiel, cutting off his train of thought at the very source. The kiss didn't last long, Brianna soon moving away from him, pressing her back even harder into the wall, trying to create more space between them than was possible.

"I'm sorry," she faltered, her tone lined with confusion.

Why had she followed him out of the house?

And why the hell had she kissed him?

Brianna was flustered, unable to solve for $X$ in the equation of her own actions, of her own thoughts. She knew that she didn't want him to get hurt, but she hadn't realized that she wanted to be the distraction from the hurt, too, the moment he could use to pretend like dinner with Nathan had never happened at all.

The person he could get lost in to make it all go away.

*Maybe they could get lost in each other—*

Brianna shook away the thought, her words mumbled and low. "I'm sorry, David. I'm so sorry. I don't know why I—I shouldn't have—"

It was David's turn to interrupt the conversation then as he kissed her again, his tongue a welcome invasion into her mouth. Brianna moaned as David's hands slipped underneath her T-shirt, his palms cupping her breasts. Brianna reached for him, too, her own palms shifting down toward his belt, eagerly pulling it through the loops on his slacks.

David's hand came down to meet hers, gently moving it away from his belt, pushing it back toward her waist. His fingers interlaced through Brianna's as he gingerly pushed down her jeans on one side. His other hand was soon on her waist, too, pushing until her jeans were on the floor, until she was standing in front of him in her panties.

And then David moved down to the floor, too.

"David . . ." Brianna whispered his name as he slid his fingers up through either side of her panties before pulling them down to her ankles. When she felt his mouth on her, she sucked in a quick breath before releasing a deep groan. There were alarm bells going off in Brianna's head, her body practically screaming at her to move away from him, to not let him taste her, to not let him ever get this close.

But Brianna found that she couldn't move. Not when David was giving her this much pleasure.

Not when there was a sensuous pressure building in her abdomen, her body already so close to going right over the edge with him. When Brianna finally went over said edge, her hips rocking against David's mouth, her fingers twisting in his hair, she'd realized the magnitude of her mistake.

She never should've let this happen. David Smith was never part of the plan.

"Where do you live?" David asked as he rose back to his feet, his hands bringing Brianna's panties back up toward her waist.

"I don't . . ."

"You don't know where you live?" David playfully smirked. "Come on. I just want to drop you off at home."

". . . Is that really all you want to do, David?" Brianna stared back at him.

"No," David admitted, the smirk still in his expression. "But something tells me you already knew that, too."

\* \* \*

". . . Whose room is this?" David leaned against the doorway to Jay's old room, everything inside still pristine and in place. "I thought you told me that you didn't have kids."

Brianna had mostly been quiet on the ride back to her apartment as a strange combination of butterflies and daggers danced around each other in her stomach. There were several times where she wanted to tell David to fuck right off, to keep his hands and mouth to himself, to stop lazily drawing circles against her thigh in the passenger seat. But whenever she caught him looking over at her, his gaze felt as warm as the sun itself, Brianna's resolve melting under the heat of it.

*Fuck.*

David was a wrench she'd never seen coming. She'd genuinely

planned on convincing him to go back to Elizabeth, of playing the role of friend and making sure Elizabeth's marriage didn't fall apart right in front of her. Because David was just a pawn in her peripheral vision, someone that she needed to keep on the chessboard until she had a chance to figure out what to do about him, if anything at all. And if she kept her proper distance, he could never be the reason her true intentions ever made it back to Elizabeth, the reason she wouldn't be able to do what needed to be done.

She just had to keep him at arm's length, keep him at bay until she knew what came next.

And yet she hadn't been able to help herself back at the unnamed apartment complex, kissing David because she'd wanted to, and because he'd been just so close.

"I don't have kids." The half-truth easily rolled off Brianna's tongue. "But I . . . I had a friend's kid staying here a lot of the time. He was at St. Jude a lot. But in between treatments, he would come and stay with me when his mom was swamped with work."

". . . Was at St. Jude?"

"He didn't make it," Brianna explained, an unexpected wave of despair hitting her all at once. "He—"

Suddenly, Brianna found it impossible to continue the conversation, her frame shaking as she wept. David's arms were soon wrapped around her, tight, keeping her in place as she cried, keeping what was inside of her from tumbling out. She hadn't meant to be crying right now. In fact, she'd rehearsed this a million times, whenever the inevitable happened, when someone asked about Jay's old room, when someone asked about the absent child whose bed was still made, whose small bookshelf was still in place.

"I'm sorry," David whispered, right beside Brianna's ear. "I'm so sorry, baby."

Brianna turned her head up toward David's, just in time to see his

203

eyes cloudy with tears, too. A second or so later, and David's mouth was on hers, all over again, as he softly pushed her toward the main bedroom. Brianna ached in so many ways at once, pain seeming to radiate throughout her very veins at the memories of Jay, of Charles, of everything that'd happened since she'd yearned to make something right, since she'd reached for everything that life still owed her with arms wide open.

But as David laid her down on her mattress, his body soon hovering over hers, the pain disappeared. And Brianna let herself fall right into it, her hands reaching for David everywhere, reaching for painlessness, reaching for something easy and light.

Reaching for a single moment where she was able to forget that there was a hole hanging behind her chest, right where her heart should've been.

*　　*　　*

"*Mom?*"

*Jay was sitting in his usual cramped way on the living room couch. Brianna had never understood how he could be comfortable in that position, his legs crossed in an unnatural way, his head leaning back against the armrest.*

*He had an English textbook laid open across his lap, his fingers tapping along its edges.*

*"Yes, baby?" Brianna replied with a warm smile. She'd been looking over her own textbook for her pharmacy classes. She'd recently decided to make a change in her career, after reading a few trending articles about there being a direct path from community college to nursing school, at least if she played all her cards right. Brianna didn't regret not going to college the first time around, always happy with her decision to keep her son instead of giving*

*him away or letting anyone rip him out of her—much to Charles's mother's chagrin—but now that Jay was older, she was ready to try.*

*"Do you like Shakespeare?"*

*"That depends. Which play?"*

*". . . These are supposed to be plays?" Jay made a sound like he was disgusted by the very concept. "I thought we were looking over movie scripts or something."*

*"Uh, baby, if you think Shakespeare was a film director, I'm a little concerned about how much attention you're paying in class."*

*"You know English class comes right after my band period," Jay whined. "And you know how much Dr. Hunter has us rehearsing the same shit over and over—"*

*"Hey! What did I say about you using that word?"*

*"Sorry," Jay apologized, slightly shifting on the couch.*

*"What's that boy apologizing for this time?" Charles walked into the living room, beaming down at Brianna. "You need me to go and get my belt?"*

*"I'm too old for that, Dad."*

*"Boy, you're never too old for a good beating." Charles chuckled. "That's life's number one rule. Someone out there is always going to be willing to kick your ass."*

*"Charles, how am I supposed to tell our son not to use curse words when you're using them, too?" Brianna offered Charles a faux pout.*

*And he bent down toward her, gently kissing the faux expression right off her face.*

*"I'm sorry, too, then," Charles said as he stood up straight. "I'm also sorry that I might miss dinner tonight. I've got a late shift on the line."*

*"Yeah, for the bazillionth time," Jay murmured.*

*"Now, what did I just say about you not being too old for a good*

beating?" Charles chuckled again as he walked over to his son on the couch. Jay playfully scurried away from him, his English textbook falling open on the floor. When Charles arrived on the couch, he sat down beside Jay, right before picking up the book and gingerly placing it back in his son's lap.

"You need to focus on this, okay? Whatever it is. You don't want to end up like me and your mom."

"You mean like you," Brianna scoffed with a smirk. "I'm going to be a nurse pretty soon. Which means you two need to figure out where you're going to live, because I'm moving out to Harbor Town with all the money that I'll have coming in. This apartment is going to be vacant ASAP."

"Oh! Big money!" Charles laughed, with Jay soon joining in on the laughter, too.

"Mom's going to blow up and act like she don't know nobody," Jay added, his own laughter overtaking his father's.

"I don't know why you're laughing so hard, boy. When your mom runs off to Harbor Town, you'll have to get a job with me at FedEx." Charles grinned. "You and me? We're going to be throwing boxes, side by side."

"That Christmas bonus is gonna hit, though." Jay grinned right back.

"Charles, stop distracting your son and get to work." Brianna laughed as she spoke. "I'll leave a plate out for you when you get home."

* * *

". . . Brianna? Brianna?" David whispered as he softly shook Brianna awake.

When she fully opened her eyes, she was still in her apartment, but everything else was wrong, wrong, wrong. She was able to feel it under her skin, the wrongness of it, her stomach hollow, her chest pitted right out. It'd been the same way she'd felt about the place ever since she'd lost Jay, ever since she'd lost Charles, too.

Even the weight beside her in the bed right now was wrong in a way she could taste on her tongue, in a way that made it so hard to breathe. Charles was a bigger man than David, the frame he'd built over years of working at FedEx giving him more of a muscular base. David, on the other hand, was all lean muscle, the body of a man who worked an office job but still regularly made time for a run, sometimes even using the gym in his office building, too.

". . . What is it? What's wrong?" Brianna turned toward David, her eyes searching his gaze in the dark of the room, the only light coming from the streetlights that were far, far away from her windows.

"You were having a nightmare, I think."

"What?"

"You were . . ." David started and stopped as he shifted closer to Brianna's side. "It almost looked like you were fighting something in your sleep. I don't know. At first, I was worried that you were . . . that something was wrong. But then, I realized that you were still asleep."

"So, you woke me up because you thought I was having a nightmare?"

"No." David smiled as he slowly shook his head. "I woke you up because I didn't want you to be in any pain. That's what it looked like. Like you were in so much pain."

". . . Oh." Brianna smiled at him in return, taken aback by his moment of kindness. "Well, thank you for not wanting me to be in pain."

". . . Can I ask what you were dreaming about?"

"It's . . . um . . ." Brianna looked away from him as she searched for the right words.

"You can tell me about it, Brianna," David said, his hand lowering to her waist, as he rested his arm across it. "You can tell me anything. I promise, I won't judge. I'm just here to listen."

". . . Okay." Brianna quietly nodded before she went on. "It's . . . it's not really a nightmare. It's more like a recurring . . . daydream."

"A recurring daydream?"

"It's like, a memory of a memory of a perfect day," she attempted to explain. "It's . . . I don't know. Like my brain trying to make up for all the bad that's happened in my life by showing me something it thinks I'd like. But whenever I have that dream . . . it hurts. It's like someone's playing a moment out in front of me and it's just . . . torture because I can't do anything about it."

"Why would you want to do anything about a perfect day? Isn't the whole point that it's perfect, as is?"

". . . Because I want to make sure the next day is going to be perfect, too." Brianna offered David a fading smile but didn't offer up anything else. She couldn't have told him about what happened that night, how Charles had surprised Jay with a new bike, how she'd helped set the whole thing up, wanting Jay not to expect his dad home from work so soon.

And she couldn't have told David about what came next, either.

The blood on her hands. Holding her child in her arms. The kind of cold that only comes from people who were already lost, bodies that no longer held a soul.

The rage she felt whenever she looked at his wife.

"You should go back to sleep," David suggested as he settled down beside her. "I'll be here to keep an eye on you, to make sure you don't have any more of those 'daydreams,' okay? I'll keep you safe."

"Ooh, that's a pretty tall order, David." Brianna chuckled, making light of the moment despite the aching that'd started behind her chest, her heart yearning for the son she'd lost.

She just missed his smile so much.

"I can handle it," David insisted before he placed a soft kiss on her forehead. "I'll keep you safe, Brianna. I'm not going anywhere."

*　*　*

". . . What are you going to tell Elizabeth?" Brianna asked as she sat up in bed the next morning. She hadn't been surprised to see David still beside her, sinking into the mattress like he was staking his claim to the spot. "About where you spent the night?"

"I'm going to tell her the truth," David joked, sleep showing in his words. "I'm going to tell her that I spent the night with the most gorgeous woman I've ever met, and that we made love in the morning, too, just before I left. You know, depending on if you think you can handle another round right now—"

"I'm serious, David," Brianna interrupted. "We have to get our story straight. If Elizabeth finds out that we—"

"I don't care if she finds out, Brianna." David shrugged off the conversation. "She was the one who cheated on me first, remember?"

"*I* care, David," Brianna replied in annoyance. "She's the one who's paying all my bills, remember?"

"Technically, *I'm* the one paying all your bills." David grinned. "So, if that's all you're really concerned about, you don't need to worry, okay? I'm going to take care of you, Brianna. Always."

"You're not getting it, David."

"What am I not getting?"

"That you can't just—" Brianna clenched her fists in frustration. "Elizabeth . . . she's fragile, David."

"Right. So fragile she had enough time to start up an affair—"

"Well, considering that you somehow found the time, too, I'm not sure that's really a fair thing to say," Brianna cut him off, despite the hurt look in David's eyes. "And you're not with her like I am, David. You don't know how close she is to . . ."

"How close she is to what?"

"You just have to try, okay?" Brianna insisted. "You have to at least give her a chance, or at least pretend like you are. If you leave her now, David, it's not going to be a trial separation. It's going to be permanent."

"Permanent, like a divorce? Which is exactly what I want—"

"Permanent like Patricia permanent, like Camilla permanent," Brianna corrected. "And I know you might not think you're in love with her anymore, David, but there's no way you'd ever want to be responsible for something like that. You're not that cruel . . ." Brianna purposely let her words trail off before she went on. "Are you?"

". . . She talked to you about Camilla?" David propped himself up by his elbows. "What . . . what did she say about her?"

"I only know the basics."

"Then you don't know anything at all."

"You know, you're doing a great impression of an asshole right now, David."

"That's not how I meant it." David shook his head. "I just meant . . . you don't know her like I do, Brianna. You might think she's fragile or weak or whatever but . . . well, fuck. You met her mom."

"What's that supposed to mean?"

"That Elizabeth is a fucking expert at spin. That she knows it's better to have a tenuous relationship with the truth at all times so no one can ever hold you to it. Or hurt you with it."

"You're not making any sense to me right now, David." Brianna frowned as she moved closer to David's side. "We just need to make sure she's okay, all right? That she doesn't suspect anything for now."

"I set up a meeting with Dr. Whitaker in a few days," he replied. "Do you think she'll at least be okay until then?"

"She will. Elizabeth will always be okay, as long as she has you," Brianna answered. "You're her anchor, David. Without you, she's . . . she's not really anything. Without you, she just floats away."

Brianna smiled when she was finished speaking, hoping that she'd convinced David to stay in the place he was always supposed to be, hoping that he'd never find his way back to her bedroom ever again, even if he had been able to soothe her every ache.

Because Brianna needed the ache.

She needed the pain to keep her on task, to guide her in the right direction.

Without the pain, she wouldn't be able to do what needed to be done.

# 22

# Elizabeth

D r. Whitaker's outfit today was tasteful.
Inoffensive.
Pristine.

It'd always been that way, though, ever since our first session. She was the kind of woman who'd filled her closet with varying shades of beige and brown, her clothing so often neutral and so often boring. Of course Dr. Whitaker's aim was to be the least interesting person in the room, so I had to assume that her commitment to such a bland color palette was just an extension of the other tasteful decorations of her office, almost like she was just another piece of furniture.

"Elizabeth," she started, in her typical, soothing tone. "What would you say brings you in today?"

I turned to look over at David, both of us sitting across from Dr. Whitaker in oversize leather chairs, the distance between us suggesting a working relationship more than a romantic one.

David's expression seemed to match the working-relationship descriptor, too, the look on his face so bored and so detached. I'd known that I'd lost him the night Nathan had come over for dinner. Within the span of one evening, my husband had stormed out on our conversation not once but twice. And when he'd shown up the next morning, he'd barely wanted to speak to me, everything about him feeling isolated and impossible to reach.

Brianna had told me that I was reading things wrong, that David wouldn't have agreed to come to therapy if he didn't want to try, that he wouldn't have come back home at all.

I wanted to believe her. I wanted to believe that, against all odds, David Smith was still in love with me, that he just needed to work through his feelings, that a few sessions with Dr. Whitaker would be enough to fill in all the pieces he felt were missing.

But judging from the way his eyes glazed over more with every passing second, it was getting harder and harder for me to keep the faith.

"David and I . . ." I paused, taking a moment to turn my attention back to Dr. Whitaker. "There was something . . . there was a revelation between us—"

"I found out that she was sleeping with another man," David casually interjected. "He showed up for dinner the other night."

"Another man?" Dr. Whitaker quirked an eyebrow, as if she hadn't known every last intimate detail of my affair with Nathan.

"Nathan Andrews. He . . . he came over to our home unannounced."

"That must've been uncomfortable for the both of you. Is that what brings you in today?"

". . . David didn't come home. After Nathan came over, David left and . . . he just didn't come home. Not until the next morning. He's never done anything like that before."

"Is that true, David? Did you stay out all night without coming home?"

"Yes." David's tone was flat, less of a tortured confession and more of a general statement.

"What do you think drove you toward that behavior?" Dr. Whitaker mused. "It sounds like avoidance to me."

"I'm sorry, are we really going to sit here and pretend like there's something wrong with *me*?" David sat up straight in his seat with renewed interest in the conversation. "I'm sorry, Dr. Whitaker, but I'm not the one who was cheating. All I ever did for Elizabeth was try to take care of her, to try to take care of us. I put so much into trying to make sure that she was okay—"

"After Patricia died," I quietly added.

". . . What?" David shot me a look of utter disbelief, as if I were speaking to him for the first time in years, a comatose patient who'd suddenly come back to the land of the living. "What did you just say?"

"After Patricia died," I repeated the phrase. "You put so much effort into me, into everything, after Patricia died. Before that, though . . . it always felt like you were looking right through me."

"Maybe I was looking right through you because there wasn't anything there to see."

"Hold on." Dr. Whitaker held up a hand in warning. "David, I'm going to recommend that we not say anything with the intention of harming or hurting. It's difficult to take back the things we say, even if we didn't mean to say them."

"I meant every last word," David's eyes cut over toward me. "I don't know when this—I don't know when we—" David looked down toward the ground before he finished with his thoughts. ". . . I'm just tired of this, Elizabeth. I don't . . . I don't know how much more of this I can take. I don't know how much more of this you can take, either."

"I don't think you should try to speak for your wife in this situation, David—"

"Aren't you tired, Elizabeth?" David brought his attention back to me. "Seriously. Don't you want to be happy? Don't you deserve that much?"

"I want to be happy with you, David." A lingering smile came to my face. "I don't . . . I can't be happy without you."

*And there was a time when you couldn't have been happy without me, either.*

I kept the last part to myself, my fingers digging into the leather armrest, my heart on the verge of crumbling to dust and blowing away with the wind.

". . . You never even apologized," David mumbled.

"What was that, David?"

"You never even said that you were sorry," David clarified further. "When it came out that you'd been having your affair, you never even apologized to me."

"Yes, I did."

"No, you didn't."

"David, I wouldn't just—of course I said I was sorry, David," I insisted. "But maybe you didn't hear me since you were already halfway out the door by that point."

"Why can't some things just be *your* fault, Elizabeth? Why are you always so fucking blameless?"

"I never said that I was blameless," I replied with a hardened edge lining my tone. "But if you would've given me a chance to explain, you would've known that Nathan and I never touched each other, not after the first night we met. It's not like I was fucking some other man, David. If anything, it'd be like me calling one of those late-night numbers and having phone sex. That's all it ever was with Nathan. It was just phone sex."

"Jesus Christ." David let out a quiet breath. "Do you even hear yourself right now?"

"To be frank, David, when your wife has spoken of the affair in the past, she's often framed it as a source of *acting out*, something she was doing in an attempt to get your attention," Dr. Whitaker continued. "Her disinterest in being physical with this other man may very well point to an interest in preserving the relationship she had with you. If she'd wanted to destroy it, we can assume she would've taken things much further."

"Oh, is that all she was doing? Just acting out?" David chuckled, sarcasm evident in the sound of it. "Well, in that case, all is forgiven. Why are we even here right now? You should be spending your time with patients who have real problems, Dr. Whitaker. Elizabeth and I are golden."

"You don't have to be such a—" I started to speak, the phrase getting stuck midair.

"Such a what, Elizabeth?" he pressed. "Go ahead. Diagnose me with whatever you need to, whatever's going to make this bullshit work in your head."

"Please, David," I whispered, my voice shaking, fresh tears slipping down my cheeks. "Please. Don't be this way. It doesn't have to be like this. It doesn't—we can go back to how things used to be."

". . . I don't know if that's what I want, Elizabeth," he admitted, the look on his face sympathetic and sad, like he was seconds away from crying, too. "I'm sorry, but I—"

David's words were interrupted by the sound of his phone ringing.

"Sorry," he apologized again as he quickly pulled out his phone before setting it back into his pocket. "I should've turned it off before I even came into the office."

"That's all right, David—" Dr. Whitaker started, but soon my phone began ringing, too, my fingers moving for it as if my body had already seen it coming. Once it was securely in my hand, I glanced down at the screen, a familiar name glowing right back at me.

". . . Janice?" I murmured down at my phone.

"She called you, too?" David hummed. "She knew you were taking today off, didn't she? You're not missing a shift by being here?"

"Well, I'm sure whatever it might be could wait until we're finished with our session—" Dr. Whitaker interjected, making a valiant effort to rejoin the conversation, but I'd already let my curiosity win out against my will to be respectful of her time.

"Janice?" I said into the phone's receiver as I picked up the call. I simultaneously held up a finger toward Dr. Whitaker, wanting to signal that I'd get back to the whole therapy thing ASAP.

*Yes, yes, I know how this looks, but please just give me a few seconds to sort this out.*

*And then we can get right back to my life falling apart.*

*Right back to my husband leaving me. Right back to the end of the fucking world.*

"Oh God! Finally!" Janice cried on the other end of the line. "Elizabeth, I need you to come to the Learning Center."

"I'm in the middle of a therapy session right now, Janice—"

"Please, Elizabeth! We need all hands on deck," she begged. "The Center's on fire. We need you to help sort things out with some of the kids and the parents. God. I think we're going to lose it all."

*　　*　　*

I'd never seen a building on fire before.

Not anywhere except the movies and TV, the blazes on the screen always looking just as perfect and coiffed as the actors standing in front of them. A building on fire was just another set piece, something to marvel at while I wondered what other projects I'd seen a particular actress in, idly trying to figure out if I'd ever seen her in anything else at all.

But right now, standing in front of a burning building, it didn't feel like a distant set piece.

It felt like watching hell come to life right in front of my eyes.

There were ashes coming off each side of the building, gently floating down to earth, landing somewhere near my feet. As for the flames, they licked at everything in sight, the concrete, the bricks, the marble. It was obvious that I'd gotten there too late to be able to save anything inside, my work belongings probably the same ashes that were gathering beside my heel.

It was also obvious that I'd gotten there too late to do anything to help at all, the kids and parents having already been sorted out and comforted by Janice and a few other employees, so many of them huddled together in the parking lot.

The only thing left to do now was to watch the destruction, to wonder about how much smoke inhalation was enough to kill, if I was chancing it with every breath I took. David was standing right beside me, his fingers lingering near mine, almost like he was going to reach out and take my palm into his at any second. I couldn't help but smile at the thought, the prospect of our closeness being restored by the destruction of a building.

*See, David?*

*This was all we ever needed to fix us.*

*We just needed something to burn.*

I reached for David's hand, yearning for the feel of it, yearning for all of our memories to swirl around inside of my head as I thought back on the seemingly millions of times that we'd held hands like this before. But just as my fingers brushed against David's, his hand was gone, his frame moving slightly to the right, putting just enough space between us for any form of physical contact to seem strained and unnatural.

I turned back toward the building then, rejection pinching at my every nerve, little needles being pushed through one side of my heart and into the other. As I stared at the building, my stomach started to churn, an unpleasant sense of *something* making its way through my veins.

*This was all too familiar.*

I crooked my head to the side as I watched Patricia's name sizzle and burn, the letters moving away from the building and leaning toward the street, hanging in the most unnatural way.

*Yep.*

*Way too fucking familiar.*

There were police sirens now, coming from somewhere behind me, followed by the sirens from fire trucks, too. And as I watched the men in red and black rush toward the burning building, there was another figure, unmoving, separate from the rest. They were standing off to the side of the flames, their presence becoming a fixture in my line of sight, like a spot on my iris that just wouldn't go away, no matter how many times I desperately blinked.

Finally, I looked over at the unmoving figure, giving it my full attention. I now realized that the figure was Brianna, her head turned up toward the burning building, her arms crossed over her chest. She looked just as helpless as the rest of us, her fascination with the fire possibly stemming from the same place as mine. I imagined that once the flames were done with, we'd settle down at a table at Starbucks and talk about it, sharing our notes on the strangeness of it, the way the sheer, impossible heat rolled so easily off the destroyed structure.

But when I blinked again, something in my stomach roiled again, too.

Because as I stared over at Brianna, the blaze between us continuing to devour everything in sight, it looked like she was smiling between the flames.

# 23

## Elizabeth

It'd been a few days since the fire, since I'd been stuck at home with nowhere to go. Without an actual office location, there was nothing for the instructors to do except email lesson plans to each other, substituting feedback and criticism for actual human interaction. And since I wasn't interested in participating in their group texts and group chats, I'd been spending my free time mostly trying not to lose what little was left of my mind.

I'd always suspected that one day I'd go completely insane. It was so often the way of intelligent women, after all, their stories commonly ending with slit wrists or an empty bottle of pills on their nightstand. Between the sleeping pills that'd become necessary for me to get any kind of sleep at night and the nearly constant panic attacks that swept through me on a daily basis, I wasn't a held-together thing anymore. I was little fragments of somethings, awake but not really alive, everything getting so much worse when I remembered that my best friend was still murdered, and my husband had one foot out the goddamn door.

There was also the fact that I couldn't get Brianna's smile out of my head.

*Had she even been smiling?*

Maybe I'd imagined it. Maybe I'd keep imagining things, too, until I accused everyone who ever cared about me of secretly being out to get me. That was the first part of going crazy, wasn't it? Becoming suspicious in ways that didn't make sense to anyone who wasn't me. Becoming paranoid that my reality wasn't *my* reality, that there were things in place I couldn't see, fingers pulling strings that I'd never be able to feel.

*Brngggggggg.*

*Brngggggggg.*

*Brngggggggg.*

I was shaken out of my thoughts by the sound of the front doorbell ringing throughout the hall. It didn't take me long to cross the living room floor and answer it, pulling the handle open without a second thought. I would've been happy regardless of who was on the other side, even if it was just the mailman with an Amazon delivery. I needed to stay out of my own head and out of my own way, and small interactions with strangers so often did the trick.

There was just something about having to pretend to be okay that made me *feel* okay, at least until the moment with the stranger had passed.

". . . Janice?" Her name fell out of my mouth as I stared back at her, genuinely thrown by her showing up at my front door. "I didn't know you were coming over—"

"We need to talk, Elizabeth," Janice replied, already stepping inside my home. "Are you alone?"

"Yes, I am," I answered. "David's at work, and Brianna said she needed to take a day to handle some personal business—"

"I need to talk to you about the fire," she interrupted, her eyes staring back at mine, every part of her seeming so serious and grave. "Elizabeth, I—"

Janice stopped herself as she took in a deep breath, her fingers shaking by her side.

"Janice? What's wrong?" I closed the front door as I spoke. "Why do you need to talk to me about the fire?"

"I knew how you felt about Jack's donation, about us renaming the Center after Patricia, too. I could see it in your face that day, when we revealed it. You seemed so . . . torn. I could tell. But Elizabeth, I never thought that you would . . ."

"Thought that I would what, Janice?" I pressed, confusion scurrying around my scrambled thoughts.

"That you would try to burn it all down," she continued. "That you would ever do something that extreme."

"Janice, what the hell are you talking about?" I shot right back. "Are you seriously trying to accuse me of burning down the Learning Center? I wasn't even fucking there!"

"The police said that it looked like arson, Elizabeth," she went on. "And that . . . you wouldn't have had to be there that morning, because it looks like the fire was actually set the night before."

"How is that even fucking possible?"

". . . It was a slow burn. Like someone didn't want to get caught at the scene of the crime. It was really smart, actually." Janice paused before she spoke again. ". . . And you're one of the smartest people I know, Elizabeth."

"I might be smart, Janice, but I don't know how to time a fucking fire!" I shouted down her accusation. "Can't you just watch the security tapes? I wasn't there, okay? You have to believe me—"

"The cameras weren't on," she murmured. "Someone had turned them off the night before. Someone who knew the access code to the building. Someone who . . . someone who knew *your* log-in code for the app, Elizabeth." Janice looked over at me, pity seeming to cloud her expression. "I'm really sorry, Elizabeth, but I have to let you go."

*I have to let you go.*

The phrase was a sudden, hard slap across the face.

A stinging harshness I hadn't seen coming, the kind of pain that left me temporarily silent and stunned.

Eventually, I regained my ability to speak. "Janice, please, you can't let me go because of something you *think* I did! I would never—someone must've swiped my info somehow—"

"It's not just coming from me, Elizabeth," she interrupted. "The owners know about what's been going on with you, ever since Patricia . . . They just think that it might be better for you to stay focused on your mental health and well-being. They think it's better for everyone this way."

"And what do you think, Janice?" I kept eye contact with her as I spoke. "Do you think it's better for everyone this way, too?"

". . . Yes," Janice admitted with a sad smile. "I think what happened with Patricia hit you a lot harder than you ever wanted to admit, Elizabeth. I should've known, too, that working with us, even after she died . . . I think you just need some more time to process it—"

"I've had time to process it, Janice!" I laughed at the pure absurdity of her response. "Someone I cared about was *murdered* and everyone's acting like things could ever go back to normal for me. This *is* the end result of processing it, of therapy and pills and all other forms of various emotional-suppression tactics, standing right in front of you." I took in a shaky breath before going on. "I'm fucking healed, Janice. This is me all stitched up. And I don't . . . I don't understand why no one's able to see that. It's not going to get better than this for

me. And now I'm being punished for having a fucking heart. I'm being punished just for reacting to things like a person—"

"Maybe we can find a way to leave a door open for you at the
Learning Center?" Janice offered. "I'm guessing all you'll need is a
clean psych evaluation from Dr. Whitaker and I can make a case for
you with the owners—"

"Fuck the owners," I spat out before I held my front door wide
open. "And honestly? Fuck you, too, Janice."

"You don't have to be so angry, Elizabeth—"

"If you don't like the way I'm talking to you, maybe you should
fire me," I said, nodding toward the door frame. "I'll see you around,
Janice."

". . . I'll see you around." Janice hesitated to move toward the
door, almost like she was worried that if she turned her back to me,
I was going to sink a knife into her spine.

*Because I'm not Elizabeth Smith to her anymore,* I thought. *Because all I am to Janice right now is a crazy woman who burned
down her office.*

Eventually, Janice made her way to the door, her footsteps slow
and measured.

And as soon as she was on the other side of it, I slammed it hard
behind her, hoping that she could feel the anger reverberating in the
motion.

\* \* \*

"Wait. So, she fired you yesterday?" Brianna started as she slid a cup
of coffee across the kitchen counter. "She can't do that, can she? It's
not like they even have evidence that it was you."

"It doesn't matter if they have evidence that it was me." I let out

225

a deep sigh. "The whole point is that it *seems* like it was me, and that's what counts. Besides, I get the feeling that the owners have been wanting to get rid of me for a while, probably ever since I first asked to start taking off mental health days, you know, to grieve the loss of a friend."

"Still." Brianna frowned. "That just doesn't seem right. Or legal."

"Tennessee is a right-to-work state." I shrugged. "I'm pretty sure they could've fired me for anything and it would've held up in court."

"God. This fucking state." Brianna rolled her eyes. "I swear to God, sometimes it's like the '60s never ended."

". . . What were you getting up to yesterday?" I asked before taking a sip of my coffee, its warmth a welcome kind of burn on my tongue. "Did it have something to do with Charles?"

"Hey, my whole life doesn't just revolve around one man." Brianna grinned. ". . . And yes. It had something to do with Charles."

"Are you two working things out?"

"Maybe? We've started talking again. I have to admit, I did miss having a man around. Even though it's also kind of . . ."

"Kind of what?"

"Weird?" Brianna lightly chuckled. "I don't know. I just didn't see this coming. I've always been such a planner. When one thing gets knocked off course, it sort of makes me feel like everything else is going to get knocked off course, too."

"Well, speaking as someone who that's *definitely* happening to, you might be right about that." I sighed again. "All it takes is for one domino to fall, and everything else is just . . . done."

I waited for Brianna's response, expecting sympathy, empathy, some sense of commiseration.

Instead, I was met with silence. I sat in it, patiently waiting for something to break it, my mind wandering about my own sorry state, figuratively and literally—

"Elizabeth?" Brianna suddenly said my name so low it was almost a whisper.

"What? What is it?"

". . . I found something. Something about Patricia. But I . . . With everything happening with your job and with David . . . I don't know if you should really get into it right now."

". . . Because you know what's best for me, right?" My eyes narrowed over at her before I could stop myself. "Because you and Janice and David and Dr. Whitaker always know what's best? And I never do?"

"That's not what I'm saying, Elizabeth. I'm not saying that I know what's best for you." Brianna shook her head. "If I thought that, I wouldn't have even brought it up in the first place. I'm trusting you to make your own decision, okay? If you're feeling up for it, we can talk about it. If you're not, we can just drop it and go back to talking about my semi-burgeoning love life—"

"I want to talk about it, Brianna," I pressed. "I can handle it. I can handle anything."

"Okay . . ." Brianna's words trailed off for a moment, her eyes moving away from me, too. "How much do you know about Jack?"

"Jack Fitzgerald?" My breath caught in my chest.

Brianna solemnly nodded. "When we were going through Patricia's social media and all of her messages . . . well, I didn't think to do it the first time, because you'd told me that she wasn't super internet-savvy—"

"What did you do, Brianna?"

"I checked her archived messages," she quickly answered. "The messages she was keeping for some reason, even if she wasn't actively checking the conversations anymore."

Brianna looked back over at me, her eyes watering as she spoke. "I found a conversation between Patricia and Jack, from around the same time that she . . . that you found her dead. It was . . . Elizabeth, I think Patricia may have been about to leave her husband."

". . . What?" I shook my head in full disbelief. "Patricia Fitzgerald was not about to leave Jack—"

"See for yourself," Brianna interrupted before she slid her phone over to my side of the table, a conversation glowing to life on its screen.

> @PatriciaFitz85 to @JackTheDon: Jack, stop. You're drunk again, and you know how much I hate it when you message me when you've been drinking.

@JackTheDon to @PatriciaFitz85: I'm not fucking drunk, Pattie. And I'm just trying to fucking talk to you. This is how you like talking to people now, right? On social media? Jesus Christ. You barely fucking look at me when I come home.

> @PatriciaFitz85 to @JackTheDon: How's Gretchen?

@JackTheDon to @PatriciaFitz85: That's not fair.

> @PatriciaFitz85 to @JackTheDon: What's not fair? Me trying to build something for myself and you being a bitter, jealous asshole? Or you fucking your assistant whenever you get bored?
>
> You know, the next time you're going to fuck a woman from work, you should make sure she doesn't leave a pair of her tights in the fucking backseat.

@JackTheDon to @PatriciaFitz85: Are
you really still holding on to that? For
fuck's sake, Pattie, I already fired her.
What do you want me to do? Kill her?

@PatriciaFitz85 to @JackTheDon:
Maybe I don't want you to do anything
for me anymore, Jack.

@JackTheDon to @PatriciaFitz85: What
are you saying, Pattie?

@PatriciaFitz85 to @JackTheDon: I'm
saying that I might ask my sister about
who she used as her divorce lawyer.
She got the house, the car, pretty much
everything.

Maybe you should lawyer up, too.

@JackTheDon to @PatriciaFitz85: If you
try to pull any of that shit with me,
Pattie, you won't be getting one damn
thing.

Can't collect on a divorce settlement
when you're six feet under.

Fucking bitch.

"Elizabeth? Are you okay?" Brianna's voice interrupted my staring at the screen, my eyes frozen in place as I read over the conversation again and again and again.

*Fucking bitch.*

*Fucking bitch.*

*Fucking bitch.*

I could hear it so clearly in my head, Jack's words slurring in an unsteady rhythm. I moved the phone back toward Brianna, my hands shaking as I brought them down to my lap.

"That fucking piece of shit," I mumbled.

"What? I couldn't really hear what you just said—"

"That fucking piece of shit!" I repeated, this time my words coming out as a scream. "Fuck!"

I screamed again, my throat not feeling capable of doing anything else. I just couldn't shake the image of Jack at the hospital, at the funeral, at our house a few weeks afterward, his face stained with tears as he openly wept on my husband's shoulder. He'd been there, every step of the way, pretending like he was grieving with the rest of us, pretending like he was a weary widower and not the one who'd strung his wife up in the middle of the night.

"I'm going to kill him," I said, matter-of-fact, like it was the right response, like it was the only response.

"Elizabeth, hold on." Brianna reached across the counter for my hand, steadying her palm against mine. "This doesn't prove anything by itself. It might look bad, but that's the same thing the Learning Center said about you and the fire, right? And we both know they were completely wrong about it, so—"

"So, what? We're just supposed to let him get away with it?"

"That's not what I'm saying, either." Brianna's palm gave my hand a gentle squeeze. "I'm just saying that we need to play our cards right here. If we go in without enough information, Jack could figure out that we know what really happened, and then he could make a run for it—"

"Wait, wait," I said, working through a thought, trying to stop my anxious brain from skipping around from one memory to another. "Jack couldn't have . . . He was drunk that night, Brianna."

"You sure?"

"Yeah, I'm sure. He was practically passed out in the back of their car after the Halloween party," I insisted. "I mean, even before he came to the party, he'd been at the bar with David—"

"And you're sure that David was at the bar, too?"

"I'm sorry, is there something you know that I don't?"

"I'm not saying that I know anything," she clarified. "I'm just saying that . . . if someone was going to kill their wife and make it look like a suicide . . . being wasted is a damn good alibi. And making sure that everyone saw that you were drunk that night, too? Well, that only makes it even better . . ."

". . . because it takes you off the suspect list," I said, following Brianna's train of thought. "Fuck, it probably means you were never even on the suspect list to begin with."

Something tightened in my chest, my world threatening to spin to a stop as dizziness settled across the folds of my brain. If it hadn't been for Brianna's palm covering mine, I would've succumbed to the darkness, to the sudden desire for nothingness behind my eyes, the yearning for an unconscious state.

". . . What should we do?" I asked, my own voice sounding distant to my ears, like I was just too far away to reach. "Brianna, what are we supposed to do?"

"I'll think of something." Brianna offered me a small smile, just as she moved her hand away from mine. "Just . . . give me some time to come up with it. I might need to listen to a few more of those podcasts until something clicks."

# 24

# Brianna

Brianna had cleaned her apartment from top to bottom, and from bottom to top, all over again. She liked to clean when she was thinking, her hands needing something to do as her thoughts wandered and returned, as she tried to work out what she was going to do next in her life, where she needed to focus and where she needed to pull back.

She'd been so busy cleaning that she hadn't noticed David peering into her apartment window, his fist only inches from knocking on her door. When she did notice him, she was startled, instinctively shifting away from David, as if she had found a lit match on the ground.

". . . David? What are you doing?" Brianna stared up at him, confused, as she opened her front door. "Why are you here?"

"I'm here because I wanted to see you, baby," he answered with a small smile. "I'm sorry. I should've called—"

"You need to be more careful. What if your wife followed you over here?"

". . . You really think Elizabeth would've followed me here?"

"I don't know, David!" Brianna pulled him into her apartment before quickly slamming the door behind him. She was immensely frustrated by David's surprise pop-in, hoping he would interpret her mood as being more about protecting Elizabeth's feelings than about him potentially unraveling everything with his carelessness. He still needed to think that she was a friend to Elizabeth, that she'd come into their lives without pretense.

He never needed to know who Brianna was behind the mirror, behind the mask.

"I told you, David. You don't spend as much time with her as I do. Sometimes, she . . . I just worry about her. And the last thing she needs is to find out that—"

David cut Brianna off with a kiss, his hands sliding around her waist.

And with that, her frustration seemed to melt away.

"I missed you," he breathed, his tone aching with sincerity.

"You just saw me yesterday." She smiled at him, just as sincere, unexpected warmth flooding through her.

"But I didn't get to touch you," he replied with a grin. "It doesn't count if I don't get to wrap my arms around you."

Brianna playfully rolled her eyes as she took a step away from him, his hands still on either side of her. "You need to brace yourself for what Elizabeth is going to tell you tonight."

"Brace myself? Why?"

"She got fired from the Learning Center."

"Oh." David lightly chuckled. "I . . . kind of assumed everyone got fired from the Learning Center, considering that there is no Learning Center anymore."

"Her boss thinks she set the place on fire." Brianna moved right along with her response. "She doesn't have any evidence for it, but it seems like she doesn't really need any, either. Elizabeth is guilty because she's guilty."

"You sound like you don't think she did it."

"Do you think she did it, David? I mean, do you really think your wife could—"

"Elizabeth."

"What?"

"You called her my wife."

"She is your wife, David."

"I don't really think that's true anymore." David's eyes went toward another corner of the apartment. "And yes, I think she could do it. I think Elizabeth could do anything she set her mind to doing. She's always been . . . built that way. Capable."

"Including arson."

"Including anything and everything." David shrugged. "I wouldn't put a limit on her."

". . . I don't understand you two."

"What do you mean?"

"I mean that she talks about you like you single-handedly saved her from disaster," Brianna explained. "But you talk about her like . . . like *she* was the disaster. Like you married a hurricane but didn't know it until it was too late."

". . . Maybe so. Maybe I was just always in the eye of the storm." He shrugged again before pressing his face against Brianna's neck, before breathing her in.

"Fuck. I want you," David whispered, close to Brianna's ear, his hands already wandering down her frame. "I want you so fucking much, baby."

Brianna smiled at David's proclamation of desire, even though her mind was several million miles away. Even as he kissed and touched her everywhere, even as he stripped her bare and made her scream and cry and beg him for more, she was never fully present with him. Being with David was usually a rare opportunity for Brianna to experience a sublime state of nothingness, but not tonight.

Not tonight.

\* \* \*

". . . I want you to stay away from her."

"What?" Brianna was half naked in her bedsheets with David's arm wrapped around her shoulders. He looked like a king, pleased with himself and the condition of his throne, as if Brianna were his most vital conquest to date.

"Elizabeth. I want you to stay away from her."

"I can't stay away from her, David," Brianna replied. "She's my boss."

"Brianna, if things are really starting to spin out of place," he continued. "If Elizabeth is really so out of her goddamn mind that she set an entire building on fire . . . what do you think she's going to do to you? If she ever finds out about us?"

"I wasn't thinking she'd ever really get the chance to get to me?" Brianna scoffed. "But thanks for the heads-up. It's nice to know ahead of time that you plan on hanging me out to dry."

"I would never do that to you," David insisted. "You know that I'm always going to protect you, Brianna. Always. And if on the off chance that she ever hurts you . . ." David's words trailed off before he went on. "If Elizabeth ever hurts you, Brianna, I'm going to make her regret it for the rest of her life."

"When you talk like that, David, it sort of sounds like you two belong together," Brianna shot back. "Why does it always have to be all or nothing with you two? Why does everything have to be so dramatic—"

"Don't."

"Don't what?"

"Don't try to push me away. Don't try to make little snide comments like that just to piss me off. If you don't want this to happen anymore, then it won't. But I can't stand the passive-aggressive bullshit—"

"I wasn't being passive-aggressive," Brianna argued. "I was just being honest. You don't see it that way because you're too close to it. Because you're too close to her. But trust me. I've got the best seat in the house."

"Let me take you out to dinner," David suddenly offered, as if he hadn't heard a word that Brianna had just said.

"You're married, David," Brianna reminded him. "Even if you don't like to admit it—"

"We can go to Southaven," he interrupted, his lips curving into a smile. "Or how about Lakeland? The farther away, the better."

"And what happens if one of your work colleagues sees you having dinner with your wife's assistant? What happens if someone tells Elizabeth about it and she goes completely berserk?"

"There are guys I work with who have *dinner* with their wives' assistants all the time. And who the hell is going to tell her? You're the only friend she has left, Brianna."

"Right." Brianna let out a shallow breath. "I'm the last woman left alive."

"Not funny." There was a warning in David's inflection, right before he pressed a soft kiss against the side of Brianna's head. "Seriously, though. Where do you want to go for dinner? It can be anywhere as long as it's not too close to Harbor Town."

Brianna looked up at David, her eyes glancing over at the man she'd somehow found herself tangled up with, the man she'd somehow turned into a precarious sort of weapon, too.

*Would he really hurt Elizabeth if she hurt Brianna?*

Brianna simply smiled at the thought, her daydreams filled with David taking her side, defending her against the consequences of her own actions, sticking up for her despite her being so clearly in the wrong. It was something she'd never experienced before, being so *wrong* and having someone take up for her as if she couldn't have been more *right*.

She then wondered if that was another reason why Elizabeth never wanted to give David up.

Because if she was a hurricane, David was his own fucking tornado, swirling around her and keeping her safe from the destruction that she caused, never letting Elizabeth really know how much damage she'd done.

How much damage she could really do.

*   *   *

"Are you sure this is the right address?" Elizabeth stared up at the brownstone. "You're really sure that Jack lives here now?"

"That's what it said on his new website." Brianna gave Elizabeth an affirmative nod. "Jack Fitzgerald. 3431 South Union Avenue."

"God." Elizabeth frowned. "Patricia would've hated this place. It's so . . . cookie-cutter."

". . . Are you good to talk to him?" Brianna gently nudged Elizabeth in the arm. "You're not going to freak out on him or anything, right?"

"No. I'm not going to freak out on him." Elizabeth rolled her eyes. "It's like you said, it's better to act like he's just . . . like he's just another wife-murdering son of a bitch—"

"Elizabeth—"

"Right, right. We're just here for a soft interrogation . . ."

". . . because a soft interrogation is the best way to catch him off guard," Brianna finished Elizabeth's thought for her. "He's not expecting to see you, Elizabeth. And if he really did what we think he did, just seeing you should be enough to rattle something out of him."

"Got it. I've got this. Don't worry about it." Elizabeth let out a heavy breath before she casually knocked on Jack's front door.

And a few seconds later, Jack pulled the door open, just as casually as Elizabeth had knocked on it. He took a moment to look each woman up and down, his face screwing up like he was completely confused.

"Hi, Jack," Elizabeth started. "Can we come in?"

"What do you want to come in for, Elizabeth?" Jack scoffed. "Didn't you tell me that we were on different sides? That we should just *be*?"

"I just want to talk to you." She smiled. "Can't we just talk?"

"You haven't spoken to me in months, Elizabeth."

". . . That's just because I didn't know what to say. I didn't know how to . . . I should've been there for you, Jack. I should've at least tried. And the fact that I didn't . . . it eats me alive each and every day."

Brianna stared over at Elizabeth, whose tone seemed so hurt, so affected . . .

Even though Brianna knew that Elizabeth couldn't care less about the man.

The realization made Brianna go still for a moment as her mind went racing about the chameleon of a woman standing beside her.

How wondrous. How terrifying.

"Fine." Jack opened the door to his home wide enough for Elizabeth and Brianna to walk right on through. "You can come in. But Kelly-Anne's going to be home any minute now, and she's not big on unexpected guests just dropping in on us."

". . . Kelly-Anne?" Elizabeth asked as she stepped inside the home.

"My wife," Jack explained as he welcomed Brianna into his home, too, his eyes trained on her frame.

". . . You're married again?" Elizabeth said, her words coming out as a whisper. "Already?"

"What was I supposed to do, Elizabeth? Was I supposed to wait around forever? For what? My wife killed herself. It's not like she was ever coming back to me." Jack's hands came up to his waist as he finished with his thoughts. "Hell, it's not like she even wanted to stay with me, in the first place. Or else she wouldn't have . . . she wouldn't have left me the way she did."

"Patricia loved you," Elizabeth shot right back. "She loved you more than anything, Jack. You were her whole world."

"Is this what you came here to do? You came here to make me feel like shit just for trying to get on with my life?"

"I'm not trying to make you feel like shit for—" Elizabeth stopped and restarted her response. "I'm sorry. You're right. I shouldn't have started off like that. I'm just surprised, that's all."

"Well, maybe you wouldn't be so surprised if you'd actually spoken to me in the last six months." Jack smiled, but his face was barely able to hide his irritation. He then looked over at Brianna, and the expression shifted into something more welcoming and sincere.

"Vera. That's your name, right?" Jack asked with a hesitation lining his tone, like he didn't want to get the name wrong.

"No. It's not." Brianna returned his smile, even as her heart started to pound behind her chest. "My name's Brianna."

*Fuck. Fuck. Fuck.*

Jack wasn't supposed to remember her.

He hadn't, right? Back at the Learning Center?

Brianna's mind raced as she looked over at the man, trying her best to keep her expression neutral and calm.

This was the kind of miscalculation that could unravel everything. The kind of miscalculation that could land her in prison for the rest of her life. If there was any trace, any connection between her and Patricia, it wouldn't take much for Elizabeth's conspiracy theory to be proven right, that Patricia hadn't died so willingly.

*Fuck.*

If Jack had remembered her, why hadn't he said anything before? Why would he just—

The answer washed over her before her mind had a chance to finish asking the question.

*AA.*

Because Jack hadn't wanted to out her as an AA member in front of Elizabeth at the Center. But now that they were in his home, with Elizabeth readily throwing accusations, it seemed as if all bets were off.

Knowing that, Brianna forced herself to take a deep breath, her body bracing for the absolute worst.

Her body bracing itself for the truth to crack her open like a goddamn wrecking ball.

". . . You sure we've never met before?" Jack squinted over at her. "Because, no offense, you're kind of hard to forget, Vera."

"My name's not Vera," Brianna replied with a small grin, her palms growing slick with sweat. "Sorry to disappoint. And I'd say that I'm pretty forgettable, actually, which it sounds like Vera isn't, so—"

"Listen," Jack said, taking a step closer to her. "You can be real with me, okay? I can understand if you were using a fake name that night. I think a lot of people use fake names at that sort of thing—"

"At what sort of thing?" Elizabeth added to the conversation as she looked between Jack and Brianna.

". . . At an AA meeting," Jack confessed. "I used to go, off and on. I was never regular with them, not until after I lost Pattie, anyway.

After that, I knew that I needed to finally get sober, once and for all. I was just tired of being a piece of shit, you know?"

Jack brought a hand to his forehead, just before letting out an unexpected dry sob.

"Fuck," Jack mumbled. "Fuck, I'm sorry. I don't know why I'm . . . All that fucking money spent on therapy and I can barely get through a whole conversation about her. I just . . . I just can't help thinking that part of why she killed herself was because of me. Because of the way I used to talk to her when I was drinking. Pattie never deserved any of my bullshit. I should've . . . I should've been better to her. I should've been better for her."

"It's okay, Jack." Elizabeth reached a hand toward him, soon resting her palm on his shoulder. "Hey, did you hear me? It's okay."

"I'm sorry about what happened to your wife," Brianna said.

"Yeah, I'm sure you're real tired of having to see me break down again, Vera." Jack lightly chuckled, lightly sobbed. "Fuck. You should've seen me at those AA meetings after Patricia died. I was sobbing my eyes out nearly every damn session."

"I told you, Jack. I'm not Vera—"

"You were talking about your son," Jack interrupted. "When you came to that meeting. You said you were worried that you started drinking too much, after what happened to him. He died, too, right? Not like Patricia, but it's not like you saw it coming, either."

"I don't have a son." It was the kind of truth that hit Brianna like a lie, like there was something so deeply rotten and wrong about saying those words out loud.

"Jesus Christ, Jack. Do all Black people just look alike to you?" Elizabeth inserted herself into the conversation, her eyes laser focused on him. "And no, they don't all know each other, either, so don't try asking Brianna if she knows who Vera is. You've embarrassed yourself enough as is."

"You're going to try to lecture me about embarrassing myself?" Jack let out a derisive chuckle. "Are you fucking serious, Elizabeth? Do you have any idea what people are saying about you, nowadays?"

"I don't give a fuck what people are saying about me—"

"You're a fucking mess," Jack continued. "That's what people are saying about you. They're saying that no one can have a conversation with you without you breaking down halfway through it. That you walk around looking like a goddamn ghost with bags under your eyes. And you're getting so skinny, it looks like you haven't eaten in weeks."

Jack took a step closer to Elizabeth before he went on.

"And I know you're the one who burned down the Learning Center."

"You don't know anything, asshole—"

"I know that you've always been a psycho little bitch, Elizabeth," Jack pressed on. "I always knew that Pattie deserved a better friend than you, too. Were you even really her fucking friend? Or were you just being nice?"

Jack paused for a moment, a sickening smirk coming over his expression. "Or was Pattie just being nice to *you*? Because no one else could really stand to be around you? The way you always moped around that house, like someone had a gun to the back of your head. No one was forcing you to stay, Elizabeth. And David would've been better off if you'd just fucking left. You were making that man miserable—"

". . . Honey?" A Black woman was standing in the doorway of Jack's home with one arm gripped around a brown grocery bag. Her other arm gently gripped her noticeably pregnant stomach, her abdomen protruding in a way that suggested that she was several months along.

"Kelly-Anne." Jack beamed as soon as he saw her. He walked up to her and took the grocery bag out of her hands, right before giving her a gentle kiss on her cheek. "Sorry about all that, sweetheart. I was just . . . catching up with an old friend."

"An old friend?"

"Hi. I'm Elizabeth." She warmly waved at Kelly-Anne, complete with a smile.

Kelly-Anne seemed to freeze, just for a second or two. She then waved back at Elizabeth before wiping her fingers underneath her eyes.

"Sweetheart?" Jack frowned as he gazed at his wife. "Were you crying?"

"I wasn't crying, Jack. I was just—" Kelly-Anne shook her head, like she was struggling to find the right words. "There was this video that just came out. Body camera footage from the police. There was this man in Houston . . . It's so awful, Jack. They were . . . kicking him . . . You can hear him screaming for his life. I just don't know why they didn't stop—"

"I told you not to watch videos like that, sweetheart. You know how fragile you are right now with your hormones. Watching things like that'll only make you upset. Only makes things worse. And anything that upsets you, Kelly, upsets the baby, too."

". . . Was it easy for you?" Elizabeth asked.

"What?" Kelly-Anne blinked in confusion. "I'm sorry, I don't think I know what you mean—"

"Was getting pregnant easy for you?" she clarified. "Because I don't know if Jack told you, but getting pregnant was a little difficult for his last wife."

"Oh." Kelly-Anne smiled. "Um, I guess you could say it was easy. It didn't take us long to get pregnant. Although it's not like we were planning for it, either."

"And is this your house?" Elizabeth gestured toward the walls around her. "Because I don't know if Jack told you this, either, but he used to live in Harbor Town with his last wife. And it seemed like they were pretty happy there."

"It's *our* house, yes," Kelly-Anne pushed back. "And I know about the home he used to have in Harbor Town, too. I also know about the old neighborhood and how toxic and triggering it was for my husband, which is why we decided that Harbor Town was off the table."

"Toxic and triggering?" Elizabeth chuckled. "For Patricia, maybe. Oh, you do know about Patricia, don't you? How she died?"

"I know that Jack's last partner tragically took her own life—"

"She didn't take her own life," Elizabeth cut her off. "Someone killed her."

". . . What?" Kelly-Anne's eyes went wide with surprise. "Jack, you never told me that—"

"Why would he tell you that someone killed his wife?" Elizabeth cut her off for a second time. "If you knew that someone killed his first wife, you'd probably be a little uneasy about being his *second*. Especially since the person most likely to kill a woman is always, *always* her intimate partner." Elizabeth shrugged after she spoke. "But you don't have to take my word for it, Kelly-Anne. You could always just ask Patric— Oh. Right."

"Fuck you," Jack growled in Elizabeth's direction. "Get the fuck out of my house."

Jack then looked over at Brianna, a scowl still on his face. "And you? You might be a fucking liar, but I still expected better from you. When we met, and we *did* meet, you seemed like you had a goddamn heart. But if you're following Elizabeth around, I don't know what that fucking makes you."

"What did it make your wife?" Brianna's voice was soft, so soft it almost hid the sharp edge of her response.

"Fuck *you*, too! Now get the fuck out of my house before I call the fucking cops!"

Kelly-Anne shot a pleading look over at Brianna, almost like they were the only two people in the room.

Brianna, innately understanding the look, softly tugged at Elizabeth's sleeve, easing her across the home's threshold.

"Brianna? Wait!" Elizabeth protested. "What the hell are you doing? We had him right where we wanted him!"

"What? With you getting into a shouting match with him while his pregnant wife is in the room?" Brianna shot back. "That's not how this was supposed to happen, Elizabeth."

"Fuck how this was supposed to happen!" Elizabeth shouted. "He fucking killed her, Brianna! He doesn't just get to move on like nothing fucking happened!"

"He won't."

"Brianna—"

"He won't, Elizabeth," Brianna cut her off as she tugged on her sleeve again, now leading her back toward Elizabeth's car. "Come on. We need to get out of here before Jack calls the cops and completely fucks us over."

# 25

## Elizabeth

I was on fire.

I'd never felt this sort of rage before, the kind that blinds, the kind that was sinking itself into my skin, over and over and over. I didn't know what to do with my hands, with my thoughts, with my soul. All I wanted to do was consume something that couldn't be consumed.

I wanted to swallow Jack Fitzgerald whole.

I wanted it so badly that I was giddy at the thought of it, absolutely delirious with an impossible desire. I wanted his shitty, understated brownstone to be empty the next time I visited, for Jack to be hauled away to jail, for Kelly-Anne to have to find a different, better father for her future child, one who wasn't so fucking pathetic, so fucking useless.

I wanted to be at every last trial. I wanted to be called to the witness stand. I wanted to talk to a jury about the angel Jack had killed, the innocent woman whose biggest crime was never being able to make it through nursing school. I wanted to tell them about Patricia's hopes and dreams, the ones I'd been able to glean from her social media accounts and the ones she'd mentioned to me in private, about finally visiting Guam or running a full 12K for St. Jude.

*God.*

I yearned for it.

I burned for it all.

"What the hell did you do, Elizabeth?" David was suddenly walking into the living room, his steps rushed, his suit seeming slightly disheveled.

"David," I said his name with a smile, temporary elation mixing with my fury. "You're home early. There's something I need to tell you—"

"No. I don't want to hear it, Elizabeth." David held up a hand between us. "I just got off the phone with Jack. Why the hell were you over at his house, Elizabeth? And he said that you were threatening his *pregnant* wife?"

"I wasn't threatening her," I replied with a breezy laugh. "I was just telling her the truth, that her odds of being murdered by her husband were high, especially considering that he murdered his first wife, too—"

"What the fuck are you talking about?" David pressed. "Are you telling me that you think Jack killed Patricia?"

"Yes."

David's jaw went slack as he dropped his briefcase toward the ground below, the sound of it hitting the marble causing me to start. He didn't say anything to me for several moments as he silently watched my frame. It looked like he was studying a painting that was hanging in a museum, a piece of art that was beyond him, above him.

". . . There's no helping you, is there?" David finally spoke.

"No helping me with what, David?"

"With anything." His answer came out flat. "There's no helping you with what happened to Patricia. There's no helping you with your-self. There's no helping you with a single bit of it, because you . . . you don't want to be helped, Elizabeth. You prefer it this way, don't you? You like things better when they're broken."

"Please don't tell me that I like things better when my friends are dead—"

"She wasn't your fucking friend!" David yelled, his fists clenching tight at his side. "You don't even remember, do you? The way you used to talk about her? Elizabeth, you could barely stand to be around her. You tried to avoid her anytime you could. You pretty much turned down every dinner invitation the Fitzgeralds ever sent to us."

"That's not true—"

"Yes, it is," David pushed. "Just because you don't want to be-lieve it doesn't mean that it's not true. You just . . . I don't know. I thought you'd gotten better since college. I thought this time would be different."

". . . This time?"

"Camilla Gibbons." David said her name like a curse.

"Why are you bringing up Camilla right now?" I quietly shook my head. "You know I don't like talking about that, David—"

"Of course you don't like talking about it." David laughed, the sound so cruel, so distant, too. "I wouldn't like talking about it, ei-ther, if I went around pretending like a dead woman was my god-damn friend. Fuck. Do you even know how psycho that is?"

"What are you talking about—"

"Camilla was never your friend, Elizabeth," David cut into my response. "She was barely anything to you. I mean, fuck, I should've known better, right? Even back then, when it happened, everyone was so surprised that you were so torn up about it. And I just . . . wrote everyone else off for you. I thought they had it all wrong. Of course Camilla meant something to you. You wouldn't have been so hurt otherwise."

He took a breath before he went on. "But a few months ago . . . I ran into someone. Brooke. One of the girls Camilla was going to rush that sorority with. She works in real estate now up in Chicago. We were waiting around for the same board meeting to start, and she had all these stories, all these memories with Camilla . . . but not one, not a single one, involving you. She didn't even know who you were."

"So what? Some bitch from college doesn't remember me and that's my fucking fault somehow?"

"You're not listening to me." David shook his head. "There's something really fucking wrong with you, Elizabeth. You carry hurt around. You fucking . . . adopt it as some kind of . . . character-building. Or maybe you're just bored. Maybe growing up with all that money but so little attention did something to you—"

"What are you trying to say right now, David?"

"I'm saying that you . . . there's just something inside of you, Elizabeth. Something that internalizes everyone else's fucking trauma like it's meant for you to have," he continued. "Something that twists it and twists it and twists it until it's all about you, until there's nothing left about the other person. Until you're all that really matters."

David took in a deep breath, his eyes still locked on mine. "It's why you can't see anyone except yourself. It's why you can't accept responsibility for anything, because you're never really wrong, because you never really mean or don't mean to do anything, because you . . . you just never really mean it. Anything you do. I don't . . . I don't know if it's an undiagnosed personality disorder or—"

"Fuck off."

"Elizabeth—"

"Fuck off, David!" I shot back, lava-hot anger rising through my

WHILE WE WERE BURNING

throat. "There's nothing wrong with me. There's nothing wrong with having a fucking heart. What you just described me as? Someone who internalizes other people's trauma? It's called having empathy. Maybe you should fucking try it sometime."

"You're out of your goddamn mind. I never should've—"

"You never should've *what*, David?" I took a few steps closer to him, closing the distance between us. "You never should've married me? You never should've wasted your time with someone out of her 'goddamn mind'? And what the hell do you think that makes *you*? Tell me, what's the best way to describe a man who only wants to fuck a woman when he thinks she's broken?"

"Elizabeth—"

"You like me broken, David. You like it when I'm just a wounded little bird for you to take care of. It wasn't lost on me that you practically fucking disappeared from this marriage when everything was finally coming together for me. When I had a job. When I had friends. When I was at a place where I could finally be happy—"

"You were never happy, Lizzie," David murmured. "You might be able to lie to yourself about it, but I was there. I've . . . been here for way too fucking long—"

"Is everything okay?" Brianna quietly entered the room. "I . . . I heard screaming."

"Everything's fine," David answered for the both of us, turning quickly from me toward her. For a moment, he reached for her, almost instinctively, like he'd done it a million times before. He seemed to change his mind, mid-reach, just as Brianna took a step away from him, as if they were both in the process of breaking a familiar pattern.

And suddenly, it was like a light bulb turning on in a lightless place, inescapable illumination revealing the truth of their every interaction, revealing the way David had changed toward me, too.

It wasn't about the affair with Nathan. It wasn't about him thinking that I lost my mind.

It was all about Brianna Thompson.

I'd known that he'd wanted her from the first time he saw her.

I'd known that there was something wrong with letting her inside my home from the first time she stood on the other side of my front door.

And here they were, the consequences of my actions, of me ignoring my gut instincts and trying to be a good feminist, trying to take one for the team.

This was all the thanks that I was ever going to get for trying to be the best person that I could be.

". . . Are you fucking her?" I asked David, keeping my voice low.

"What?"

"Are you fucking Brianna?" I asked again, this time cutting a look over at her, her expression filling with concern. I then brought my focus back to David, his own expression filling with something that seemed so much like pity. "God. You're fucking pathetic."

David laughed at the accusation. "Would it even matter if I was, Elizabeth? I thought this was an open marriage. Or do affairs not count when you're the one fucking someone else?"

"I wasn't *fucking* someone else—"

"Why can't you just be honest with yourself?" David's voice was raised but steady, like a taut arrow behind a bow. "Why can't you just . . . why can't you just be honest with *me*, Lizzie?"

David brought a finger to his chest as he spoke, his eyes locked on mine.

"It's me, Lizzie," he nearly whispered. "I've been here since . . . I'm the only one who's ever . . ."

"I am honest with you, David," I said as I took a step closer to him. "Always. Nothing's ever going to change that."

"You really believe that, don't you?" The sadness behind his eyes was crystal clear now, tears nearly forming in them. "You really think you've been good to me? That we've been good to each other?"

"That's because we have been, David." I placed a hand on the side of his cheek. "We've always been perfect together."

"No," David murmured as he slowly slid my hand away from his face. "We've never really been anything, Lizzie. I don't think . . . I don't think we've ever even seen each other. Not until today. Not until right now. And honestly . . . I don't think there's anything here left to see."

It was the last thing he said to me before he offered me a sad smile.

Before he quietly began to head upstairs to our bedroom, his walk urgent, his steps not missing a single beat.

# 26

## Elizabeth

D avid? David!" I called out as I followed right behind him, only stopping when he stopped, which happened to be outside of the closet at the far end of the hall.

He didn't say a word to me as he pulled out one of our large suit-cases, the kind we'd only use when we were going on weeklong vaca-tions. He snapped the handle of the suitcase up, extending it before he rolled it back down the hall. He then stopped at his next destina-tion, which was our bedroom, his movements becoming methodical as he laid the suitcase open across our bedsheets.

"Where are you going?" My question was frantic and unfocused. "Where the hell are you going, David?"

"I'm leaving, Elizabeth. We both know it's time."

"David—"

"Stop, Elizabeth." David looked over at me as he spoke, his ex-pression strained. "There's nothing you can say to me right now that's going to change my mind." He then turned away from me as he threw a set of clothes into the suitcase. "I can't do this anymore,

Elizabeth. I can't keep pretending like I can help you, like I can save you—"

"I never asked you to save me."

". . . You're right," he admitted. "You never asked me to save you. You never asked for any of this. But I didn't, either—"

"David—"

"But I still can't pretend anymore, Elizabeth," he went on. "I don't . . . I don't think I know you at all, and I'm not sure I ever really did."

"David, don't do this. Don't go," I pleaded. "She's never going to love you like I do, David. She can't. Whatever you think you have with Brianna isn't—it's not—"

"She's the only reason I stayed with you, you know," he softly interrupted. "Brianna is the only reason I tried to make things work for as long as I did. She was worried about your mental health. That if I tried to leave you before you were ready, you were going to fall apart."

David gently placed a polo into his suitcase before he went on. "Honestly? I think Brianna Thompson might be the only real friend you've ever had. And if you want to keep talking to her, hanging out with her . . . I'm not going to stop you. I know you'll need someone, Elizabeth, even if that person can't be me anymore."

". . . Do you love her?" My voice cracked as I asked, everything in me feeling like it was held on by a single tattered thread.

"It doesn't matter, Elizabeth," he answered, his own voice still so soft and so gentle, like he was putting a young child down for bed. "None of that matters anymore."

*None of that matters anymore.*

*You don't matter anymore, Elizabeth.*

*You are nothing and nowhere and no one to me.*

*You're halfway to halfway gone.*

Fire blazed through my veins as I glanced down at the suitcase on the bedsheet, as I took in David's calm, inerratic posture and pose, nothing about him suggesting that leaving me was going to be in any way difficult for him to handle. It seemed more like he was standing in the self-checkout line at the grocery store, his main concern that he'd gathered up all his things, not wanting to forget an errant bag of apples or milk he needed for his coffee in the morning.

Although, even if he forgot something, he could always just come back.

Was that all I was to this man I'd given so much of my life to?

I was just another *option*. A place that he knew would welcome him without any sort of hesitation, no matter what he'd said or done—

*No.*

It was worse than that. I wasn't even a real option to David anymore. I was a grocery store that he visited when he happened to be on the other side of town, a place he had no intention of returning to, even if he forgot an item on his list. Whatever David needed from now on, he'd be getting somewhere else, somewhere that to him felt a lot closer to home.

The fire inside of me raged as I grabbed on to the suitcase, knocking it off the bed. David looked at me like I was wild, his features only growing more frustrated as I turned the suitcase over onto its front, letting all of his packed clothes tumble out onto the bedroom floor.

"You're not leaving me, David," I commanded before I shot a look in his direction. "You . . . you can't leave."

"Please, Elizabeth. Don't make this any harder than it has to be—"

"But it's not really that hard for you, is it?" I let out a laugh that was tinged with nothing but pain. "God, did you ever even love me, David?"

"More than anything in the whole wide world, Elizabeth," he answered with a small smile. "But it's over now, Lizzie. And you have to let me go."

". . . I don't know if I can do that, David," I replied, tears already streaming down my cheeks. "I don't know if I . . . if I know how to let you go."

"I won't make it hard on you. The divorce. You can have half of everything, straight down the line. You can even have the house, if that's what you want. Whatever you'll need to make things easier for you—"

There was a pair of scissors.

There was always a pair of scissors, tucked away near the front part of the suitcase. I'd made sure to bring them on every vacation after our first disastrous trip to Mexico. The first night we'd made it to Guadalajara, there'd been packets of road snacks that David had picked up at a gas station on our way in, and a few glass bottles of brightly colored alcohol. We spent the majority of our first evening on vacation struggling to get the various packets open, finding creative ways to attempt to open the alcohol, too, their tops screwed on so damn tight.

The scissors had been David's idea. He'd grabbed them from a convenience store, telling me that the place was all out of bottle openers because of other forgetful tourists like us, who'd neglected to bring their own. But he had a feeling that if we tried, we'd be able to use the scissors to get the bottles open, too, if we wanted it badly enough.

We just had to want it badly enough.

And the scissors could make anything happen.

Like tearing into a pack of jerky-flavored potato chips from Texaco.

Like forcing David to stay by sinking their blades into his skin.

For a moment, David stared over at me like I was a complete stranger, his gaze shifting wildly from the scissors sticking out of his abdomen and back to me, my hands spotless, free of any trace of the blood he might have expected to see on my fingers.

And then he screamed.

"David? David!" Brianna suddenly rushed into our bedroom, her own scream soon swirling into David's.

*Huh.*

They sounded good together.

Like a song I never wanted to admit that I genuinely liked whenever it came on the radio.

"What did you do?!" Brianna screeched over at me, even though her attention was fully focused on David, her hands going down toward his. It looked like she was trying to hold him together, like she had the sole capacity to keep him from bleeding out on the floor. "What did you do, Elizabeth?!"

"I didn't do . . . I don't . . . I don't know."

"We have to get him to the hospital," Brianna's arms wrapped around my husband's torso, David's head resting against her shoulder. "Call 9-1-1."

I didn't move a muscle as I watched them together, David still screaming, Brianna trying to comfort him the best that she could.

"It's okay, David. You're going to be okay," she murmured. "I'm here, okay? Just don't move. And don't try to pull it out, no matter how much it hurts."

David nodded and winced as he reached a hand up toward Brianna's cheek, softly brushing his fingers against it.

Like he was trying to comfort her, too.

"Call 9-1-1!" Brianna shouted at me this time, her eyes wild as she waited for me to move. "Elizabeth! Please!"

". . . What are you going to tell them?"

"What?"

"About what happened?" I asked. "What are you going to say when they ask what happened to him?"

". . . You want to work on your alibi?" Brianna's voice was low. "While your husband is bleeding out on the fucking floor?"

"He's not my husband anymore. I don't know who he is."

". . . Then that's what we'll say happened," Brianna suggested. "That you thought David was an intruder. That you're on meds for your anxiety, but lately you've been experiencing . . . side effects? We can say that seeing David scared you because he wasn't supposed to be home this early."

Brianna let out a shaky breath before she finished with her thoughts. "We can say that it wasn't your fault, Elizabeth. Okay? We won't let . . . Nothing's going to happen to you, okay?"

"Okay."

\* \* \*

I wanted David to be dead.

I hoped for it, even as I watched him wheeled away toward the ambulance, Brianna right by his side as if she were his doting wife. I hoped and prayed and wished for him to die before they made it to the hospital, before anyone could slide the silver out of his skin and attempt to stitch his insides back together.

Because I wanted to be dead, too.

The world wasn't going to make any sense if David was alive and I was dead, or if David was dead and I was still somehow breathing.

I made my way back into our house after the police had come and gone. They hadn't asked me a lot of questions after I explained that I was medicated, after Brianna had told them that there wasn't any altercation, that it was all just a huge misunderstanding. In an ironic way, after stabbing my husband, I'd gathered some clarity about the situation I'd been so desperate to avoid.

He'd been right about Brianna. She really was my only friend.

And I'd found a way to fuck it all up by hurting the man I was pretty sure she'd been fucking behind my back.

But every friendship had its ups and downs.

A few hours passed with me alone in the house. I didn't really know what to do with myself.

What was I supposed to be doing with myself as I waited to hear the news of my husband's death? As I waited for Brianna to text me with an update about his hopefully terminal condition? I'd had my fill of reality TV during the first hour or two of waiting, watching bored housewives take out their frustrations on each other, pretending to give themselves meaning with catty fights and unnecessarily dramatic talking-head segments.

By hour three, I'd convinced myself that I needed to take more Paroxetine. I'd been calm enough while talking to the police, but as the clock ticked on, I found that my nerves were becoming too frayed and too sharp. I didn't like being nervous, even when it suited the situation. Nervousness was the first step to paranoia for me, to me wondering if there was something waiting around the next corner, to wondering if I was going to be snatched into the dark—

Jack.

I was standing in my bathroom, staring back at my own face in the mirror, when everything clicked together, all at once.

*Jack knew.*

Jack had to know. He knew that I was looking into what happened to Patricia. He knew that he needed to connect me to the arson at the Learning Center, his gift a convincing enough connection, something that would give me an artificial motive.

The only thing I couldn't figure out was how he'd known about the affair, how he'd been able to bring Nathan back into my life.

Although it wasn't a stretch for me to believe that somehow Jack and Nathan had crossed paths, that Nathan was out for blood and willing to do anything it took to cut me deep.

If this was Jack's attempt at keeping me off his trail, it was a respectable one.

But I was still coming for him.

. . . Or maybe I wasn't.

My eyes scanned our medicine cabinet, passing right by the Paroxetine and landing on the sleeping pills that Brianna had gotten for me instead.

*How many sleeping pills did it take to die?*

Whenever I'd seen women kill themselves on screen, they always downed the entire bottle.

But I didn't have an entire bottle left.

A part of me was curious enough to Google the answer, while another part of me felt like being adventurous, living and more than likely dying in the moment. The latter part of me won out as I switched on the faucet, soon grabbing a small cup that we kept by the sink. When the cup was full, I turned off the faucet and emptied the rest of the sleeping pills out onto my palm.

And then I swallowed them down, one by one, taking a sip of water after each swallow.

I chuckled to myself as I kept my eyes on the mirror, amused by my own dramatic death scene. It felt performative, like there was an audience waiting to critique each of my choices, waiting until I fell to the floor to decide whether I was any good of an actress.

*Huh.*

Maybe I wasn't any better than those housewives on TV.

When I was finished with the pills, I slowly sank to the floor. I placed my hands in my lap as I waited for the end to either come or not come, to either fade into oblivion or end up doubled over the toilet. It was boring, really, wondering if I was going to be dead within the next few minutes. And as I counted the tiles on the bathroom floor, I realized why playing Russian roulette was such an attractive form of almost-suicide.

Because otherwise it was about as exciting as filling out paperwork at the DMV.

"Elizabeth? Elizabeth!" Brianna's voice rang out through my home.

I didn't say anything in response. My mouth was starting to feel dry, and I didn't have anything to say, anyway. Why put myself through the discomfort of speaking?

Weren't one's last moments supposed to be peaceful?

"Elizabeth!" Brianna screamed my name, clearly making her way through every room in the house. Her footsteps stopped when she came to the bathroom, our eyes locking, mine from the floor and hers from the doorway.

"What did you do, Elizabeth?" Brianna's gaze quickly cut from the empty bottle of sleeping pills and back to my frame settled against the wall. "What did you do?"

I shrugged off the question. "Is David okay?"

"Elizabeth, did you take all of those pills at once?"

"Is David going to be okay, Brianna?"

"Elizabeth!" Brianna screamed. "Did you take all of these pills?"

"Yes," I answered, my tone calm. "Please, Brianna. Just tell me how David's doing—"

I didn't get a chance to finish my sentence, not before Brianna's hands were on me. Her body was pressed close to mine on the floor as she held an arm around my waist. She used her other arm to balance herself against the wall, her fingers soon prying open my lips, her digits pressing down hard at the back of my tongue.

I choked on the feel of her fingertips inside my mouth, the invasion so unexpected that it made me lurch forward. My choking turned to coughing, and seconds later my coughing had turned to vomiting, bright orange goo spewing out of me, the sleeping pills scattered among the liquid. Brianna moved her hand away from my mouth then as she pulled me closer to her chest, cradling my head against her shoulder.

"I'm sorry," I started, my body shaking with tears I couldn't explain or understand. "I'm so sorry, Brianna. I don't know what . . . I don't know why . . ."

"It's okay."

"I'm sorry about . . . if I said anything hurtful about you and David . . ." I continued, my vision completely unfocused, my irises so blurry and stained. "I just feel like . . . I feel like I'm losing my mind, Brianna. I feel like I'm losing everything, all at once. I don't . . . I don't know what I'm supposed to do. I don't know how I'm going to . . . I don't know how I can even . . ."

I could barely get through my sentences, sobs threatening to interrupt my every syllable. "Everything just hurts so much, Brianna. Everything hurts so much."

". . . Good."

*Good?*

"I don't think I . . . What did you just say?"

"I said 'good,'" Brianna repeated the sentiment, her hold on me now feeling less like a source of comfort and more like a prison I didn't have the energy to escape. "How else do you think you should feel, Elizabeth? After you did what you did? Did you really think you still deserved to feel anything other than what you're feeling right now?"

". . . After what I did? Brianna, I don't know what you're talking about—"

"Elizabeth, you killed my son."

27

# Brianna

*Then*

Brianna and David stood in the kitchen, his frame dangerously close to her own.

He'd been talking about wanting kids, oblivious to Brianna's pained body language, her eyelids slightly fluttering as she thought about the death of her own child, the death of her own heart.

Just then, his phone rang out between them.

"I should probably get that," David mumbled. "And then I should probably go to bed."

"Good night, David," Brianna replied with a warm smile.

"Good night, Brianna." David didn't take his gaze away from her as he spoke . . .

And Brianna's gaze lingered on him, too.

But once David was out of the room, Brianna shifted back toward her original purpose, going through Elizabeth's phone as quickly as she could. When presented with the initial password screen, she simply entered the correct combination, remembering Elizabeth's password all too well.

D-A-V-I-D-0-4-8-5

After she was logged into the device, Brianna scrolled through Elizabeth's call history, knowing that if she'd called Patricia that fateful afternoon, it would've been over a year ago. While scrolling, Brianna noticed several phone calls from around three months ago, from a phone number that'd been saved under *Work*.

But strangely enough, the number wasn't reminiscent of any numbers that Brianna would've associated with the Learning Center at all.

Which meant that Elizabeth was hiding something, something that Brianna might be interested in shining a light on if she ever had the time.

But right now, all she cared about was finding out the truth; all she cared about was finally finding out what happened to her son.

Brianna then continued her scrolling journey all the way back to the day her life had been changed forever.

And on that day, there'd been only two phone calls logged on Elizabeth's device.

The first call was to Patricia Fitzgerald.

The second call was to 9-1-1.

And there it was, Brianna's original theory come to life, the one where Elizabeth called Patricia to talk about Jay, to let her friend know about the dangerous little Black boy she'd seen on Maywood that afternoon. She might have gotten their roles reversed, assuming Patricia called 9-1-1 instead of Elizabeth, but the result had still been the same.

Different ingredients. Same shitty cake.

But as Brianna stared down at the phone again, a wave of shock hit against every nerve in her system.

Because the first call to Patricia Fitzgerald was a *missed* call.

Patricia had never even called Elizabeth back.

So when Elizabeth called 9-1-1, Patricia had nothing to do with it . . .

*Patricia Fitzgerald never had anything at all to do with what happened with Jay.*

Which meant that Brianna Thompson had killed an innocent woman.

*       *       *

Brianna stood at the kitchen counter, still mindlessly scrolling through Elizabeth's phone, even though she already had her answer.

She waited to feel something deep and sad.

Something that would've hidden itself under her bones, creeping up on her in the middle of the night, a gnawing guilt somewhere stuck in her stomach for a lifetime.

She waited to feel anything even resembling it.

But the only thing she felt was an impossible burning, the anger that already resided inside of her seeming to hit a fever pitch. When she thought about Elizabeth working at the Learning Center in Whitehaven, working so closely with Black children . . .

When she thought about the way the woman even carried herself like she was a good person, like she was a living, breathing safe space . . .

All Brianna was able to see was red.

Because Elizabeth Smith was nothing short of a modern-day monster. She was a wolf in sheep's clothing, embedding herself with just the right words, the right beliefs, the right qualities, so that no one would know what was really buried in her core, not unless they dug as deep as Brianna had done. Elizabeth had known the risks and consequences of calling the police on a Black person, of calling the police on a Black child, and she'd chosen to do it anyway.

Even worse, she'd chosen to do it under a fake name.

*Patricia's name.*

Elizabeth had avoided taking accountability for what she'd done, inadvertently passing the fate she deserved on to another. And all the while, she was carrying on like she had any right to be hurt, as if she had any right to play the victim when Patricia would've never been harmed if it hadn't been for Elizabeth choosing her as an alias—

Brianna stilled just as a thought crossed her mind, just as her hand tightened its grip around Elizabeth's phone.

There was a legacy of women just like Elizabeth, privileged white women who were allowed to ruin the lives of women like Brianna on nothing more than a hunch. Sometimes even less. Women like Elizabeth were allowed to accuse and cast aspersions whenever they felt like it, and women like Brianna were supposed to waste their lives trying to make up for the imagined sins they'd committed, trying to ease the fragility of white women who seemed so easily bruised.

And in the end, women like Elizabeth always seemed to win. They never had to live with the consequences of their actions, allowed to continue in their day-to-day as if nothing had the power to hurt them or stop them. They were powerful in their absolute ignorance, in their absolute refusal to place themselves as part of The Problem, eager to bring up the rights owed to women while just as eager to call the police on a Black boy with a brand-new bike.

But Elizabeth wasn't going to win this time.

Brianna was going to make damn sure of it.

And by the time Brianna was finished with her, her pain was going to be enough to make up for old and for new, the kind of generational hurt that passes down through children and bloodlines. Brianna was going to make consequences stick for Elizabeth, in a way that nothing else would've ever been able to, in a way that only Elizabeth could've done to herself by admitting fault or offering to take the blame.

It'd been wrong to kill Patricia, Brianna knew that now, even if she *had* actually been the one who called the police that afternoon.

Because a life for a life wasn't the right answer.

The answer was a life exchanged.

# 28

## Brianna

*Now*

I don't understand . . . I don't understand . . ." Elizabeth's breaths seemed erratic as they reverberated from Brianna's grasp around her. "Why would you . . . How could you . . ."

She then went still as she looked up at her. "You think I killed your son? Brianna, I would never—"

"I know you called the police on him, Elizabeth."

". . . What?" She violently shook her head. "What are you talking about?"

"I saw it in your call log." She stared down at Elizabeth, watching as the woman's eyes went wanton and wild. In that moment, Elizabeth reminded her of a scared animal, a cat that'd been carted off to some shelter, unsuspecting.

A helpless little thing.

Elizabeth's favorite role to play.

"Brianna, I wouldn't—"

"I saw the transcript of the call, too," Brianna continued. "You called in under Patricia's name."

"But I didn't—it's not like—" She stuttered and stammered. "You don't understand. Patricia thought that a kid's bike had gone missing. I was just trying . . . I just wanted her to like—I wanted her to feel like I was at least trying. And it's not like I'd ever seen Jay with a bike like that before—"

". . . What did you just say?" Brianna's voice went low.

"I wanted her to feel like I was trying—"

"No." Brianna held up a finger. "You said that you'd never seen Jay with a bike like that before." Her grip around Elizabeth only grew tighter. "Are you saying that you knew my son?"

"No! I didn't know him!" Elizabeth insisted. "I just . . . I'd seen him around the neighborhood on his old bike. And I . . . I just noticed that something was different that day. Brianna, if I'd known, I never would've—"

Just then, Brianna's arms went limp, something in her soul going limp all at the same time.

Elizabeth scrambled away from her then, until she was nearly halfway across the room.

". . . Wait," Elizabeth murmured. "You saw the transcript of the call?"

"Yes."

"And you saw that I called under Patricia's name . . ." Elizabeth murmured again before her eyes opened wide. "Brianna, did you . . . did you hurt Patricia? Did you know that she was going to get hurt? Oh my God."

Elizabeth let out a sob before Brianna even had a chance to respond. "Fuck. Just tell me. Just tell me! Was it you? Or was it Jack? Is that why he knew you? Because you'd been fucking stalking him, following him around. Did you watch as he killed her? Did you know this whole time?"

"Jack had nothing to do with Patricia's death, Elizabeth," Brianna corrected. "That man's a lot of things, but a killer isn't one of them. He's just a really mean drunk, which makes it really easy to put a target on his back, too."

". . . So, what?" Elizabeth nearly whispered. "What does that mean, Brianna? Does that mean that you were the one who killed her—"

Elizabeth went quiet, cutting off her own words. She then spoke again. "I don't even understand . . . How did you—"

"I'm not going to dignify that with a response."

"This isn't about dignifying anything—"

"You don't get it. I don't owe you *anything*, Elizabeth. Not a single goddamn thing." But despite this fact, Brianna still winced away from the memory.

A woman pleading for her life.

A sparkling street.

A lolling tongue.

Guilt coursed through Brianna's veins in that same instant, a permeating sadness that'd fizzed around her mind, too easily swam through her cells.

*God.*

It was heavy, heavy, heavy.

"Vanessa? What about Vanessa?" Elizabeth was still sobbing, her voice shaking as she asked the question. "The sleeping pills? Your friend? Fuck, Brianna. Was anything you ever told me ever true? What . . . are you? Who are you?"

". . . I was just trying to make things right," Brianna answered, the weight of her guilt threatening to pin her to the bathroom floor.

*God.*

*Oh my God.*

*My God, will you ever forgive me?*

Nina's words echoed all around Brianna, coming back to her like fresh wood thrown on the fire, like a needle slipping underneath her skin.

*If you hurt yourself . . . you can't be with him in heaven.*

*And that boy . . . he's still going to need his mama.*

*He's still going to need you, Brianna, no matter what you think.*

What if she'd hurt someone else? What if she hadn't meant to do it? What if all she'd wanted was Jay back in her arms, away from pain, away from Harbor Town, away from Patricia, away from Elizabeth, away, away, away, away—

"What the fuck is wrong with you?!" Elizabeth screamed, her words followed by desperate gasp after desperate gasp for breath. "You weren't making anything right by killing Patricia! Or by trying to ruin my life. You were just being a fucking sociopath!"

At that, Brianna was pulled from her thoughts, pulled away from Jay.

And she couldn't help but laugh and laugh and laugh.

"What's so fucking funny, Brianna?"

"You," Brianna answered, her eyes sharp and focused. "You're funny, Elizabeth. Really. Truly. You and your utter inability to take responsibility for anything, ever. It's honestly pretty impressive, the way you wrap yourself up in a perfect little delusional bubble. The way you always frame yourself as the victim, as the one who's hurting, even when I'm telling you that you, *you*, cored me from the inside out. You . . . took everything from me, Elizabeth Smith, and yet . . . you're the one with tears in your eyes."

Brianna lightly chuckled again, the sound warm and fond. "David was right about you."

". . . David?" Elizabeth's tone was lined with pain. "Did David help you with this?"

"No." Brianna shook her head. "Like I said, he was never part of the plan. He . . . just kind of happened."

"Right. You just happened to end up fucking my husband—"

"Maybe I wanted to hurt you?" Brianna guessed as she playfully shrugged. "Somewhere, deep down. Or maybe I just wanted to feel something again. Anything. Maybe David was just that. Something to feel."

"Does he know that?" Elizabeth scoffed. "Does he know that you were just fucking him to try to hurt me?"

". . . I don't think that's quite right, either," Brianna murmured. "I don't know. I don't know what I feel about David. Maybe I'll have to figure out what to do about him later—"

"You stay away from him, you bitch—"

"Or what?" Brianna pressed. "What are you going to do if I don't stay away from him, Elizabeth?"

She moved closer to Elizabeth then, close enough to destroy any gap left between them, her face inches away from Elizabeth's.

"Tell me. Tell me what else you could ever do to me," Brianna continued. "Tell me how you're ever possibly going to hurt me worse than you already have."

"Brianna . . ." Elizabeth closed her eyes as she let out a loud sniffle. "Brianna. Please. I know how you feel about me right now, but maybe we can just—"

"Oh, no. You have no idea how I feel about you right now, Elizabeth. You couldn't."

"Brianna—"

"But you'll be able to, soon enough," Brianna went on. "You'll get to learn what it's like to wake up every morning and be in so much pain that you don't know how you're going to make it through the rest of your day. You're going to try to tell people how much pain you're in, how it feels like everyone and everything is against you, and they're not going to believe a word. They probably won't even listen to you, not when all you are is the woman who stabbed her husband. The woman who goes around accusing the only Black woman in her life of trying to ruin it. Changing out her pills? Setting a building on fire and getting her blamed? Stealing her husband? Do you have any idea what you sound like?"

". . . Changing out my pills?" Elizabeth's voice shook as she spoke. "Brianna . . . you did something to my pills?"

"Relax. It was nothing that could've hurt you," Brianna answered. "But you should really get into the habit of looking at your pills. Making sure the numbers all match the same ones as yesterday. Or else you might find yourself a little more anxious than usual. Although that's usually what happens when you're taking placebos."

"Fuck you." Elizabeth let out a broken sob. "So, was that it? The big bad list of everything shitty you ever did to me?"

"Nathan."

"What?"

"Nathan was the last shitty thing I ever did to you," Brianna replied. "Or, I guess, the last shitty thing you ever did to David. You weren't even trying to hide it, were you? Not really. Some part of you wanted David to find out about it."

Brianna paused, a thought occurring to her, before she went on. "Actually, maybe that one was more of a favor. Helping you tell David the truth."

"And what? You told him to act like a total asshole during dinner?"

"You think Nathan and I were working together?" Brianna scoffed. "The only thing I did was pretend to be you when I texted him an invite to dinner, and the rest he thankfully did himself. What's with you, Elizabeth? Why do you keep assuming some man had to help me with any of this? Just because you don't know how to stand on your fucking own doesn't mean the rest of us are just as helpless—"

Brianna held up a hand, correcting herself in the moment. "Sorry. I forgot that your helplessness was learned. Right? Someone taught you this whole little routine of yours?"

"Fuck off!" Elizabeth whimpered. "I'm not doing a routine. I'm fucking hurt. You're fucking hurting me, Brianna. And what about Charles?"

"What about him?"

"I thought you . . . You told me you loved him. Was he . . . was he even real? Or was that just another one of your lies?"

"Charles is real."

"Then how could you do this to him?" Elizabeth's eyes slowly opened. "How could you . . . Are you really going to leave him for David?"

"He left me first, Elizabeth," Brianna clarified. "He didn't like where I was headed, who I was becoming. He thought that I was . . . holding on too tightly to everything. To my grief. To my anger, too."

Brianna then let out a laugh, the effort lined with genuine amusement.

"But honestly? After all this, Elizabeth, I'm starting to feel a whole lot better. Aren't you—"

Brianna winced when she felt something slice across the palm of her hand.

Her blood soon followed, slowly appearing against her skin, like syrup being drizzled into a coffee shop mocha.

She then noticed the small razor blade in Elizabeth's hand, the one she was now clutching between her shaking fingertips. Without much deliberation, Brianna pulled the tiny weapon away from Elizabeth and into her own grip, the blade resting against her middle finger.

And then she pushed Elizabeth hard against the bathroom wall, the razor blade held up against the trembling woman's neck.

"Don't," Brianna whispered. "Don't turn me into something I'm not, Elizabeth."

"You're already a fucking killer, Brianna—"

"Jesus Christ. You're never going to get it, are you?" Brianna continued. "I already told you that I don't want you dead, Elizabeth. All I ever wanted was . . . I just wanted you to feel it. I wanted you to understand."

Brianna pressed the blade into Elizabeth's neck, her eyes locked on the other woman's.

". . . Do you feel it, Elizabeth? Do you get it yet?"

"I get that you have your fucking razor blade held up to my neck like a psycho—"

"It's not my fucking blade!" Brianna shouted before she let it fall to the floor. "It's never been my fucking blade."

Brianna took in a deep breath as she finally stood, already moving away from Elizabeth.

"Where the hell do you think you're going?"

"To the hospital. To check on David," Brianna answered. "By the way, that's the last of your questions that I'm ever going to answer, so don't bother trying to text or call me. Ever again. Besides, by the time you try to, my numbers will all be different, anyway."

"Fuck you! I could fucking sue you," Elizabeth weakly threatened. "I could ruin your life in court, Brianna. You have no idea who the fuck you're dealing with. You have no idea what kind of fight you've just started—"

"With what money?"

"What?"

"Think, Elizabeth." Brianna stared down at her with something resembling pity in her eyes. "How are you going to sue me? How are you going to do anything? You don't have David anymore. And if you try to take me to court before the divorce . . . he's going to leave you with nothing. You get that, right?"

"That's not true—"

"Elizabeth," Brianna cut her off, her tone stern. "It's over. Okay? This is finished with. You just need to let go."

Elizabeth stared at her then, completely silent, her eyes seeming to look Brianna up and down.

She then pointed to a spot next to the bathroom mirror, and Brianna's gaze followed the trail to a seashell-white cabinet.

"There's some gauze in there. And wrap. For your hand," Elizabeth whispered. "I think we have some Band-Aids, too."

". . . Thank you," Brianna replied as she quietly moved toward the cabinet. She proceeded to wrap her hand while keeping a keen eye on Elizabeth, the woman crumpled in the corner of the room.

A few moments later and there were police sirens, echoing right outside of Elizabeth's window, too-bright reds and blues emanating from their vehicles, illuminating every dark space in the room. Elizabeth started, but Brianna casually shook her head, attempting to offer her some momentary comfort.

"They're not here to take you away," she said. "They're here to protect you. I had a feeling you were going to try to do something stupid tonight, after what happened with David. It's just a wellness check."

"Oh," Elizabeth murmured, halfway underneath her breath. "Then thank you, too."

The room went silent then as the two women stared at each other. It wasn't lost on Brianna that even after harming each other, they'd both offered protection, too, some sort of refuge from the pain. Brianna idly wondered if in another lifetime, one where Elizabeth was more capable, more cohesive, they really could've been friends, really could've been there for each other when they needed each other the most.

But Brianna knew that she'd never be able to forgive Elizabeth.

Not in this lifetime.

Not in the next one, either.

And maybe never at all, her rage carried down through her descendants, her pain felt even by a great-great-granddaughter passing by one of Elizabeth's relatives in the street.

\*  \*  \*

*Was this being happy?*

Brianna didn't know anymore. Once upon a time, she would've been able to recognize it, the warmth in her veins, the almost dizzying delight.

But now she didn't feel much of anything. There were no emotional signifiers for anything other than rage and pain, the feelings she'd been feeding off of ever since she'd learned Patricia Fitzgerald's name, although now there was something new swimming in her stomach, too.

The guilt. The shame. The regret.

Even still, in the moment, she knew that she wasn't *unhappy* as she sat next to David's bed at the hospital, his hand gently reaching out to hold hers. He'd gotten out of surgery a few hours ago, the doctors worried that the scissors had landed in something vital inside of him.

Brianna hadn't been so worried, though.

And she didn't know if it was because she was overly optimistic about the hospital's lifesaving capabilities . . .

Or if she didn't really care, either way, if David Smith survived.

She would've been hurt by his death, sure, but not as hurt as she should've been. Because she'd already reached the maximum amount of pain in her life.

Because her heart was already permanently broken.

". . . What happened to your hand?" David murmured as he stared down at her wrapped palm.

"Oh. I . . . cut it on something."

"How?"

"By rushing down here to see you," Brianna lied. "By not being careful about packing an overnight bag for the hospital."

"You packed an overnight bag?" David weakly smiled. "You're going to stay here with me tonight?"

"Where else am I supposed to go?" Brianna smiled. "Am I supposed to run off to Hawaii or something— Actually, you know what? That's a pretty good idea. Where's your debit card?"

"Ha. Ha. Very funny." David lightly chuckled as he reached for her other, uninjured palm, gently taking it into his own. He then winced before letting out a shallow breath.

"Fuck. It hurts to laugh. It hurts to do anything. I feel like I got hit by a fucking—"

"Hurricane?" Brianna joked.

And David tiredly rolled his eyes. "Is she— Is Elizabeth going to jail?"

"For what? Stabbing you?"

"Yeah. That." David winced again. "I'm not going to press charges. I mean, I wouldn't. I wouldn't do something like that to her, get her in trouble for . . . I'd never want to hurt her over something she didn't really mean to do."

"You think she didn't mean to hurt you?"

"I think she just wanted me to stay."

". . . You'll pretty much forgive her for anything, won't you?"

"I'd pretty much forgive you for anything, too." David smiled as he spoke. "That's what you're supposed to do, right? When you love someone?"

*When you love someone?*

*David loved her?*

Brianna had never entertained the idea of being loved by someone else, by someone new. And with the way she was hardly able to recognize her own emotions anymore, she didn't know if she'd ever even be able to tell if she loved someone back.

But maybe this was it.

Maybe this was love.

Or at least, the way she'd know love from here on out, the hollow kind of love, the empty kind that might've felt good to say but left no residue in her chest.

"Hmm." Brianna smiled again before she tilted her head to the side. "You know, with the way you just phrased that, David, it kind of sounded like you're in love with both of us—"

"Past tense and present tense," he clarified. "I did love Elizabeth. With everything that I had."

"And now?"

"And now . . ." David trailed off as he struggled to lean over toward Brianna. She decided to meet him halfway, her lips pressing against his in a tender kiss. When the moment was over, Brianna leaned back in her seat.

Yes, maybe this was love.

Neat, corporate love.

The only love she could handle anymore.

"Speaking of Elizabeth . . ." It was Brianna's turn to let her words trail off as she tried to find the right way to respond. "I went back to your house while you were still in surgery."

"Why?"

"Because something told me to check on her. I'm glad I did, too, because Elizabeth . . . she tried to kill herself, David."

"What?" Shock and terror lined David's voice. "She tried to do *what*?"

"It's okay. I helped her. She'd taken a bunch of sleeping pills, so I just . . . I helped her induce vomiting before they could get too far into her system. And I made sure to call 9-1-1 on the way over, too, just so they'd be there to take her to the hospital, just in case."

"You helped her induce vomiting?" David sounded like he was in disbelief. "Really?"

"Right." Brianna warmly smiled. "This is the part of the affair where we actually start getting to know each other."

Brianna then playfully shifted their hand-holding into a proper handshake.

"David Smith, my name is Brianna Thompson, and I'll be going to nursing school in a few months. Or at least as soon as I find a program where they'll take my credits."

"Nice to meet you, Brianna." David grinned as he shook Brianna's hand right back. "Has anyone ever told you how beautiful you are?"

"Just this one guy I met at work." Brianna grinned in return before she leaned toward David, once again giving him a soft and tender kiss.

It was okay that she felt nothing when she kissed him.

Not even the passion from before, the way he was able to blunt her rage, the way he was able to blunt her sadness, too.

She didn't need to feel anything when she kissed David because she was never going to need that from him ever again.

Now Brianna needed something different, something else.

She needed a reminder of the past, of the wrong she'd done. By being around David, he was inadvertently never going to let her forget, never going to let her let the guilt slip away from her skin. There might even be times when he'd still want to visit Jack, want to bring Brianna around a man who'd never be fully certain if he'd met her before or not, Brianna always having to pretend, always having to dance around it.

She'd be forced to look David in the eyes, every so often, and remember. Remember Harbor Town. Remember Patricia. Remember Elizabeth, too. Remember how far her rage and sadness had carried her, how it'd brought her to the brink, how it'd pushed her off the edge of no return. She needed to remember to never let herself ever go that far again, to never become what she'd been, blinded by it, changed by it.

But just like she needed a reminder of her past, she needed a shield from it, too. Brianna knew that David was always going to take her side, that he seemed to define loyalty by protecting the women he loved from their own mistakes, their own fuck-ups and sins. Much like with Elizabeth, if Brianna was ever accused of the worst of the worst, David wouldn't believe it. He tended to be blinded, too, just like Brianna, emotions clouding judgment, clouding everything.

And Brianna knew that, no matter what, David was going to keep her safe.

Physically. Mentally. Emotionally.

In all the ways that always mattered.

And maybe that would be something better than love.

Or, at least, Brianna was willing to hope.

# The Happiest of Endings

Elizabeth Smith was a broken woman.

While she'd managed to never spend a single day in prison, courtesy of David not pressing charges, and courtesy of him getting the Learning Center not to press charges, either, she might as well have been thrown into solitary confinement.

That was how alone she always felt. That was how desperate she always felt.

She'd been right to fear that she wouldn't know how to live without David. It felt like being half alive, at all times, Elizabeth mostly having to pretend at any emotion other than crushing depression. She was still seeing Dr. Whitaker, David agreeing to let her *have* the therapist in the process of their divorce. He'd also agreed to let her have anything else she'd wanted, too, the house, her car, the majority of their material possessions.

David seemed intent on letting Elizabeth have everything except what she really wanted:

Him.

It was like he'd taken on an extreme form of ghosting her, not even allowing her contact with him without a divorce lawyer being in the room. It was torture, knowing that every message she sent was blocked, that every phone call was set up to go straight to voice mail. Suddenly, she'd become a nonfactor in his life, something she'd never thought she could possibly be.

She was finally, fully, the grocery store on the other side of David's town. The one place he'd never go back to, the sort of place he'd eventually forget ever existed.

David had disappeared from social media, too, which meant that Elizabeth hadn't even been granted the chance to occasionally glimpse his life, her view of him permanently blind and blurry. She'd tried finding ways around it, searching for secret accounts, attempting to track him down under old usernames she remembered from their time in college together.

But David Smith was just gone.

The only thing Elizabeth had left of him was his last name.

"Lizzie, are you okay?" Nathan stepped into the kitchen, his presence feeling like a shock to Elizabeth's system.

*He wasn't supposed to be home this early.*

She then spared a look at the clock in the corner, realizing that it was after six p.m., that she'd somehow once again lost an entire day to memories of David, memories of a life she'd so often felt stuck in, too.

She yearned for David's touch just as much as she yearned for the trap of it.

Not that Nathan's touch was awful. It was just never going to compare, like trying to draw a line between a Louis Vuitton purse and a cheap handbag from the flea market on Highland. She'd still decided to move in with Nathan, though, after they dated for a few weeks, post her divorce, post her selling the Harbor Town house, too. It was almost like he'd been waiting in the wings for Elizabeth, sending her a message at just the right time, wondering if she'd be interested in catching dinner with him, when the ink on her separation papers hadn't even fully dried.

Nathan was just what it seemed like she needed. He was a well of nothing but love and support, encouraging Elizabeth to go back to work if that was what she wanted, to have another drink if that was what she wanted, to skip going to the gym if that was what she wanted.

Elizabeth wondered if he would've given her the okay to blow her brains out, too, *if that was what she wanted.*

"Lizzie?" Nathan repeated her name, concern rising through his voice.

". . . I'm fine," Elizabeth lied before faking a wide smile. "Sorry. You know how my pills can make me a little spacey sometimes."

"But they're working for you, right?" He smiled in return. "That's all that matters. As long as you stay on the right path—"

"What did you want for dinner?" she hastily interrupted, knowing that if she ever had to hear the phrase *on the right path* again that she was going to stab herself in the neck with a butter knife. "I could whip us up a pretty mean lemon-and-raspberry salad—"

"A salad?" Nathan chuckled.

"What's so funny about a salad?"

"Nothing, usually," he continued with a smirk. "But there is something pretty funny about wanting us to eat salads on Halloween."

*Halloween?*

Elizabeth grimaced, her eyes closing as she realized that Nathan was right.

It *was* Halloween.

The holiday had barely made a dent on her social calendar, since she was no longer in the know about all the parties happening in the neighborhood. Elizabeth had quickly learned that there was a queen bee in Nathan's Cordova suburb, Suzanne Weber. She was classically beautiful and classically mean, in that familiar way that Elizabeth had become accustomed to in high school.

And, keeping in the tradition of mean girls everywhere, Suzanne had *neglected* to invite Elizabeth to her annual Halloween party. Elizabeth couldn't pinpoint what it was, exactly, whether Suzanne's snub was due to the splash it made in the news when she was accused of burning down the Learning Center or the rumors about how her marriage had ended with David's blood on the floor.

Either way, the lack of an invitation meant that Elizabeth had officially lost her social capital all over the city. She wasn't a real person anymore, not in Harbor Town, not in Midtown, not in Cordova.

Not anywhere.

". . . Are you sure you're okay, baby?" Nathan murmured.

"I'm going out, I think," she replied, already heading toward the front door.

"Where are you going—"

Elizabeth slammed the door hard behind her, right in the middle of his sentence, no longer interested in continuing the conversation.

\* \* \*

Maybe it was fate.

Maybe it was just an extended form of torture, some higher being wanting Elizabeth to suffer more than she already had for things she'd never even done.

But right now, Elizabeth was sharing a parking lot with David's Lexus, the license plate as familiar to her as the back of her hand. She'd gone breathless at the sight of it, confusion flooding her veins before it was replaced with the pure adrenaline of unexpected joy. She didn't know whether to honk to try to get his attention or if it would be better to approach him slowly from the side of the vehicle, not wanting him to realize it was her until it was too late for him to speed away.

But just as Elizabeth planned to make her grand reintroduction, she spotted Brianna walking through the parking lot. She looked mostly the same, still just as stunning, like she'd walked off the front cover of a magazine devoted to health and beauty. There was a woman walking right beside her, matching her gait, both of them laughing loud, the sound of it carrying through the night air. The woman next to Brianna seemed to be about the same age as her, even though the corny, toddler-like witch costume she had on made Elizabeth think that she was much younger at first glance.

Elizabeth squinted to get a better view of Brianna's costume, wondering what she'd decided to be for Halloween. When Elizabeth finally recognized the costume, her eyes went wide, her heart beating so fast inside her chest it felt like she was going to explode into a million pieces, parts of her flying across the parking lot all at once.

*Brianna was dressed up as a nurse for Halloween.*

"Fucking psychopath," Elizabeth whispered before ducking lower in the driver's seat of her car, not wanting Brianna or her friend to catch sight of her as they continued through the parking lot. Brianna and the stranger didn't stop walking until they were standing on either side of David's car. Just then, Elizabeth was able to gain an even better look at Brianna's outfit, her eyebrows furrowing when she spotted the nametag pinned to her shirt.

**Brianna Thompson**

**St. Jude Children's Research Hospital**

**Residency Staff**

Brianna wasn't dressed up like a nurse for Halloween.

Brianna was just a nurse.

"Fucking psychopath," Elizabeth repeated, her stomach roiling as she imagined Brianna being responsible for anyone's health and well-being, knowing that she was extraordinarily capable of taking a life.

Wasn't that against the code of conduct for health professionals? Being fucking murderers?

Elizabeth idly wondered about the process of reporting something like that to a higher-up, of alerting the hospital staff at St. Jude that they'd hired a burgeoning serial killer, a woman capable of more evil than anything they could ever see coming.

Her thoughts soon shifted, though, as Brianna moved the jacket that she'd been holding in front of her and neatly folded it on the backseat of the car.

And that was when Elizabeth saw it.

Brianna wasn't just a nurse.

Brianna was a *pregnant* nurse, her baby bump only a few months along. As soon as it was exposed, Brianna's friend sprinted over toward Brianna's side of the vehicle, playfully rubbing a hand across her stomach.

"Oh my God! I swear I can already feel her kicking!"

Brianna rolled her eyes before she beamed back at her friend. "That's not even possible right now, Vera. Which is something you would know if you studied those nursing textbooks that I let you borrow."

"Hey, I never said I wanted to be a nurse." Vera's laughter punctuated her words. "You're the one who's trying to push everyone to get like you, now that you have a good man and a good job. I'd be happy with only *one* of those things, and if I have one, why the hell would I ever need the other?"

"Honestly, Vera, I can't with you." Brianna laughed now, too. "I don't know why I even put up with you."

"Because you loveeeee me," Vera sang the phrase before she nodded down at Brianna's protruding stomach. "Have you and David figured out what you're going to name her?"

"David was thinking about Meredith—"

"You're going to give a little Black girl an old-white-lady name?"

"Uh, your name is Vera, right?"

"Right, which is how I know that's a bad idea." Vera frowned as she walked toward the other side of the Lexus. "Why not try something hip right now? Ooh, what about Anastasia?"

". . . Anastasia's not a bad name," Brianna admitted as she opened the driver's-side door.

But before she had a chance to step inside the car, Elizabeth was standing right beside her, her hand pressed against the roof of it.

". . . You're pregnant?" Elizabeth's voice sounded as broken as she felt, tears already crawling down her skin. "You . . . you and David are having a baby?"

"Elizabeth . . ." Brianna said her name with a lilting tone. She cast a look over at Vera, giving her friend an assuring nod before she turned back toward Elizabeth.

She then held out her arms for Elizabeth, who cautiously stepped into them, letting Brianna wrap her in a tight embrace.

"I thought I already told you, Elizabeth . . ." Brianna started, her tone shifting from lilting to as threatening as the dark of night. "I'm done answering your questions."

"Please. I just want to know—"

"If you ever come around me or my family ever again, it'll be the last thing you ever do."

"Brianna, please. I just want to talk to you," Elizabeth cried. "I just want—"

"What are you not getting, Elizabeth?" Brianna cut her off, her arms still wrapped around her as if they were dear, dear friends. "What you want doesn't *matter* anymore. Nothing you want is ever going to matter again. You get what other people think you deserve."

Brianna then pulled away from Elizabeth, now smiling over at her.

"Don't be such a stranger, okay? We should keep in touch," Brianna said, her continued smile coming off as nothing but bared teeth to Elizabeth, a threat covered up with false kindness.

"Right. I'll . . . I'll text you later tonight," Elizabeth lied right back to Brianna, aware that this was all for show, all for the sake of the woman sitting and waiting for Brianna in the car.

And as Brianna finally settled behind the driver's seat of the Lexus, Elizabeth watched as she drove out of the parking lot, still yearning for the life she used to live, the one that Brianna had seemed to so effortlessly settle into herself.

But there was another yearning, too, some small part of Elizabeth that she hadn't been able to kill, no matter how many times she'd tried.

The part of her that yearned to be back in Brianna's arms.

The part of her that yearned for the friend she'd never really had . . .

And the only friend she'd ever truly lost.

# ACKNOWLEDGMENTS

I have to start by thanking my mom, who always believed in me and encouraged me to write down my craziest and zaniest ideas. Mom, your belief in me made me think that this was even possible, and I could never thank you enough for your faith in my words and for teaching me how to trust the process. I love you, always and always. (Oh, and thank you for getting through those rough first drafts, too!)

I'd also like to thank my agent, Lauren Abramo, for working on this book with me for over a year and being extraordinarily patient with me as we got it together. Thank you, Lauren, for being a true advocate for me and helping me bring my best work to the page. Also, thank you for explaining literally everything to me about publishing (no, seriously).

To Danielle Dieterich, Ashley Di Dio, Sally Kim, and the rest of the team at Putnam who took a chance on an unlikable female protagonist and her very problematic nature—thank you so much for going on this journey with me. Bringing a book from production to publication feels like a miracle and I'm so lucky that I had the chance to work alongside you all and watch you work your magic.

To my family, friends, and loved ones, my partner who supported me through the writing process and kept me sane, to Harriet and Victor for letting me rant about my latest idea for a book, to Kristen and Alys for letting me rant in general. And to everyone who's had a hand in my getting here, I want to thank you from the very bottom of my heart.

Here's to the next one.